Twisted Lives

Tamara Merrill

CALI Press

Coronado, California

CALI Press
PO Box 2213
Coronado, CA 92118
www.TamaraMerrill.com

Publisher's Note: This is a work of fiction. Names, characters, places, and incidents are a product of the author's imagination. Locales and public names are sometimes used for atmospheric purposes. Any resemblance to actual people, living or dead, or to businesses, companies, events, institutions, or locales is completely coincidental.

Book Layout Spark © 2017 BookDesignTemplates.com

Cover Illustration Basic Bear Designs: AdobeStock_1042820339
Edited by: Lisa Wolff

Twisted Lives/TamaraMerrill -- 1st ed.
ISBN Paperback   979-8-9895976-1-1
ISBN Hard Cover   979-8-9895976-2-8
ISBN eBook   979-8-9895976-3-5
ISBN Audio   979-8-9895976-4-2

Dedication

For all those who have endured the pain of abuse, you are not alone. Your strength, resilience, and courage in the face of darkness inspire hope and healing. May this book be a reminder of your worth and a beacon for a brighter tomorrow. You are not alone.

National Abuse Violence Hotline

Call: 1-800-799-7233

Website: thehotline.org

CONTENTS

PROLOGUE: Lost

The wind whipped her hair across her face and tore at her coat; giant old-growth trees bent before the onslaught and turned the snow into a bitter, stinging fury. She dropped to her knees and wept. He was dead. He had to be dead, or if not dead, freezing to death. She'd never find him in time.

The dog, his dog, ran circles around her, yipping and urging her to rise. The dog raced toward the tree line, plunging in and out of the deep banks of fallen snow.

She struggled to stand, her feet slipping on the ice hidden beneath the snow.

Her head throbbed; each breath was a battle. Using her bare hands for leverage, she forced herself to rise. Her legs quivered. She lost her balance and fell again. She needed to rest.

The dog stopped, whirled, and ran a few paces toward her, barking and whining.

She spoke, her voice husky and harsh from last night's abuse. "Ajax, find Jeremy."

The dog looked back and forth from her to the woods. He whined and then barked loudly, urging her to come.

She cleared her throat and managed to repeat the command, "Find Jeremy."

Ajax spun away and dashed toward the trees. She pressed her ungloved hands into the icy snow and fought to stand. Determined to follow the dog, she pushed herself upright, shaky and trembling. She blew on her icy fingers and shoved her hands into her pockets. Her knees quaked as she forced herself to take one step and then another. The throbbing in her temple caused her eyes to blur. She rubbed her face with her icy hand, lifted her eyes to the sky, and implored the empty woods, "Please, he has to be here!"

The headache made it impossible to think straight, to remember. When she'd opened her eyes and found his bed empty, she'd known at once that something was wrong. Jeremy wasn't a quiet kid. Most mornings were filled with his banging about and her telling him to hush. Was it possible he'd left the house and she hadn't heard a thing?

Why hadn't Ajax barked when he opened the door? She tried to concentrate. *Jeremy knows better than to go outside without permission. Something doesn't make sense.*

She squinted, peering through the whirling white until she located the dog's trail. Listening for his bark, she slogged through the snow, the leather soles of her shoes sliding on the hidden ice. Her head throbbed. She admitted to herself, last night's vodka wasn't helping this morning.

She called her son's name over and over, praying for a response each time. Hearing nothing over the constant roar of the wind.

Ajax whined, barking at her as if telling her to get it together.

The wind lifted the snow, throwing the icy crystals into her mouth and eyes.

She shivered and fought on.

Rodney will kill me if anything happens to Jeremy. He is still so angry and blaming me for the past. This time it really is my fault. How could I not have heard a six-year-old get up, dress, and leave the house? Too much vodka last night? She pushed that thought away and shouted Jeremy's name again and again.

Ajax entered the trees.

In her rush to find Jeremy, she had dashed out of the cabin unprepared for the cold and ice. Hastening her steps to catch up caused her feet to slip. She grabbed a holly branch; thorns pierced her palm. She whimpered and sucked at the blood.

The dog disappeared.

"Damn it," she swore aloud. "This isn't fair."

Was Jeremy dressed for the snow? His bed had been rumpled and unmade, she was sure of that, but did he have his jacket? She tried to picture the coat rack next to the door.

No picture came.

The pounding pain in her head increased. Her stomach lurched, and she spat out the bile that rose to her throat.

Ajax barked in the distance.

Her head came up.

His bark grew excited and frantic.

He's found something. Please, God, let it be Jeremy. Let him be all right.

She broke into a shuffling, clumsy run. Deadfall, buried in the snow, grabbed at her feet. Falling hard, the wind was knocked out of her chest.

The world tilted, and the light faded.

***

She moaned and pushed Ajax aside, sat up and remembered.

"Jeremy!" she shouted. The woods remained silent. The sun was higher in the sky. She was sure of it. She had no idea how long she'd been lying in the deep snow.

"Ajax," she said, and the dog cocked his head to listen. "Find Jeremy."

Ajax sat down and then lowered himself to a fully prone position.

"Oh, Ajax," she said sadly, "what have I done? Where is my son? We have to find him before it's too late."

Ajax whined.

The world spun as she moved to get up; her head ached. She searched for a handhold, found a branch, and levered herself to her feet. She heard a car approaching and realized that they'd reached the county road. She waved her arms to attract attention.

CHAPTER ONE

NOW DAY 1: Thursday 01/25 MORNING

It had to be a nightmare, nothing else made sense, she thought, watching Rodney pace across the cabin floor. She could see his lips moving and the sheriff's lips responding, but their low voices didn't reach her. She couldn't understand. *Why is Rodney in my house?* she wondered.

She tried to speak, but her tongue felt too big for her mouth. Her head hurt. She rubbed at her forehead and was surprised to feel a bandage. *What is happening? Where is Jeremy?*

Her eyes closed and she drifted off to sleep.

***

When her eyes opened again, it was dark in the cabin. She reached out to turn on a light, but the lamp wasn't where it should be.

She heard a voice: "Hush, dear. Everything is alright. Go back to sleep."

Obediently, she closed her eyes and felt the darkness overwhelm her.

She whispered, "Jeremy."

***

She woke screaming and shot upright in the bed.

The light was too bright.

She felt a sharp prick in her arm and fell back into a warm, dark place.

She thought she heard voices and then they, along with her fears, faded and she dreamed of nothing at all.

***

Her eyes opened. The window was outlined by the sun. But the window was in the wrong place. She struggled to rise.

Strong hands pushed her back and the voice murmured again, "Hush, darling one. Everything is okay."

But it wasn't.

Something was wrong.

She tried to think but felt the prick of a needle in her arm. She slept.

***

She woke and started to lift her head but remembered the voices and the prick. She lay still, listening to the quiet. *Is there anyone in the room? Where am I? Where is Jeremy?*

At the thought of her son, she felt strong hands touch her arm. *Did I say his name aloud?*

She forced her breathing to slow and the hands lifted. *Where am I? What is going on? Jeremy? I must find him!*

She wanted to scream Jeremy's name, but she forced herself to stay quiet. She kept her breaths slow and even, pretending to sleep, listening carefully for any voice or any sound that might provide a clue.

Little by little, she turned to her side, hoping that it would look like she was merely moving in her sleep.

A woman's voice: "I think she's waking."

She lay perfectly still. Footsteps moved away and she risked opening her eyes the tiniest bit. An IV pole stood next to the bed. A plastic bag filled with clear liquid hung from the hook, its tube extended down to the port in the back of her hand. *Hospital? What happened? Where's Jeremy?*

The footsteps were approaching again.

She closed her eyes.

A hand stroked the hair off her forehead. "Time to wake up, Sarah. Someone is here to see you."

Jeremy? Her eyes flew open.

"There you are, darling."

Rodney? Why is Rodney here? And why is he calling me darling? Cautiously, she turned toward his voice.

"Where's Jeremy?" she asked. Her voice sounded rough, and she realized how thirsty she was. She struggled to pull herself up.

"It's okay, Sarah. Everything is going to be okay." Rodney ran his hand gently up and down her arm and bent close to kiss her. His lips brushed against hers.

She recoiled, but with her head pressed against the pillow there was nowhere to go.

She stared into his eyes. That look hadn't changed. He still hated her. But the gentle hand on her arm and soft kiss didn't seem like hate.

A nurse moved into view behind Rodney. He stood and turned slightly. "She's awake."

"I can see that." The nurse smiled at Rodney, before turning to Sarah. "Would you like a drink of water, dear?" she asked.

Sarah licked her lips and nodded. Rodney stepped back and the nurse held a straw to her lips. Sarah drank.

The nurse stroked her arm. "You've had a nice long sleep and your lovely husband has been here every minute. I'm just going to take your vitals and then we'll get that IV out of your hand."

She stared at the nurse. Nothing made sense. "How did I get here?" she asked.

"You had a nasty fall, darling. Don't you remember?" Rodney slipped back into view.

"Fall, where?"

"Down the stairs. All the way down the stairs."

"There aren't any stairs in the cabin." She turned her puzzled gaze toward the nurse. "I was in the cabin—there aren't any stairs."

"You had a blow to your head," the nurse explained. "Your memory's a bit foggy. I'm going to let the doctor know you're awake. He'll be in shortly." She patted Sarah's hand and turned away.

"Did you find Jeremy? Is he okay?" She tried to sit up, but Rodney's strong hands pushed her back.

"Why in the world would I need to find Jeremy?" Rodney spoke calmly and sweetly, but his gaze remained hard and uncaring as he watched her reaction. "Jeremy is right where he belongs."

She frowned. "He wasn't in the cabin when I woke up this morning. Ajax led me to the road." She struggled to remember more. "It was so cold, and I was afraid that he didn't have his jacket."

"I think you had a bad dream while you were unconscious. Who's Ajax?"

"The dog," she stammered, "you know he's the dog."

"Whoa." Rodney's lips curved in a smile, but the smile didn't reach his eyes. "We don't have a dog."

"Of course, we have a dog. You gave him to Jeremy on his fourth birthday."

Rodney shook his head. "Not true, Sarah." He turned away as the door opened. "Doctor," he greeted the man entering the room. "She's awake but very confused. She thinks we have a dog."

"That's not unusual. People are often confused for a few days after a bad concussion. But," the doctor chuckled, "I don't think I've ever heard of someone remembering a dog that isn't there." He picked up her wrist and held it as he watched the monitors. "Everything looks fine," he said and laid her hand back on the bed. "We'll let you out of here as soon as they do the paperwork. Don't worry; your memory will straighten itself out."

She sat up as the doctor left the room. "Okay, Rodney. What's going on? Where is Jeremy?"

"Jeremy is fine. He's at home waiting for you. He's been worried, of course. He saw you fall."

"I didn't fall down a flight of stairs." She spoke firmly and chose her words carefully. "Jeremy wasn't in the cabin this morning. I was trying to find him."

"I think you need to stop talking like that. People will think you're crazy."

"But..." She closed her eyes. *He's calling me crazy again, just like before. Am I crazy?* She opened her eyes, forcing herself to stay calm. "What hospital is this? How long have I been here?"

"That's a much more sensible question. You've been here a few days."

"How did it happen? How did I fall down these stairs?"

"You'd been drinking. Quite a bit, it seems. I didn't realize how drunk you were. You insisted on reading Jeremy a story even though it was past time for him to be in bed. You simply lost your footing at the top of the stairs and fell to the bottom. You could have been killed." He spoke flatly, stating the facts as if he'd rehearsed them, or had told them many times.

"I don't remember any of that. Why were we in your house?"

"*My* house? Don't you mean *our* house? It's where we live. Where else would you be?"

"We're divorced, Rodney. You know that."

"Divorced?" He shook his head. "You need to forget that notion. Of course, we aren't divorced. We love each other."

She scrambled to take in this information. *I know this isn't true,* she thought. *Something is very wrong.* "Rodney, nothing makes sense."

"You heard the doctor. In a few days, after the concussion is healed and the medication wears off, your memory will straighten it-self out. You've been asleep for days. That alone can leave a gap in your memory, and…" He paused and watched her closely as he added, "I've read that many patients with a head injury never remember the events right before or after the trauma."

She thought she noticed a threat in his voice. *He doesn't want me to remember.*

She stayed silent, avoiding eye contact.

"Let's get you up and dressed so we can get out of here. I kept Jeremy home from school today and he's waiting to see you."

At the thought of seeing her son, her mood shifted. She pushed her concerns aside and forced a smile. "Do I have clothes around here somewhere?" she asked.

"That's my girl. I'll get the nurse and see what's taking so long."

Rodney disappeared, and a moment later a nurse entered the room with clothing over her arm. She placed the clothes on a chair and said, "Here you go, dear."

Sarah recognized the voice; this was the woman she'd heard in her sleep, or was it? She seemed familiar.

"Do you know what happened? Were you with me when I was asleep?" she asked. "Did you give me shots that made me sleep?"

"Don't be asking too many questions, dear. You know what they say about curiosity and the cat." The nurse shook her head slightly and touched her finger to her lips in a shushing motion. "Just put on these clothes and go home with that lovely husband of yours. And, if I may suggest something, you need to get help with your drinking problem. Next time you might not be so lucky."

Am I getting paranoid? she wondered. That sounded like a threat, too.

She put on the unfamiliar bra and panties, pulled on yoga pants and a tee shirt that she didn't recognize, and used a brush she'd never seen before to tidy her hair. She looked in the mirror. *At least I remember myself and Rodney and Jeremy.* She shook her head and considered her other weird memories. *And I'm sure we're divorced; I'm positive about that.*

Rodney appeared at the door with a wheelchair. "Hop in, darling. It's time to go home."

"I can walk."

"I'm sure you can, but it's a hospital rule."

She sat in the chair and lifted her feet onto the rests. She heard the nurse say, "Off we go" and felt the familiar prick in her neck.

CHAPTER TWO

NOW DAY 1: Thursday 01/25 AFTERNOON

"Damn," she muttered.

"Are you awake again, darling? We're almost home."

The prick in my neck. What was that? Had he given her a shot of something? Or did the nurse? She forced herself to pay attention.

Looking out the car window, she tried to concentrate. *Where are we? Nothing looks familiar. Home? This can't be home. Jeremy and I live in the cabin. Whose home does he mean?* She closed her eyes. *How did we get here?* She couldn't remember leaving the hospital or getting in the car.

As if he could read her mind, Rodney said, "Don't worry about gaps in your memory. The doctor said it could happen any time."

He glanced at her and smiled slightly. "Anytime at all, whenever things need to be controlled, you'll forget."

Was that another threat? What the hell was he doing?

They turned into the driveway and pulled to a stop.

Jeremy! her mind shouted, but she forced herself to stay quiet.

Sarah pushed the door open and stepped out of the car. The world seemed to tilt, and for a moment she thought she would faint. She took a deep breath and felt Rodney take her arm. They moved together across the snowy drive.

The front door opened, and a boy stepped out.

Sarah stopped in mid-stride. "Rodney," she demanded, "who is that?"

Rodney looked around at the snow-covered trees and lawn, then frowned. "Who, Sarah?"

"That boy." She pointed toward the child on the porch.

"Jeremy?" Rodney watched her carefully. His lips lifted in a slight smile. "What's wrong with you? That's our son. Jeremy."

"No, it's not!"

"Of course, it is." He winked, and Sarah felt her stomach clench. "Don't tell me you can say you remember a dog and a divorce, but you don't recognize your own child?"

"I'm not crazy! You know that's not Jeremy and you know we're divorced! What are you trying to pull, Rodney?"

Rodney didn't answer. Instead, he wrapped an arm around her and pulled her in tight to his side—too tight.

Sarah struggled to move away, but the arm became even tighter.

"Just calm down, darling. You don't want to upset Jeremy, do you?"

She twisted her body, but his grip was firm.

"Get control of yourself, or I'll have to help you." He glared down at her, his face frozen in a sneer.

She recognized that cold tone. It was the voice he always used when he was displeased with something she'd done. Sarah knew he was one step from full-blown, violent anger. She stopped struggling and nodded. His grip loosened.

"All right then. Say hello to your son and then we can go inside."

Sarah watched the boy walk toward them. There was a strong resemblance, but she was sure he was taller than Jeremy, his eyes were darker, and he moved differently.

"Hello, Mother," he said.

Not my son! His voice was wrong, and this kid was older.

Rodney's grip tightened again, and Sarah forced herself to croak out a hoarse, "Hello."

"Hug your mother, Jeremy. She's had a rough couple of days."

The boy stepped forward and hugged her around the waist. He took her hand and urged her toward the front door. "Are you still sick, Mother? Father has been taking very good care of me, but I missed you."

Sarah tried to catch Rodney's eye, but he kept his gaze on the house. Sarah bit her lip. Her thoughts raced. *What kind of game is Rodney playing? Surely, he doesn't think that I'll go along with this. Where is Jeremy?*

She wanted to scream.

Rodney approached as the boy released her hand. He put his arm around her again but felt her stiffen, and his grip tightened as he propelled her up the front steps, across the wide porch, and into the living room.

"Rodney." Sarah stopped and looked around her. "This is not your house. I've never been here before."

"That's enough, Sarah. I don't care how hard you hit your head. You need to stop talking like that. People will think you're crazy."

She bit down on her lip and tried to stay calm. If she'd learned anything at all while she was married to Rodney, it was that disagreeing with him would only make things worse.

"I think I need to lie down." She attempted a smile. "You'll need to tell me where my room is."

"I'll take you, Mother."

Rodney released his hold and the child slipped his hand into hers and pulled her toward the stairs.

She wanted to pull away, but Rodney was watching closely, and she didn't want him to give her another of those shots.

At the top of the stairs a welcoming seating area was arranged. On a slim table, beneath a window, Sarah recognized the family picture taken in Yosemite two years ago. It was the right picture, but Jeremy was different. She was sure of it. She paused and picked up the framed print. The child's face was too round, and Jeremy had never had that haircut.

"That was a lovely vacation, wasn't it," the boy said. "I was only four, I think, so I don't really remember much, but you've told me all about it."

Sarah shook her head and put the picture back on the table. Something wasn't right. *Jeremy doesn't talk like this boy. He never calls me Mother.*

The boy gestured to a room down the hall to the left. "That is my room, and you and Father have the room at the other end of the hall. Father said you'd like to sleep alone until your head is better. So, you'll be in the guest room."

He dropped Sarah's hand, walked ahead, and stopped at an open doorway. He gestured for her to join him. "Here we are, Mother. I hope you have a nice rest."

Sarah stepped past him. "Thank you," she murmured and closed the door behind her gently, resisting the urge to show her frustration by slamming it.

She examined the room. It was lovely, but as impersonal as a hotel room. The large bed, centered between elegant nightstands, was covered in a soft beige quilt, a brown cashmere throw folded at its foot. Two slipper chairs, upholstered in brown-and-beige-striped silk, bracketed a round table that held a silver lamp and another picture. She recognized this picture. It was Jeremy on the day they brought him home from the hospital. A perfect picture of a perfect family; she and Rodney looked like the proud parents that they were.

Sarah crossed to the windows and pulled back a drape. The property seemed to be surrounded by a dense growth of tall pine trees. A broad lawn swept away from the house, and rolling drifts of snow reached down toward an icy gray river. The long driveway extended toward what must be a street. She couldn't see another house, at least not from this window. Movement caught her eye and she watched as Rodney exited the front door and crossed to the car. The trunk opened and he removed a suitcase.

Rodney looked up and their eyes locked. Neither of them moved. Sarah shivered at the cold, angry glare he was giving her. This was the Rodney she knew. Her hands trembled as she dropped the curtain and stepped back.

****

Panic twisted Sarah's stomach. Her heart raced. Where was Jeremy? Why was Rodney pretending they were still married? Who was that boy? Where were they? The questions came one after another, but there were no answers. Her stomach heaved, and she rushed into the adjoining bathroom and threw up a thick stream of yellow bile.

She couldn't remember the last time she'd had anything to eat. *What day is this? I'm so scared.*

Sarah shivered and leaned her forehead against the vanity mirror, taking deep breaths and trying not to cry. The tears came anyway.

"Jeremy, where are you?" she whispered to her reflection.

Clinging to the rim of the sink, she stared at herself. *What kind of mother loses her son and doesn't even know how long he's been gone?*

Sarah splashed cold water on her face and patted it dry. Pulling open a drawer, she found a brush and some hair ties. She twisted her hair into a ponytail and realized that it was lank and oily and needed to be washed. How long had it been since she'd had a shower?

The bedroom door opened.

Startled, Sarah jumped and turned to see Rodney posed in the doorway. He was the picture of casual elegance, dressed beautifully, she noted: his khaki slacks had a perfect crease, and his button-down collared shirt had exactly the right amount of starch. The shirtsleeves were carefully rolled, twice. Not a hair on his head was out of place.

"Are you feeling calmer now?"

Sarah nodded.

"You must be hungry. Our housekeeper, Mrs. Hendricks, will have dinner ready in about an hour, so I don't think it's a good idea for you to snack." His hard gaze roamed over her body. "You've gained weight and it isn't becoming."

Sarah stared at him.

"I'm sure you'd like a cocktail. Why don't you take a shower and get cleaned up? I'll bring you a vodka tonic. That is still your drink of choice, right?"

"Rodney," Sarah finally managed to say, "I don't want a drink or dinner. I want to know what is going on. Where is Jeremy?"

"He's downstairs playing a video game."

Sarah turned toward the door and then realized he meant that other boy. She turned back; her hands clenched into fists. She struggled to sound calm. "Where is my *son*, Rodney? What have you done with him?"

"*Our son*," he emphasized the words, "is downstairs waiting for his poor, injured mother to get her act together enough to have a nice family dinner. Take your shower."

He turned as precisely as any military man on parade, exited, and without looking back, closed the door behind himself. Sarah lifted her arm to throw the hairbrush at the door and caught herself just in time. She remembered that when they were married and Rodney acted this way, the only thing that worked was to follow his orders without question. Maybe a shower would clear her head.

***

Sarah stood under the scalding water. She scrubbed at her skin and shampooed her hair. Everything in the shower stall was scented with roses, a smell she found cloying. She'd always preferred light, lemon-based products. She rinsed again and again.

Someone had placed clothing on the bed for her. Not her own clothing, but delicate, gauzy undergarments, a silk shirt, silk trousers, and ballet flats, everything in the palest of eggshell tones. Not her style at all. She crossed the room and opened the closet. Empty, entirely empty, not even a hanger in sight. Sarah pulled open a dresser drawer. It, too, was empty.

She clutched her towel around her more tightly, strode across the room, and pulled open the door to the hall.

The boy stood in the hallway. "I was waiting for you, Mother. Father said to bring you down for dinner."

Sarah gaped at him. He was just a kid. Why in the world did he feel so sinister?

"You should put on the clothes Father laid out for you. He won't like it if we are late for dinner."

Sarah retreated. Whatever was going on, she told herself, she'd be better able to confront Rodney if she was wearing more than a towel. She dressed quickly and joined the boy in the hall.

***

Silently they entered the dining room together. "Ah, there you are." Rodney held out a chair and indicated she should sit. Jeremy stood behind the chair directly across from her. Rodney moved to the head of the table. "You look lovely, Sarah. I've always thought shades of white were your best color." He cocked his head and considered her carefully. "Do you like the trousers, darling? They are Chanel and quite slimming on you."

"Where are my clothes, Rodney? If this is my house and I live here, why is my closet empty?"

Rodney chuckled. "Goodness. You really don't remember, do you?" He rose and walked to the buffet.

Sarah watched his reflection in the large mirror. She could see the cruel twist of his lips as he poured two glasses of wine. He picked up one and swirled it lightly, then raised it to the light and admired the rich, garnet color.

He caught her eye in the mirror. "I assume," he picked up both glasses and turned around, "that you don't remember destroying all your clothing. You must have blacked out again. Your drinking is really out of control, Sarah. We are going to have to teach you some restraint."

Sarah started to protest her innocence but then snapped her lips shut. She needed to figure out what was going on. Her marriage to Rodney had been horrific and now, somehow, she was caught in his trap again.

CHAPTER THREE

BEFORE: 9 Years Ago

Sarah met Rodney at work during a business breakfast. As a very junior member of the marketing team, Sarah's job was to take notes, refill coffee cups, and be sure everyone had their choice of bagel, doughnut, or fruit. Her boss didn't introduce her and no one on the client's team acknowledged that she was in the room.

Like in every other meeting, while listening to her boss's sales pitch, she'd had plenty of time to assess each member of the client's team. Instead of concentrating on the conversation, she indulged herself by appraising the clothing and shoes that the other women were wearing. She made notes on items to look for on the racks of the local consignment shops and discount stores next weekend. Sarah knew that her small, five-foot-two-inch stature and cheerleader looks caused many people to overlook her skills and education and to assume she had no career goals. To gain credence at these meetings, she was determined to assemble a professional wardrobe at a bargain price.

Just yesterday, she'd complained to her best friend, Claire, that she wasn't being taken seriously at work. Claire, a tall redhead with a no-nonsense, take-charge manner, was a very successful real estate agent, and she had not understood. Sarah wasn't surprised. She felt certain no one had ever taken Claire anything but seriously. She could wear a gunny sack and she'd still be tall and beautiful. Sarah drew a stick-figure cartoon of Claire wearing a paper bag. She almost smiled but caught herself in time as her boss's tone penetrated her daydreams. She listened to him introduce Rodney Blake and extol his accomplishments. Glancing up, she noted that this Rodney guy was quite good-looking and seemed to be in charge.

Sarah made a few desultory notes and then doodled on her notepad. She composed a brief shopping list based on a website she'd read that stated that both men and women in the workforce are more impressed by blue than by any other color: "khaki pencil skirt, navy blazer." She drew lines through her list and scribbled, "BORING." As Rodney spoke, she sketched a caricature of him, and added a speech balloon filled with, "Fee! Fi! Foe! Fum!"

Her boss called for a break, and Sarah flipped her pad shut and rose to socialize with those pouring second cups of coffee.

"Hello," Rodney said as he approached. "I'm Rodney Blake."

"Sarah Ross." She extended her hand politely.

Rodney took her hand and held it a moment too long, before saying, "I noticed that you've been taking notes, and I wondered if you might be willing to share them with my team."

Sarah blushed. There was nothing even remotely worthy of sharing on her pad. "I don't think I can really add anything to the handouts," she stammered. "I'm mostly here to keep track of any questions that your team asks us and, so far, there haven't been any."

Rodney laughed. "Okay. But then, I have to ask what you've been writing?"

Gary, her boss, appeared next to Rodney. "Sarah's a doodler." He laughed.

Sarah cringed.

"She can't think without a pencil in her hand," Gary continued. "When she joined the team I thought it meant she wasn't paying attention, but our psychologist told me some people concentrate by doodling. So, I decided to let it go and," he placed his hand on Sarah's shoulder, "she is developing into a really fine, little promotions assistant."

Sarah wanted to punch him. She forced herself to smile, excused herself, then walked away and struck up a conversation with one of the women. The meeting resumed and Sarah forced herself to listen without doodling.

When the meeting ended, Rodney approached her. He smiled and she noticed how his eyes crinkled at the corners—not really crow's-feet, but he was older than she'd thought.

He said softly, "It was a pleasure meeting you, Sarah Ross. Perhaps next time you'll allow me to see your notes."

Sarah blushed again and remembered the touch of his hand.

Rodney's smile deepened. "Don't worry," he said, "your secrets are safe with me."

Sarah hated her blush, but there was no way to control it. "I have no secrets," she managed to say.

Gary clapped Rodney on the shoulder, forcing his attention away from Sarah.

She made her escape.

***

The next morning, Rodney called and asked her to lunch.

Sarah considered saying no but her interest was piqued, and he was an attractive, albeit older, man.

From that day on, he courted her. The fifteen-year difference in their ages melted away as he introduced her to his sophisticated world full of wealthy and powerful people.

Claire told her to enjoy the ride but to keep her wits about her.

Sarah rolled her eyes at her best friend and declared that she was in love.

Claire didn't believe in "meet cute" or love at first sight and spoke out against both.

Six months later, when Rodney proposed, on a dive trip in the Bahamas, Sarah accepted without reservation.

Arriving back home, she'd called Claire. "Guess what?" Sarah bubbled.

"Is this my old friend, Sarah?" Claire responded. "It's been so long since I spent any time with her that I'm not sure I'd recognize her voice."

"Claire, don't be like that. I sent you an email just last week."

"Two weeks ago, actually, and you ignored my invitation to meet for dinner."

"Rodney and I were planning a trip and the time just got away. I'm sorry. You know you're my best friend."

"I like to think I am, but we talk so seldom that I hardly know you anymore."

"I miss you, too. But Rodney makes plans for almost every day." Sarah giggled. "Sometimes we have lunch and dinner together. Please, don't be mad at me. I have something I want to tell you. Meet me for a drink after work, okay?"

CHAPTER FOUR

NOW DAY 1: Thursday 01/25 EVENING

Sarah glanced around the dining room, avoiding Rodney's eyes, looking for something to say in response to his disparaging remarks. She forced herself to stay calm and act like everything was okay.

Rodney placed a glass of wine in front of her. "Sarah." His tone turned her name into a command.

She looked up, met the cold fury in his eyes, and gulped.

"Welcome home, darling." He tilted his glass toward her and took a sip.

"Jeremy," Rodney moved his gaze from Sarah to the boy, "tell your mother about school. She's been gone a few days."

"I've started a new school."

"Jeremy is only six," Sarah blurted, staring at the boy.

The boy looked at Rodney.

Rodney nodded.

"Yes, I'm six," the boy said carefully, "but Father says I'm very bright. I go to a special school in the city that is just for boys like me. My reading skills are above average and I've adjusted well."

Sarah couldn't take her eyes off this boy. He sounded so strange, not like a kid at all. He had to be at least a year, maybe two or even three years, older than her son. *But that isn't old enough to tell such detailed lies, is it?*

"Father takes me into the city with him in the morning. After school I attend the sports program, and a driver brings me home at six."

"Unless I'm done with work early," Rodney added. "If I can, I pick Jeremy up at school and we come home together." His lips twisted in a tight smile as he considered Sarah. "Mrs. Hendricks has agreed to come early and stay late until you feel better, darling. The doctor thinks it would be a good idea that someone is here all the time. You shouldn't be alone until your memory has returned and we can be sure that there are no lasting effects from your head injury."

Sarah's hand trembled as she reached for her wine glass. She needed to stall before she said the wrong thing. The wine was too sweet and left a strange aftertaste in her mouth. "What is this?" she asked, indicating the wine.

"Don't you like it?"

"It's rather sweet."

"It's a Maryhill Zinfandel. I think it will be excellent with the lamb chops we are having tonight." Rodney took another sip. "It doesn't seem overly sweet to me."

Sarah paused, remembering how much Rodney hated to be questioned, how he never tolerated any hint of criticism. She spoke carefully. "It's fine. And it will be perfect with lamb. Thank you." She took another sip and set the glass to the side.

"Do I like lamb chops?" the boy asked Rodney.

Rodney chuckled. "No," he answered. "But I believe you are having chicken."

"Good." Jeremy smiled at Rodney. "Thank you."

"Your manners have certainly improved," Sarah commented.

"I'm getting older now, Mother. And Father likes me to behave at the table."

"Don't worry, Sarah. I'm sure he's as rough-and-tumble as always when he's with his friends."

Sarah caught the frown Rodney directed at the boy. *What was that all about? Whoever this kid might be, he certainly isn't my son.*

The dinner, served by the housekeeper, tasted wonderful. Sarah hadn't realized how hungry she was. She couldn't remember the last time she'd eaten. "How long was I in the hospital?" she asked.

"It doesn't matter. You're home with me now."

Sarah wanted to argue. It did matter. Why was Rodney avoiding all her questions? Instead, she finished her wine and allowed him to pour her a second glass. When dessert was served, Sarah received a slice of papaya instead of the chocolate tower that was placed in front of Rodney and the boy. She felt Rodney watching her reaction. He knew she hated papaya.

"Eat up, darling. I know you want to lose weight, so I've instructed the staff to help you."

Sarah laid her fork down and finished her wine. "I'm very tired," she said, still determined not to argue. "If you'll excuse me, I'd like to go to bed now."

"Certainly." Rodney rose politely.

The boy followed his example and sprang to his feet.

"I hope you feel better soon, Mother."

"Thank you." She turned her head toward the boy and the room spun. For a second, Sarah was afraid she'd fall. She seized the back of her chair to steady herself.

Rodney grabbed her arm. "I'll take you to your room."

Take me? Sarah let go of the chair. "I'm fine."

Rodney's lips twisted into a sneer. He placed his hand on Sarah's back and moved her to the door. "Say good night to your son."

Sarah looked at the boy and managed to say, "Good night."

Rodney's hand tightened as he steered her out of the dining room and marched her up the stairs and down the hall to her bedroom.

Sarah didn't protest or try to get away. Her heart pounded in her chest and the walls seemed to undulate. She rubbed her eyes with her free hand.

"Feeling done in, darling?" Rodney purred. "A good night's sleep will help."

He let go of her arm and Sarah stepped into the bedroom. The bed was turned back and a pure white nightgown lay ready.

"Tomorrow," Rodney said.

Was that a threat? "What happens tomorrow?" Sarah asked.

The door closed and she heard the lock click into place. Rodney didn't answer.

CHAPTER FIVE

NOW DAY 2: Friday 01/26 MORNING

Sarah jerked awake. "What the—!" She pushed herself to a sitting position. Her eyes roamed the room. It hadn't been a bad dream; she was in a strange bedroom. And Jeremy was gone.

Sarah grabbed her hair with both hands and pulled on it. "Enough," she said to the empty room. "I'm not an idiot. That kid is not my son, and whatever Rodney is trying to pull, I've had enough of his bullshit."

She stood, strode to the window, and pushed back the heavy drapes. The drifts of snow seemed deeper. It must have snowed again last night. One set of tire tracks marked the long driveway. She could see no other sign of life. Sarah shivered and rubbed her arms, lifted one hand, and placed her palm flat against the glass. "I'll find you, Jeremy," she vowed. "Try not to be afraid. Mommy's coming."

Crossing the soft carpet, Sarah reached for the doorknob. She remembered the sound of the lock turning and hesitated. *Surely, he won't leave me locked in all day.* The knob didn't turn. Tears filled her eyes and she brushed them away, impatient with herself.

Sarah lifted her fist and knocked. She pressed her ear to the door and listened carefully. Somewhere a vacuum hummed. *I'll shower and get dressed and then, if I have to, I'll go out the window.*

Sarah washed her face, brushed her teeth, and took a quick shower. She found makeup in the cabinet but put on only moisturizer, lip gloss, and mascara.

She studied her face in the mirror. The bruise on her forehead had a greenish hue. *It must be at least a week old*, she thought. *I remember leaving work on Friday. I picked up Jeremy at after-school care and I let him choose a frozen dinner when I stopped to buy vodka.* She searched her memory. *He chose a potpie, the one in the green box.* Sarah pulled her wet hair up into a messy ponytail and crossed the room to the closet.

The large empty space yielded one pair of soft gray woolen slacks and a white cashmere sweater. "One outfit at a time, I guess," she said. The dresser drawer held one pair of light gray socks, one bra, and one pair of panties. "What game is he playing?" she asked her reflection.

Sarah dressed in the clothing and searched for shoes. She found only a pair of soft white cloth slippers, neatly placed by her bed. She slipped her feet into them and approached the door again. Pressing her ear to the wood, she heard nothing, raised her hand to knock, and then dropped it to the knob. The knob turned easily.

If Rodney put the clothes in my room, he must have snuck in while I was in the shower! A shiver ran up her spine. *Or, last night while I slept! Either way, this is creepy. I need to figure out what is going on.*

She forced herself to take deep breaths, in through her nose out through her mouth. She slowed her breathing and brought up her last memories of being with her son. *Jeremy ate dinner and I had a drink. We played Cootie for a while and then I let Jeremy watch TV. A normal Friday night.*

She stepped into the hall, looked in both directions, and turned toward the stairwell.

Silence.

"Okay, I can do this," she whispered and headed downstairs.

***

"Good morning, Mrs. Blake."

Sarah jumped and clung to the handrail.

Mrs. Hendricks stood watching her from the bottom of the stairs. "Sorry, I didn't mean to startle you."

"It's fine. and please, call me Sarah. I haven't been Mrs. Blake for a long time."

Mrs. Hendricks smiled slightly and shook her head. "Mr. Blake said you might still be confused. If you go into the dining room, I'll bring you coffee and your breakfast."

An image of the stark, elegant dining room flashed through her mind. "I'm more a kitchen kind of girl."

Mrs. Hendricks frowned. "Mr. Blake won't like that."

"He's not here, is he?"

The housekeeper shook her head. "You just missed him."

"All right then. Let's go to the kitchen. Lead the way."

Reluctantly, Mrs. Hendricks followed Sarah's order and led her down the hall past the dining room and into the spacious kitchen. Sarah took in the granite countertops, the gleaming appliances, and the Italian tile backsplash. Nothing looked familiar.

Sarah seated herself on a bench in the cozy breakfast nook. Cradling the mug of coffee Mrs. Hendricks placed in front of her, she considered the situation. She needed information, and right now, there was only one source.

"This is excellent coffee," she said, smiling at the housekeeper.

"Thank you. Mr. Blake said you'd want only toast and half a grapefruit for breakfast. Is that enough?"

Sarah nodded. "Have you worked for Rodney long?'

"No, just a few days. He hired me while you were in the hospital."

"How long was I in the hospital?"

Mrs. Hendricks looked surprised. "I'm not sure. You should ask Mr. Blake."

"Not being able to remember is so hard." Sarah dropped her eyes and swiped away pretend tears.

"Don't worry, dear. I'm sure it will all come back to you. I don't know exactly when you had your accident, but I'd guess a couple of weeks ago."

Mrs. Hendricks set Sarah's meager breakfast on the table and refilled her mug.

"Jeremy is a lovely boy." She smiled at Sarah. "Charming manners, and not any bother at all."

Except that kid is not Jeremy. Sarah gazed out the window at the snow-filled yard and composed herself. "Do you live in?" she asked.

"Oh, no. Mr. Blake takes care of the boy's breakfast. I come at two in the afternoon and stay until after dinner. I tidy up, make the beds and do laundry, and things like that."

Sarah looked at the clock. "It's only nine-thirty."

Mrs. Hendricks chuckled. "I'm sure Mr. Blake explained that I'd be here with you in the daytime until the doctor is sure you're okay."

Sarah nodded. "Did you unlock my bedroom door?"

Mrs. Hendricks looked confused. "I don't understand."

"When I woke up, my bedroom door was locked."

"I don't think so. Why would that be? Maybe you turned it the wrong way."

Sarah picked up the slice of unbuttered toast and took a bite. *I have to get out of here before he starves me to death.* Sarah smiled at the housekeeper. "Is there a newspaper around here?"

"No. If one is delivered to the house, Mr. Blake must take it with him to work."

"Television?"

"In the office, but Mr. Blake doesn't want you to be upset. He asked that I keep that door locked until he says otherwise."

"Telephone?"

Mrs. Hendricks looked surprised. "I'm sure you have a cell phone, don't you?"

"Of course," Sarah said. "I had a cell phone, but I think Rodney took it."

"Now, why would he do that? I'm sure you just mislaid it." Mrs. Hendricks filled a glass with water and placed it on the table. She pulled a small bottle from her pocket and shook out a tablet. "The doctor wants you to take one of these pills after breakfast."

Sarah held out her hand for the bottle. She examined the blank label. "What are they?"

"Mr. Blake didn't say, just that you need one to keep the headaches away."

"Just leave it by the water. I'll take it when I finish my breakfast."

Mrs. Hendricks complied.

Sarah glared at the pill. *Like hell I'll swallow that.*

She waited for Mrs. Hendricks to turn her back and busy herself at the sink. Then Sarah slipped the pill into her pocket and left the kitchen.

She headed down the hall to the stairway. On the right, she passed the open doorway of the dining room. To her left were heavily curtained French doors. *Maybe that's Rodney's office.* No light or shadow penetrated the curtain. She twisted the knobs, but the doors were locked.

Stopping in the entry, Sarah gazed into a large living room and then walked to the double doors of the front entrance. Through the sidelight, the veranda and the snow-covered yard stood empty. She felt certain it was the same view she'd studied from her bedroom window. She glanced up and admired the large crystal chandelier. This whole place looked like a hotel.

She turned around and faced the stairs.

The wide hallway to the left stretched past four more doors, every one of which was tightly closed. Sarah climbed the stairs to her room, taking time to examine the layout of the house.

One of those doors must be a coat closet, she reasoned. *Or perhaps, in a house this big, everyday coats are kept somewhere else. Maybe there is a mudroom off the kitchen with warm jackets, boots, hats, and gloves. If I can find my coat and boots, maybe I can leave.*

The stairway turned, and her view of the first floor disappeared.

Sarah paused before climbing the final steps and looked down through an ornate leaded glass window into what she surmised must be the backyard. Here too, the snow lay unbroken by footsteps, but it was a different view from the one she'd seen from her bedroom window. Shadows slanted across the snow toward the woods.

West, she decided. *If the backyard is west, the house must face east. Not that I know where I am, but I think my bedroom window faces east.*

Sarah finished the climb and stopped at the top to listen. She could hear a radio playing in the kitchen but could sense no movement from anywhere in the house. Wherever Rodney was, he was not in the house.

Her bedroom door stood open. Making a quick choice, she hurried to the room that the boy had indicated was his.

The door was unlocked. Sarah took a shuddering breath and stepped inside. The room was large, with a window seat tucked into a bay window.

Oh, Jeremy would love this, she thought, looking around. A set of bunk beds, perfectly made, with blue ripcord duvets pulled smooth and pillows carefully tucked into matching shams, stood against one wall. *If,* Sarah thought, *this was really Jeremy's room, Gaffy would be placed on the bed waiting for him to come home from school.* She lifted a pillow to check for the scruffy, well-loved stuffed giraffe that was Jeremy's constant companion. The giraffe was not there.

Canvas bins lined a storage unit on the far wall. She pulled out a red bin and stared at the LEGO kits piled inside. Not one appeared to have been opened. She knew Jeremy always ripped a new kit open right away, even if he wasn't going to put it together until later. Quickly she searched the other toy bins. None contained loose LEGOs. "Impossible," she muttered.

There were plenty of games and puzzles, and one bin held art supplies, but nothing looked used, and nothing looked like anything Jeremy played with or asked for. She opened the closet and took in the array of brand-new clothing. Sarah removed a pair of slacks from their hanger and examined the tag—size eight. *I bought Jeremy size-six jeans just a few days ago. Or at least I think it was only a few days ago. I need to find out what day it is!*

She glanced around for a calendar but found none. The bookshelves were filled with colorful books and robot figures. Sarah shook her head. Jeremy was afraid of robots. This absolutely couldn't be his room.

She pulled a copy of *Encyclopedia Brown, Boy Detective* from the shelf. It, too, was brand new. Not the worn, dog-eared copy she read aloud while Jeremy curled up beside her on the bed. Tears streamed down her face, and she brushed them away.

Exiting the boy's room, Sarah tried the other doors along the upstairs corridor. They were all locked except for her bedroom. Not even an extra bathroom was open.

I have no idea where I am, she thought. *Nor what day it is. But there must be a way to figure out at least those two things.*

Sarah stepped into her bedroom, crossed the room, entered the bathroom, and flushed the pill down the drain. Then, catching a glimpse of herself in a full-length mirror, she stopped and considered her reflection. Her dark blond hair had escaped from its scrunchie and hung in curly tendrils around her face. Impatiently she pulled the hair tie out and twisted her hair into a tight knot at the nape of her neck, smoothing away every trace of curl. "How can I look so normal when everything is so wrong?" she asked herself.

She pulled at her sweater and ran her hands over her slacks, twisting back and forth to see herself from all angles. The clothes were flattering and they fit exceptionally well, but they weren't her style and they weren't comfortable. "Better than nothing, I guess," she shook her head, "but I'd rather have my old jeans and boots."

Turning from the mirror, Sarah searched the room again, hoping to find anything at all that would explain what was happening. She opened each dresser drawer, but they were as empty as they'd been the night before. On an ornate writing desk against the wall between the two large windows, someone had arranged a small clock, a vase filled with dark red roses, and a candle in a charming vignette.

Sarah strode across the room and opened the desk drawer. Empty. She lifted the clock. It was digital and should have told the date and time, but the numbers were frozen at 04:06. The battery compartment was empty. "Damn, Rodney!" She threw the clock on the unmade bed, grabbed the roses, and thrust them into the bathroom wastebasket.

04:06? Our wedding date was April sixth! Is this a coincidence or a message? Sarah's heart raced and she willed her hands to stop shaking. She picked up the clock, carried it to the desk and returned it to its place.

Slamming the bedroom door behind her, she stormed downstairs.

Mrs. Hendricks looked genuinely concerned as Sarah rushed into the kitchen. "Is everything alright, dear? You don't have a headache, do you?"

Sarah shook her head. Either the woman was a great actress or she didn't know anything. "No, I'm fine. I was just thinking I'd like to go out and get some fresh air."

"It's below zero out there. I'm sure Mr. Blake would want you to stay inside."

I don't really give a damn what Rodney wants, Sarah thought.

She smiled at Mrs. Hendricks. "I've been confined for too many days. I need to stretch my legs."

"Well, don't go too far."

"I won't." Sarah moved to the kitchen door. "Do you know where my heavy coat is?"

Mrs. Hendricks shook her head and made a tsking sound with her tongue. "You really can't remember this house, can you?"

"I can't. I don't think I've ever been here before."

"You poor thing. I guess Mr. Blake is right. You do need me to ensure your safety until he gets home each day. Just wait until I finish tidying the house, then I'll find your coat and take a walk with you."

Sarah bit her lip and forced back the sharp retort that sprang to mind. *This woman is my jailer. A very polite jailer, certainly, but my jailer, nonetheless. First, I need to convince her I'm sane and healthy. Then, I need to figure out a way around the orders Rodney has given her.*

"Do you know if there are any books in the house?" she asked. "I'd like to read while I wait."

"I'm sorry, dear. Perhaps tonight you could ask Mr. Blake to unlock his office. I believe all the books are in there."

"I'll just pop up to the boy's—Jeremy's—room and borrow one of his and then wait in my room."

"Lovely idea. I'm sure reading something you know your son enjoys will be a comfort. I need to finish Mr. Blake's bedroom and bath and do a few things. I'll only be an hour or so, and then we can get that fresh air."

"Thank you." Sarah forced herself to sound sweet instead of sarcastic. "You go ahead. I'll just pour myself another cup of coffee and take it upstairs with me."

CHAPTER SIX

NOW DAY 2: Friday 01/26 AFTERNOON & EVENING

Mrs. Hendricks left the kitchen, and Sarah let out a sigh of relief. She watched as the housekeeper walked past the stairwell and down the hall until it branched to the right and she disappeared from view. *Rodney's bedroom must be down there. I thought the boy told me that the master bedroom was upstairs at the end of the hall. He should know where his dad sleeps.*

Sarah poured her coffee and carried the cup back to the stairwell.

She paused at the bottom of the stairs and listened. The loud hum of the vacuum reached her ears.

Carefully, Sarah placed her cup on the flat top of the newel post and walked silently down the hall and around the corner. Double doors opened wide to a magnificent large bedroom.

Sarah covered her mouth to stop the sound of her gasp.

It was bigger than her whole cabin. The brocade comforter and all the furniture—in fact, everything in the house—looked expensive. Where was he getting this much money? He earned a lot, but not this much.

She moved silently to the doorway and peeked in. The bedding had been flung back as if Rodney had just exited the bed. A tall pier-glass mirror stood in the corner. Mrs. Hendricks was reflected in the glass, her back turned to the bedroom door. Sarah took a chance and stepped into the doorway just far enough to scan the room.

A bathroom door stood open, as did the door to a large closet. She craned her neck to see into the closet. The space appeared to be filled with men's clothing. Against the far corner, a desk was covered in files and loose paper.

The vacuum stopped. Sarah scurried away, her heart pounding. *I need to get back into that room*, she thought. *Those papers may tell me what is going on.*

***

Safely sheltered in her room, Sarah leaned against the closed door and forced herself to calm down. A knock caused her to jump. Her whole body trembled. She bit her lip and managed to ask, "Who is it?"

"Just me, Mrs. Blake."

Sarah turned and opened the door.

Mrs. Hendricks extended a coffee mug. "You left your coffee on the stairs."

"Thank you." Sarah reached for the mug, her hand still trembling.

The housekeeper frowned. "You look very pale, Mrs. Blake. You'd better sit down. I'll just put your coffee on the table for you." She walked past Sarah, entered the bedroom, and crossed to the table. She placed the cup on a coaster and glanced back over her shoulder. "Come sit down. The coffee will perk you up. Drink it before it goes cold."

Sarah stayed by the door. "I want to get a book from the boy's room."

She turned and fled.

In the boy's bedroom, she pulled a thin volume from the shelf, took a deep breath, and walked slowly back to her bedroom. Mrs. Hendricks was making the bed. She looked up and smiled.

Sarah murmured, "Thank you," as she crossed the room and sat at the table.

She lifted the mug to her lips and took a sip. The coffee had cooled too much to drink.

Sarah set it down and picked up the book. Running her finger over the title, *A Wrinkle in Time*, she smiled. *If I really wanted to read a book, I made a good choice.*

Mrs. Hendricks finished the bed. She turned to Sarah and said, "You read a bit, and I'll finish in here later, okay?"

Sarah nodded. She waited until the housekeeper exited. Then she opened the book. A piece of paper was folded in half and tucked between the dust jacket and the inside cover. Sarah set the book on the table, extracted the paper, and unfolded it. She skimmed the typed list:

1. Jeremy Blake – age 6, well mannered, privileged, attends Anderson Academy, grade 1, very bright
2. Rodney Blake – father
3. Sarah Blake – mother, has been in hospital, mental problems
4. Mrs. Hendricks – housekeeper
5. No cell phone or computer or personal items allowed in house

She read it again and then again. It sounded like a list of reminders. But why would the kid need reminders, and why would he hide it? She read it one more time, then she folded the note into a smaller square and placed it under the table lamp. Picking up the cold coffee, she carried it to the bathroom and dumped it down the drain.

A residue of brown sludge remained in the cup.

Sarah touched it with the tip of her finger. It felt sticky.

She tasted the sticky substance with the end of her tongue. Bitter, but mostly it tasted of coffee. Sarah rubbed her temples and stared into the cup. *Maybe I'm paranoid, but I'm sure there's something wrong with this coffee. What did Hendricks put in it and why?*

Sarah returned to the bedroom, placed the cup back on the coaster, and picked up the book.

Instead of reading, Sarah thought about what she'd discovered. Nothing made any sense. As a list maker, Sarah's first thought was to write down her impressions. She searched her bedroom and attached bathroom room for paper and pen but found nothing except an eyebrow pencil and Kleenex.

She slapped the vanity counter and muttered, "Damn it! Think! The kid must have paper and pens."

Leaving her room, she paused as she passed the stairwell and listened. She heard movement in the kitchen area and quickly walked down the hall toward the boy's room.

Sarah twisted the doorknob. It didn't turn.

"Unbelievable!" She wrenched the knob again. "Shit! It's locked."

Furious, she turned back, stomped down the stairs, and headed for the kitchen.

As Sarah entered, Mrs. Hendricks looked up and smiled. "There you are. I was just coming to get you." She held up a pea coat and a bright red scarf. "I found this. It looks nice and warm."

Sarah took a deep breath and forced her anger away. She reached for the coat. "Thank you."

"You're welcome, dear. There are gloves in the pockets, but I couldn't find any boots. I'm afraid you'll need to stay on the veranda."

Sarah looked down at her feet. "I don't have any shoes."

"Of course you do. Did you look in your closet?"

Sarah gestured toward her slacks and sweater. "This was all that there was in my closet."

"Surely not."

Sarah nodded. "Yep. No shoes. One outfit."

Mrs. Hendricks clicked her tongue and shook her head. "Heavens. I wonder where your clothes are?"

In the cabin. Aloud, she said, "Me, too."

"There must be a reason. Why don't you ask Mr. Blake tonight? I'm sure he can explain it." She shook her head and clicked her tongue again. "It's below zero out there, so you certainly can't go out in socks and slippers."

"Where did you find the coat?"

Mrs. Hendricks flushed. "It's mine, dear. I looked in all the closets, but I couldn't find your coat."

"Because I don't live here." Sarah sank onto the bench in the nook. She propped her elbows on the table and held her head in her hands. Tears threatened and she forced them away.

"Of course you live here. You just don't remember, but you will," Mrs. Hendricks said.

Sarah muttered, "Yeah, right."

Mrs. Hendricks stretched out her hand and patted Sarah on the back. "Your husband is a lovely man, dear. You need to be patient a bit longer, just until your poor brain heals."

"There's nothing wrong with my brain!" Sarah frowned at the housekeeper and shrugged off her comforting hand. "I need a pen and a piece of paper." She stood and looked around the kitchen. She crossed to the counter and pulled open the top drawer. *Success!* she thought, pulling out a yellow legal pad. She rummaged a bit but didn't find a pen or pencil. Her shoulders slumped.

Mrs. Hendricks watched and then pulled a pencil from her pocket and handed it to Sarah.

Sarah mumbled her thanks and returned to the breakfast nook. She pulled the pad of paper close and stared at the blank page.

Finally, she wrote: *I am Sarah Blake, née Ross.* She paused and then, pressing the pencil into the paper, drew a line of question marks.

Sarah tapped her pencil on the table and stared at the question marks she'd drawn across the pad. She had to figure this out. She wrote: *Where is Jeremy?—Why would Rodney do this?—How do I get out of here?* She sighed.

Mrs. Hendricks turned from the sink and studied her. "Is everything all right, dear?" she asked. "Can I get you something?"

Sarah ripped the paper from the pad and crumpled it into a ball.

"Does Rodney work in Seattle?"

Mrs. Hendricks smiled. "Of course not. His office is in Wenatchee."

Sarah doodled on the yellow pad as she considered how to ask her next question. *Wenatchee makes no sense at all,* she thought. *We lived in Seattle when Jeremy was born and that's where we lived when I divorced him. My cabin is by Alta Lake, so maybe fifty or sixty miles from this house, if this house is in Wenatchee.*

"I remember when we lived in Seattle. His office was downtown, by Pioneer Square. He was so happy there I'm surprised he moved."

Mrs. Hendricks lifted an eyebrow. "Wenatchee is a lovely little city. I'm sure you both thought it was a good place to raise your son."

Sarah glanced down at her pad and wrote: *Divorced, 2 years ago.*

"Is this house really in Wenatchee? The house is surrounded by woods and it's so quiet."

Mrs. Hendricks's eyes darted around the room. She crossed her arms and then looked toward Sarah. "Why are you asking these questions?"

Sarah dropped her eyes, bit her lip, and then pretended to wipe away a tear. She kept her eyes on the table as she answered, "I'm trying to remember. I know Rodney wants me to." She sniffled. "Everything is just so confusing."

"You poor thing." Mrs. Hendricks crossed the kitchen and settled into the breakfast nook across from Sarah. "Maybe I can help you."

Sarah looked up and produced a grateful smile. "That would be wonderful." She picked up the pencil. "Please, help me remember. Maybe if you tell me a few things about this house I'll recognize something."

Mrs. Hendricks folded her hands on the tabletop. "I can't see what it would hurt. Although Mr. Blake told me not to let you get too excited."

"Did he say why the rooms are all locked?"

Mrs. Hendricks nodded. "That's for your own good. Your husband is afraid you'll hurt yourself again."

"Again?"

"Your accident," Mrs. Hendricks said and then paused.

Sarah's breath caught in her chest, and she was filled again with the terror of plowing through the snow, following Ajax, calling for Jeremy. She covered her mouth with her hand and forced her breathing back to normal. When she was calm, she asked, "Do you know what kind of accident I had?"

Mrs. Hendricks nodded. "You drove your car over an embankment." She stretched out a hand and covered Sarah's hand with her own. "Deliberately."

Sarah froze. Her mouth opened in surprise. She began to tremble. "But," she started to protest and stopped herself. *I'm positive Rodney said I fell down the stairs.*

"It's alright, dear. You're safe now."

Not hardly, Sarah thought, jerking herself back under control. "I was just surprised. I don't remember wanting to commit suicide. Jeremy and I like living in the cabin."

"There *is* no cabin. Mr. Blake told me you might talk about that but it isn't true. You live here, in this lovely home, with your husband and your son."

Sarah tilted her head and looked around the kitchen. "Tell me about this house. Please help me remember. How long have we lived here?"

"I don't know that. I only know that the house is on the edge of the Wenatchee National Forest. You and your husband own twenty acres out here and your home is in the middle of your acreage."

Sarah's mind raced. *Alta Lake is part of the same recreational area; maybe I'm closer to the cabin than I thought.* "Why do you know how much land this house has?" she asked carefully.

Mrs. Hendricks chuckled. "Mr. Blake mentioned it when he interviewed me. I think he was concerned that I might find it too isolated."

Sarah stood. She picked up the crumpled wad of paper and walked to the window over the sink. Looking outside, she said, "It *is* kind of isolated." She opened the cabinet under the sink and dropped the paper into the garbage.

Mrs. Hendricks applauded. "See, you knew right where to find the garbage!"

"I guess I did," Sarah agreed. "Do you think it would be okay if you walk me through the house and just tell me what's in each room?" She caught Mrs. Hendricks's eye and asked shyly, "Maybe I could just peek inside and see if I remember anything else."

Sarah waited as Mrs. Hendricks made the clicking noise with her tongue that was becoming familiar.

Finally, the housekeeper pushed her hands against the tabletop and stood up. "Let me grab my keys. I don't think Mr. Blake would mind a quick look-see."

Sarah kept her head, turned toward the kitchen doorway. But she watched from the corner of her eye as Mrs. Hendricks opened the upper cabinet to the left of the sink, shoved aside a stack of bowls, and retrieved a set of keys.

"Come along, dear. We'll give you a quick memory tour, and then I need to begin the dinner preparations."

Sarah's heart was pounding so hard in anticipation that she was surprised Mrs. Hendricks didn't turn to look at her. She picked up the pad and pencil from the table, took a long steadying breath, and followed the housekeeper out of the kitchen.

***

Later, with Mrs. Hendricks safely in the kitchen, busy with dinner preparations, Sarah settled herself in one of the slipper chairs in her bedroom and flipped to a clean page in the yellow pad. She drew a large rectangle and stopped to look out the window. The driveway was still empty.

During their walk through the house, Mrs. Hendricks had unlocked each room and provided only a quick glimpse of what lay behind each door.

Sarah closed her eyes and tried to remember what the house had looked like when they'd arrived yesterday. All she could recall was that it was enormous and brick, with a long veranda; a house she'd never seen before. An image of the boy standing on the snowy porch in front of large double doors filled her mind. She shook her head and said, "It doesn't matter. I can do this."

She carefully considered the blank rectangle and then drew a smaller rectangle at the midpoint and labeled it—stairs. Across from the stairs, she drew a symbol for the set of double doors she knew were directly opposite the stairwell; doors that opened to the front yard. Sarah added the other rooms she'd seen on the first floor— kitchen, living room, dining, office, and bedroom—labeling each. *Not great*, she thought, *but I think this will help.*

Sarah studied her drawing and placed an X to depict each locked and unexplored room. She quickly added the layout for the kitchen.

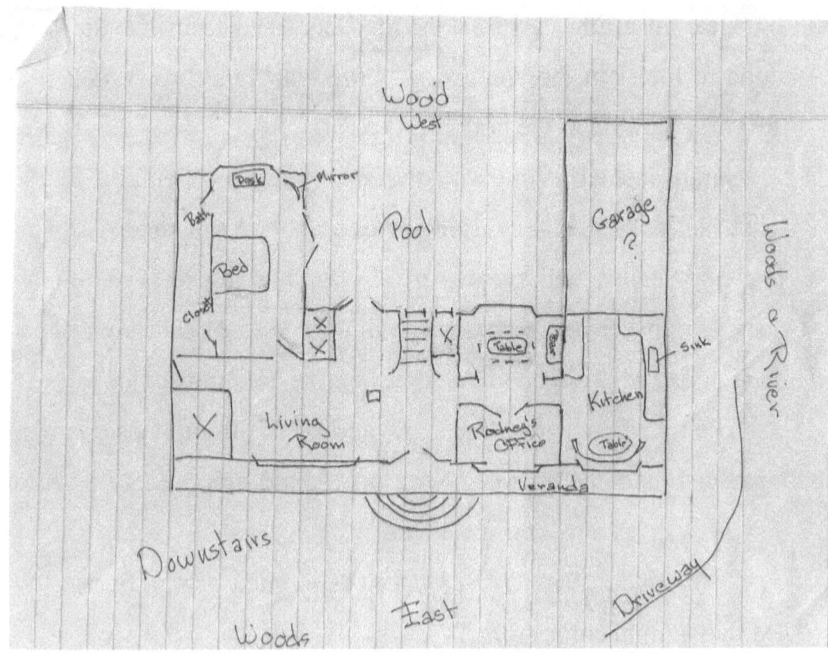

Then, keeping an eye on the drive, she drew a second rectangle and sketched in the second floor, adding X's for the locked areas.

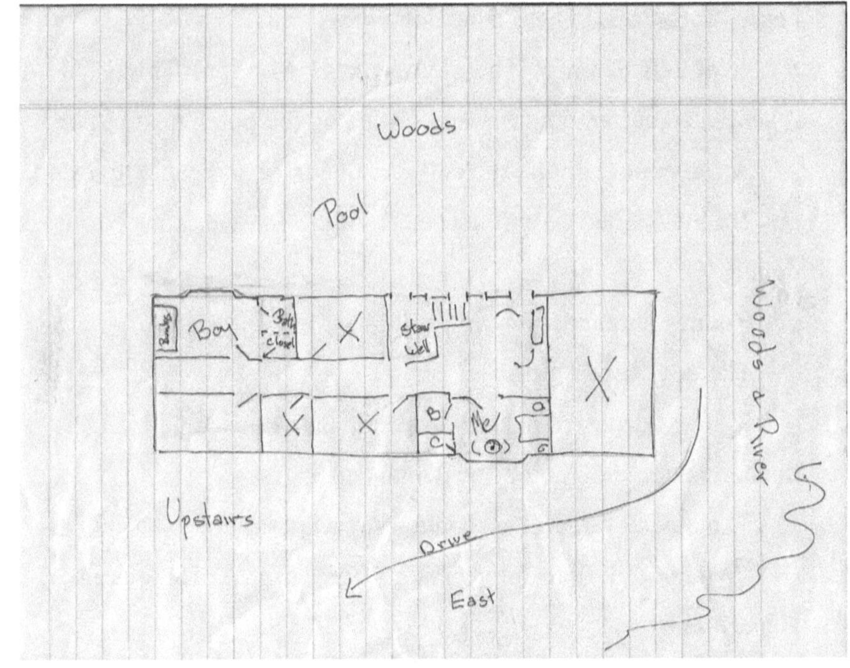

Hearing a dog bark, Sarah lifted her head from her drawing and stood to look out the window. A large black and brown dog stood in the yard, barking at the house. "Ajax!"

Sarah pushed at the window, attempting to open it. She tried to twist the locks, but they didn't budge. "Stay right there," she called. The dog leaped and twisted in circles, barking and yelping. Sarah rushed from her bedroom and ran down the stairs. She flung open the front door and dropped to her knees on the cold threshold.

The dog flew across the snow and up the front steps. He barreled into Sarah and she wrapped her arms around him. Tears flowed down her cheeks. "I knew you were real!"

"What is all this?" Mrs. Hendricks loomed behind Sarah. "Where did that animal come from?"

"It's Ajax," Sarah said. "It's Jeremy's dog."

Mrs. Hendricks gave a small gasp and pressed her hand to her heart. "It can't be. There is no dog in this house."

"Not *this* Jeremy! The *real* Jeremy! My son! This is his dog." Ajax licked at Sarah's tears and settled on the porch next to her.

A car swung around the curve in the drive and came to a stop. The boy Rodney called Jeremy leaped from the car and hurried to greet the dog.

Rodney shouted, "Jeremy, stop!"

The boy froze. "Yes, sir."

Rodney slammed his car door. His face flushed with anger. "What the hell is going on here?" he demanded.

The boy stayed still as Rodney strode past him.

"Where did that filthy thing come from?" He glared at Mrs. Hendricks.

The housekeeper blanched and stammered out, "Mrs. Blake says it's Jeremy's dog."

Rodney seemed to grow taller as he demanded, "You believe her? There was no dog in this house before; why do you think that that thing belongs to Jeremy?"

Mrs. Hendricks's mouth opened and closed, but no sound came out.

Rodney looked down. "Get up, Sarah."

Sarah didn't move.

"Now!" He stretched out a hand.

Sarah took it and allowed herself to be pulled to her feet. She knew Rodney could feel her trembling and bit the inside of her cheek to stop the flow of tears.

Rodney looked back over his shoulder. "Come here, son. Is this your dog?"

The boy approached slowly, dragging his feet and watching Rodney carefully. He shook his head. "No, sir."

"Thank you." Rodney gave a curt nod. "Go inside now and do your homework. Your mother and I need to have a talk."

The boy squeezed past Sarah and Ajax. He reached out to pet the dog but withdrew his hand without touching him, then disappeared from view.

Rodney glared at Sarah, his hands set on his hips, his fists clenched, and asked, "Did you women hear that? Jeremy does not have a dog."

"The real Jeremy does!" Sarah's eyes narrowed as she faced Rodney.

Rodney's face contorted. His hand shot out and he grasped Sarah's upper arm. "What is wrong with you? You have to stop this nonsense. Imagine how our son feels when you say things like that."

"Things like the truth?"

Rodney's grip tightened on her arm.

Sarah gasped at the pain.

He turned his gaze to the housekeeper. "Get rid of this mutt. I'll deal with you later."

Keeping a tight hold on Sarah's arm, he marched her from the porch, across the entry, and to his office. Sarah struggled to break free when he reached into his pocket for the key, but Rodney's grip tightened.

He unlocked the door and swung it open, banging it against the wall, and pushed her into the room. "Sit!" he demanded.

Sarah sank to the edge of a chair and sat trembling, twisting her hands together, trying to control her fear. Her breath came in ragged gasps.

Rodney towered over her, his fists clenched.

"You need to stop causing trouble, Sarah. I'm tired of being embarrassed by you. You know damn well that you're my wife, and that kid is our kid. If you can't get on board with reality, maybe you'd like another trip to rehab." He stepped back and unclenched his fists.

Sarah took a deep breath and stared down at her hands. "I don't understand, Rodney." Slowly she raised her eyes and studied him. "Why are you doing this?" she asked.

Rodney cocked an eyebrow and swept his hand through the air. "This?"

Sarah's eyes didn't leave his face. "You know what I mean. Why am I here? Whose house is this, anyway? I can't believe it's yours."

Rodney sneered. "It's our house, darling." He reached out and cupped her cheek. "I'm not doing anything, Sarah. You are a suicidal alcoholic, and I am your loving, loyal, long-suffering husband."

"But, Ajax—"

"Shut up about that damn dog!" He pulled his hand away and stepped back. "Get up. You need to apologize to Jeremy and Mrs. Hendricks, and then I'll take you to your room."

Sarah shook her head.

"Now, Sarah."

Her stomach lurched at the memory of other times when she'd defied him. She stood and wrapped her arms tight around herself.

He kept one hand on the small of her back and propelled her to the kitchen.

Mrs. Hendricks stood at the range, stirring something in a large kettle. She looked up and smiled at Sarah.

Rodney glanced between the two women and frowned. "How did you get outside? Who unlocked the door?"

Mrs. Hendricks gasped; the spoon clattered to the floor. She took in Sarah's pale face and trembling hands, then she steadied herself, looked Rodney squarely in the eye, and said, "I washed the sidelights this morning, inside and out. Unfortunately, I must have left the door unlocked. I'm sorry, Mr. Blake."

"I warned you about that." His icy gaze narrowed, and his lips thinned. He moved to close the gap between himself and the housekeeper.

Sarah interrupted. "For heaven's sake, Rodney. The door was locked."

Rodney halted his move and turned back to Sarah as she continued: "I simply turned the bolt and opened it. Are you trying to keep me a prisoner," she cocked an eyebrow and twisted her lips, "in my own home?"

"Of course not." Rodney's angry tone disappeared. "I'm just worried about you. I want to keep you safe."

Sarah nodded, keeping her eyes fastened on his. "An egress door that doesn't open from the inside certainly wouldn't be safe."

"You're right, darling. I don't know what I was thinking." He dropped his voice to a whisper and hissed, "You aren't likely to go farther than the doorway without shoes."

"Mrs. Hendricks." He turned back to the housekeeper. His lips parted in a charming smile. "I apologize for my behavior. I certainly didn't mean to sound angry. I'm just so worried about Mrs. Blake's health."

Mrs. Hendricks nodded her acceptance.

"All of this excitement has been too much for my wife. I think it would be best if she eats dinner in her room tonight." Rodney took Sarah's hand and turned her toward the kitchen door. He looked back over his shoulder and asked, "Did you get rid of that dog?"

"Yes, sir. I shooed him off. He ran into the woods."

"Good. If you see him again, I expect you to call animal control. I don't like a strange dog hanging around the property."

Mrs. Hendricks picked up the dropped spoon and placed it in the sink. She kept her eyes averted and didn't respond, as she pulled open a drawer and extracted a clean spoon.

Sarah felt Rodney's hold on her hand tighten. She walked with him out of the kitchen, past the dining room, and to the stairwell before she said, "That dog is Ajax, and you know it. You gave him to Jeremy for his fourth birthday."

"You really are crazy, Sarah. Jeremy never saw that dog before in his life. You heard him say so."

Sarah climbed the stairs with Rodney one step behind. She wanted to scream.

Rodney said in a low voice, "You need to calm down, Sarah. All of this arguing will get you nowhere."

They reached the top of the stairs. Rodney took her arm again and walked beside her to the bedroom door. He gave her a little push and she stumbled through the doorway. "Oh dear, have you been drinking again?"

Sarah turned, her eyes flashing in anger. "You know I haven't. You pushed me."

Rodney chuckled, shaking his head.

A movement caught Sarah's attention. She slipped her eyes to the side and thought she saw the boy's door close.

Rodney turned to see what she was looking at. The hallway was vacant and silent. He stepped forward. Sarah stepped back. "Your dinner will be up in an hour or so. Why don't you take a nice warm bath and slip into something more comfortable." Rodney lifted his arm and cupped her shoulder with his hand.

Sarah was unable to stop her shiver.

He grinned as he slowly slid his hand down her arm, brushing against the side of her breast. "You need to be careful, darling."

The door closed behind him. Sarah heard the key turn in the lock. She stumbled to the bed and sat shaking; sobs wracked her body.

***

Mrs. Hendricks opened the under-sink cupboard to retrieve the dish soap. The flash of something yellow in the wastebasket caught her eye. She bent and pulled out Sarah's crumpled note. A step sounded in the hall, and she pushed it into her pocket.

"We need to have a talk," Rodney said.

When the housekeeper didn't speak, he continued, "I thought you understood how precarious Mrs. Blake's condition is."

"I do. She is very confused and frightened."

Rodney shook his head sadly. "You know she has nothing to fear. The doctor feels that by keeping her here, safe, in familiar surroundings, her memory will return. It is very important that we don't confuse her with too much information at one time. That is why it is imperative that you keep the rooms locked. The doctor believes that if she is exposed to too much stimulation, too fast, she may never recover."

"But, nothing is familiar to her. Maybe she needs to see something she can remember."

"Mrs. Hendricks, I believe the doctor knows best, don't you?"

She nodded rapidly.

"Good. When Sarah remembers that Jeremy is her son, she will be ready. She needs to stay in this house, protected until then. Understood?"

"Yes."

"Very well. If you can't handle this job, I'm sure I can find someone else." He watched her for a long moment and then said, "I'll be in my office. When dinner is ready, I'll take Sarah's tray up."

***

Mrs. Hendricks turned back to the stove. She touched the paper in her pocket, making sure it was concealed.

Upstairs, the boy turned on a video game and waited to be called to make an appearance.

Sarah forced her tears away and went to the window. She stared out at the broad, snow-covered lawn. Tracks led away from the house and into the woods. She strained to catch a glimpse of Ajax.

Nothing moved.

CHAPTER SEVEN

BEFORE: 9 Years Ago

Claire relented and agreed to meet Sarah after work. Sarah arrived early and waited at the Marcus Hotel bar, her hands folded around the stem of her vodka martini. The new diamond on her finger caught the light and flashed off the back bar mirror.

"That's some rock," Claire said, slipping onto the barstool next to Sarah. "I'm guessing that's your big news."

Sarah blushed and nodded. "Rodney asked me to marry him. And, I want you to be my maid of honor."

Claire signaled the bartender and ordered before asking, "Are you sure that that's what you want?"

Lifting her glass, Sarah took a careful sip and turned to face Claire. "Don't act that way."

Claire accepted her drink from the bartender. "What way?" she asked as she spun on her stool so that her knees pressed against Sarah's. "I asked a simple question. Are you sure that you want me at your wedding?"

"Of course I do. You're my best friend."

"Did you clear your invite with Rodney?"

Sarah looked away.

"I didn't think so." Claire set her drink on the bar and drew in a calming breath before saying, "Your husband-to-be doesn't like me."

"That's not true!" Sarah finished her martini and wiggled the empty glass toward the watching bartender, signaling for another. "You don't really know each other."

"I know enough. Your darling Rodney has made it perfectly clear he doesn't want you spending time with me."

"Claire, don't be jealous. I know I've neglected our friendship, but we're in love. Rodney and I like to spend time together."

"You've known the man, what—six months?"

"Seven," Sarah said.

"I stand corrected. Seven months. And you're going to marry him?"

"I am. I want to. My mom thinks I should."

"You're twenty-six; he's forty-one. What do you have in common?"

"I'm twenty-seven. He loves me, and I love him."

Claire shook her head. "That wasn't what I asked, but—" Claire stopped speaking as she caught sight of Rodney crossing the room.

Rodney spun Sarah's stool around and kissed her. "Hello there, what are you two beautiful ladies up to?"

Sarah blushed. Laughing, she said, "Rodney, what are you doing here?"

"I was lonely," he said. "I missed you, so I thought I'd take you both to dinner." He kept his hand on Sarah's shoulder as he turned to Claire. "Lovely to see you again, Claire. Have you been giving Sarah your congratulations?"

Claire gritted her teeth and then forced a smile. "Hello, Rodney. We hadn't gotten that far yet."

"I just asked Claire to be my maid of honor." Sarah reached out and touched Claire's hand. "You have to. I can't get married without you."

Rodney stood behind Sarah. He placed one hand on her shoulder and spun her stool to face himself.

"Darling," he said. "I thought we were just having a small ceremony with only family."

Sarah cocked her head to the side and smiled at Claire. "Claire's my best friend. She's family."

"Best friends are people you've known all your life. Didn't you two meet in college?"

"Actually," Claire said, setting her glass carefully down on the bar, "Sarah and I met at a club, not at college, about what?" She paused. "Two years ago, right? Remember you were dating that adorable guy. Todd?"

Sarah nodded rapidly, a small smile playing across her lips.

Rodney withdrew his hand from her shoulder.

Sarah frowned and looked at him.

"Todd wasn't anybody important."

Rodney signaled the bartender. "Allow me to pick up your tab, ladies. Claire, will you be joining us for dinner?"

"I don't think so. You two go ahead."

Sarah pleaded, "Claire, come on. It'll be fun. Rodney knows all the best places to eat."

The bartender stopped in front of the threesome. "Another round?"

"No thanks," Rodney said. "We're leaving." He pulled a credit card from his wallet and handed it over.

Claire lifted her glass and drained it quickly. "I'm staying. I'll have another."

Sarah faced Rodney. "I didn't even have time to talk to Claire yet. It's been months since we spent time together."

The bartender handed Rodney's card back.

Rodney waited.

Claire patted Sarah's hand. "You go, Sarah. I'll call you for lunch next week."

"You'd better." Sarah slid off her barstool and hugged her friend. "You didn't answer. Will you be my maid of honor?"

Claire looked directly at Rodney as she answered, "I'd love to. Have you set the date yet?"

"Soon, very soon," Rodney said. He wrapped his arm around Sarah, dropped a kiss on her hair, and turned her toward the door. "We need to hurry, Sarah. I have a reservation at Balthazar."

Claire watched them walk away.

"That her dad?"

The bartender's question pulled Claire's attention away from the couple. She smiled at him. "Nope, fiancé."

"To each his own, I guess."

Claire nodded and shrugged. She laid a twenty on the bar.

The bartender grinned. "No need. He was acting kind of like a jerk, so I put your drink on his tab."

Claire laughed. "Thanks!"

***

The following week, Claire left two messages for Sarah. The first on Monday, suggesting lunch on Wednesday; the second on Tuesday, again suggesting they meet for lunch on Wednesday. Sarah didn't return either message.

Finally, Friday afternoon, Claire called again, and this time Sarah answered.

She greeted Claire by saying, "I'm so sorry, it's been one of those weeks."

"Hey, not a problem. How are the wedding plans coming along?"

"I need to talk to you about that."

Claire stayed silent, waiting for Sarah to continue. When the silence dragged on, she asked, "Are you okay?"

Sarah spoke in a whisper. "I think so. It's just that…"

"Just what?"

Sarah gave a small sob.

Claire glanced at the clock on her computer. "It's almost three-thirty. Can you get away now?"

Sarah's voice trembled as she said, "Yeah. Okay. But I'll only have a few minutes. I can't be late."

"I can be at your office in about ten minutes. We'll just grab a glass of wine at the café next to you."

"No, meet me in the lobby, okay?"

"Sure, see you in a few." Claire shut down her computer and grabbed her purse. "I wonder what that's all about," she said to herself as she checked her makeup. "Everybody wants a happy hour glass of wine on Friday night. Sarah certainly sounds like she needs one."

***

Watching Sarah exit the elevator, Claire noticed how tired she looked. Instead of commenting, she hooked her arm through her friend's and said, "So, spill. Tell me what's up."

"Rodney will be here to pick me up a five fifteen. I can't be late."

"Okay." Claire looked around the lobby for a quiet corner. "Do you want to sit?"

"No. Can we walk?"

"Sure." Claire unhooked her arm from Sarah's. "Lead the way."

Sarah gave a little laugh. "I'm sure it's fine, but I didn't tell Rodney I was going to see you today, and he doesn't like surprises."

"In all honesty, you didn't know you would see me until ten minutes ago."

Sarah nodded and swallowed hard. "I know, but—" She shook her head. "It's okay. I'm just being silly." She looked around and then waved toward a grouping of chairs. "We don't need to walk. Let's sit over there."

Claire followed her across the lobby. They sat, and Sarah pulled out her phone. She glanced at the time. Claire said, "So tell me about your wedding plans."

Sarah fidgeted, opening and closing the clasp on her handbag. "Rodney doesn't want a wedding."

Claire raised an eyebrow. "I thought getting married so fast was his idea."

"He wants to get married, but he doesn't want any guests or anything. He doesn't have any family or friends that he wants to attend. He thinks it will look weird if the only family is mine." Sarah's eyes filled with tears. "I don't know why that upsets me. I love him, and that's what matters." She pulled a Kleenex from her bag and wiped carefully under each eye to ensure that her mascara hadn't smudged.

"I always wanted a big wedding. My mom and I used to talk about it all the time. When I was a kid, she'd let me wear her veil and her white satin high heels." Sarah swiped away another tear. "I wanted you to be my maid of honor and all my high school friends to be my attendants. I thought my groom would wear a morning coat and a top hat. I wanted an amazing gown with lace, and beads, and tons of crystals. The bridesmaids would wear shades of pink, and all the flowers would be pink and white, with lots of candles and champagne."

Claire smiled. "Sounds lovely. So why not have that wedding? You and your parents have enough friends to fill up the church."

"Rodney doesn't want it." She sighed and gave her head a shake. "He says he did all that the first time he was married, and he isn't willing to do it again."

"But, it's your first marriage."

"Rodney says it's our wedding, that it really is just for us, and that a bunch of people will just cost a lot of money. He hasn't met many of my friends and he thinks being surrounded by strangers would ruin the day."

Claire bit back her retort and settled on asking, "Why doesn't he have any friends or family?"

"It isn't that he doesn't have any. He knows lots of people." Sarah frowned. "Rodney doesn't like to talk about his past. I do know his childhood was kind of rough. His parents divorced when he was young, like maybe four or five, and he went to live with his grandmother. She died when he was nine and after that he was in foster care."

"You said he'd been married before. When was that and what happened?"

"He was nineteen and she was seventeen. They were just too young, and it didn't last very long, less than two years. He doesn't talk about that either."

Claire nodded. "Wow! Maybe I need to cut him some slack. I just figured he didn't like me but it sounds like he might have good reason to be cautious about relationships."

"He tells me all the time that he loves me and that he loves spending all his time with me. We are happy, Claire. Please be happy for me."

"If you're happy, I'm happy." She smiled at Sarah and asked, "What does Rodney want to do?"

"He booked a cruise for April fifth, and when we are out to sea, the captain will marry us." Sarah's lips twisted in a tight smile. "He says it'll be more romantic and will a make good story to tell our children. But I don't know. Do you think it sounds romantic?"

Claire avoided the question. "April fifth is only ten days from now."

Sarah nodded rapidly. "I know. That's the other thing; he wants to get married right away and not wait until I have time to plan a big wedding. I gave my notice today."

"You're quitting work? I thought you loved your job."

"It's not really a career or anything, and Rodney wants to have children right away, so I'd be quitting anyway."

"Sarah, it's the twenty-first century. You don't have to get married, or quit work to have children, or do what some man wants you to do."

"I know. But this is what I want to do." Sarah looked down at her phone again. "I'd better go outside and wait for Rodney. He hates it when I'm late."

They stood together, and Sarah gave Claire a quick squeeze. "I'll call you when we get back, and when you get married, Claire, I want to be your maid of honor, promise?"

"*If* I get married, you mean. And if I do, it won't be for a long time. But I'll remember your request."

Sarah walked a few steps toward the door, then turned back. "Be happy for me, Claire. Okay?"

Claire forced a smile and waved her off. "Go. If this is what you want, I'm happy for you. When you are home from the honeymoon, I'll invite you and Rodney over for dinner."

"Thank you." Sarah hurried back and hugged Claire again. "You guys will like each other once you get to know each other."

The smile left Claire's face as she watched Sarah leave the lobby. "Not likely," she muttered.

***

Sarah adjusted the slats of the plantation blinds that covered the three tall, wide windows in the living room until they were all at precisely the same angle: one-quarter open, slanted upward. She longed to swing them aside and gaze out at the world, but Rodney would be home any minute.

She looked around the room to ensure that everything was in place. Lifting a tapestry sofa pillow, she plumped it and returned the pillow to its position on the left end of the sofa, then pushed the top down an inch with the side of her hand. The crease she'd created was off-center. Sarah repeated her movements, taking care to crease the pillow in the exact center.

Glancing at the mantel clock, she caught a glimpse of her reflection in the mirror above the fireplace. She gazed at herself for a moment. She looked very sad and watched her image as she forced a smile. The smile didn't reach her eyes.

"You need to talk to Claire," she told her reflection.

The front door opened. Sarah took one last look at the room and hurried to greet Rodney.

"Hi." Sarah smiled and tilted her face up to receive his kiss.

Rodney ignored her gesture.

"I made coq au vin for dinner. It'll be ready at seven."

Rodney frowned. "I'm ready to eat now."

"But, yesterday, you said you wanted to eat at seven."

"For God's sake, Sarah. Must everything be an argument with you?"

Sarah blinked her eyes rapidly to keep back her tears. "I'm sorry. I must have misunderstood. Let's have a glass of wine together and then you can relax for a few minutes while I finish dinner."

"Since I have to wait for dinner again, I'll watch the news. Bring me a scotch." He turned away and took two steps toward the den. His eyes swept over the living room.

Sarah held her breath.

He kept walking.

She went to the kitchen, opened a cupboard, and took down a heavy-bottomed whiskey glass. In the pantry, she studied the shelf of alcohol. The Johnnie Walker Blue was missing. She bit her lip. *There was plenty last night. Maybe I put it away in the wrong place? I know it's here somewhere.*

"What's keeping you?"

Rodney's voice made Sarah jump.

She spun to look at him.

He stood slouched against the door frame of the pantry. His eyes looked cold.

"I can't find the scotch," she admitted. Her voice trembled as she continued, "There was almost a full bottle last night."

"If there was," he lifted one eyebrow, sarcasm filling his tone, "it would still be there." He paused. "You don't need to lie to me, Sarah. If you forgot to buy scotch, just say so."

"But I didn't forget," she protested.

"Well, there is only one person here who went shopping today, and I happen to know that I wrote scotch on the to-do list last night."

Sarah hesitated. She knew she'd gone to the grocery to buy the chicken and pearl onions for tonight's dinner, and she'd stopped at the cleaners to retrieve Rodney's shirts and his gray suit, but there hadn't been a list. She bit her lip and tried to remember seeing a to-do list this morning.

"It doesn't do any good for us to make a list if you don't use it, Sarah." Rodney straightened and looked at her sternly. "We agreed that we'd keep the list right there," he gestured, "on the counter next to the garage door."

Sarah nodded. She did remember that.

Rodney took the three steps to the counter and picked up a notepad. He held it up for Sarah to see.

Printed carefully, in Rodney's handwriting she read:

TO DO

- *Dry cleaners*

- *Chicken*

- *Pearl onions*

- *Scotch*

- *Lunch with Claire*

- *Dinner ready at 6*

"You didn't even read it, did you?"

Sarah shook her head. She knew that list hadn't been on the counter that morning.

"What else did you forget today?"

"Nothing," she mumbled.

"Did you have lunch with Claire?"

"No. We didn't have a plan to meet. I don't know why that's on the list."

"Claire called me today to ask if I knew where you were. She certainly thought you had a lunch date."

"Really? That's so weird." Sarah's brow creased in a frown. "Why would she call you instead of me?"

Sarah held out her hand for the notepad.

Rodney ripped off the page and crumpled it.

"It's too late now." He frowned at her, then turned and left the kitchen.

Sarah poured herself a glass of wine and sipped as she tore lettuce for a salad. She found herself thinking about her marriage. Rodney wanted to start a family right away and had insisted that she quit work and stay home. Claire thought she was crazy to agree, but her mom argued that there was "no time like the present." It had been fun to set up the house and learn to cook, but she still wasn't pregnant, and Rodney was getting impatient.

She glanced at her phone; no messages from Claire. *Surely, if we were supposed to meet for lunch, she'd have called me before she called Rodney.* She opened her calendar app. There was a doctor's appointment tomorrow to get the results of her fertility test, but there had been nothing for today. She shook her head to clear away her worries. She poured herself a second glass of wine, drank deeply, and pulled the casserole dish from the oven.

The rich smell of the coq au vin filled the kitchen. She popped the bread in the oven to warm and carried the casserole to the dining room table. Rodney appeared in the doorway and smiled at her. Her heart lifted. She smiled back and set the dish on a trivet.

"Smells good in here," he said. "Do you want me to pour the wine?"

"Please. I'll just get the bread and be right back."

Relieved by the lack of anger in Rodney's voice, she took the bread from the oven and arranged it in the bread basket, exactly the way he liked. She finished her glass of wine, placed the empty glass in the dishwasher, and carried the bread to the table.

Rodney had dimmed the lights and lit the candles. He held Sarah's chair for her and then seated himself. He lifted his full glass in a toast.

Sarah lifted hers.

They tapped the rims together, creating a soft clink.

"To my beautiful wife," Rodney said. "And, to hearing good news tomorrow."

Sarah sipped and forced a happy smile. She picked up her salad fork and began to eat.

CHAPTER EIGHT

NOW DAY 3: Saturday 01/27

The throbbing of her temples woke Sarah. She dug the heels of her palms into her eye sockets and pushed against the pain. It brought a moment of relief, and then the headache overwhelmed her again, and a rush of nausea came with it. She stumbled from the bed and sank to her knees in front of the toilet.

Her stomach lurched; she coughed and gagged. A stream of yellow bile burned her throat and erupted into the bowl. Sarah closed her eyes and rested her head against the cold porcelain. *What the hell? How do I have a hangover? I didn't drink last night.*

The memory of Rodney bringing dinner surfaced. He'd still been angry about the dog. Sarah rubbed at her temples and pushed herself to her feet. She ran the cold water tap, rinsed the foul taste from her mouth, and splashed her face, hoping to clear her head.

Sarah struggled to remember. He said she'd upset Jeremy and Mrs. Hendricks with her foolishness. But he hadn't mentioned anything else. She was sure that was right. Instead, he'd stood waiting, his back against the closed door, watching until, at his insistence, she'd choked down all of the creamy polenta. Rodney hadn't pressed her to eat the chicken breast or the green beans.

At least, I don't think he did. She dried her face and opened the medicine cabinet, hoping for some Tylenol. *Did he put drugs in the polenta? Am I nuts? Why does he need me to sleep?*

The shelves were empty.

"Damn it." Sarah slammed the cabinet shut and went back to the bedroom.

The bright sunlight streaming through the fully open drapes caused the pain in her temples to move behind her eyes. She staggered across the room and reached up to jerk the drapes closed. A movement caught her attention.

Something was in the woods.

She was sure of it.

"Ajax," she said, and she cupped her hands on the cold glass and pressed her face against them, hoping to get a clear view.

The glare from the bright sun on the pure white new snow was blinding. All of the footprints from last night had disappeared. She focused on the woods.

The undergrowth swayed. *Is Ajax out there, or is that the wind?* She concentrated. "Shit!" Exhaling sharply, she jumped back. *That's not a dog. That's a person.*

Again, Sarah leaned forward and pressed her face into her cupped hands. She stared at the woods, willing someone to appear.

A tall man stood, mostly concealed in the brush, wearing a winter camouflage parka and pants with a matching beanie pulled low over his ears. He peered at the house through binoculars. As she watched, he moved the binoculars across the front of the house and raised them slightly.

He's looking in the windows! Sarah stepped back and concealed herself with the heavy drape.

Questions tumbled through her mind. *Is Rodney having someone watch me? Or is someone watching Rodney? Does he know? Maybe they're watching that kid?*

Sarah moved the drape just enough to peer between the wall and the curtain.

The woods were empty and still. She rubbed at her eyes and scanned the trees; there was no movement. Nor any trace of an intruder. Not even a footprint or a bird. Sarah stepped away from the drape and stood boldly in the center of the window. "I dare you to come get me," she said.

Nothing moved.

"I know I saw a man," she said. She stood for several seconds scanning the woods and yard. Then she turned away and sank down on her bed, tears flooding her eyes. She brushed them away. "You're stronger than this," she told herself and got up to take a shower. "Since the bastard didn't leave me Tylenol, I need coffee."

***

Sarah turned off the water and reached for a towel. Hearing a slight sound from the bedroom, she stopped and listened. Nothing. Wrapping herself in the towel, she stepped out of the stall and entered the bedroom. Rodney sat in the striped chair near the window.

Sarah gasped. Anger flushed her cheeks and she glared at the intruder.

"Did I scare you, darling?" His lips twisted in a cruel smile as he cocked his eyebrow.

"What are you doing in here?"

"My house, my wife." He gestured to the table. "I'm here to share a lovely cup of coffee with you. I was afraid you might have a headache this morning, and I wanted to help."

"My head is fine," Sarah declared, even as she winced at the glare from the window.

"Sit down." Rodney waved to the second chair.

Sarah took a step forward and stopped. "I'd rather get dressed first."

"Be my guest. I'll just sit here and enjoy the view." He picked up a coffee cup and sipped.

Sarah stomped to the closet, opened the door, and stepped inside, slamming the door behind her. *I'll be damned if I'll let him watch me dress.*

Two choices hung in the closet: a pair of soft-looking, well-worn jeans and another pair of those perfect wool trousers, this time in a creamy beige. She moved to the wardrobe and opened the top drawer: again only one set of bra and panties—creamy beige covered in lace— and one pair of socks. Still no shoes, but the same soft house slippers were lined up on the empty shoe shelf.

This time he'd left two tops, a beige cashmere sweater and a dark green sweatshirt. Sarah quickly dressed in the jeans and sweatshirt, pulled the socks over her bare toes, and shoved her feet into the slippers. She ran her fingers through her hair and returned to the bedroom.

Rodney lifted his cup in a salute. "I knew you'd choose the mundane. Your taste hasn't improved, then, has it?"

His criticism struck a nerve, and Sarah felt herself bristle. She went on the attack. "Game's over, Rodney. I'm tired of this, and I want my son back."

"Our son is at school is eating breakfast, and you need to calm down and learn some manners." He poured a cup of coffee from the silver pot. "Sit down and drink this coffee."

"Why? Do you want me in a drugged stupor again?"

"For heaven's sake, Sarah. That's the last thing I want. I was very disappointed when I stopped in to say good night last night and found you passed out."

"I didn't drink last night!"

Rodney shook his head slowly and pointed to an empty vodka bottle in the wastebasket. "Don't lie, Sarah. That says different. I'm not sure how you got it." He squinted and frowned as he looked at her. "I suppose you stole it when Mrs. Hendricks wasn't watching. I'll need to tell her to keep a closer eye on you."

Sarah stared at the empty bottle. Her stomach lurched again. She closed her eyes to stop the wave of nausea. *Did I drink that?*

She shook her head and looked at Rodney. "I didn't drink that?"

"You probably don't remember." He finished his cup of coffee and set the empty cup back on the tray. Then, reaching into his pocket, he pulled out two white pills and handed them to Sarah. "Here. These will help."

Sarah balled her hands into fists.

"It's just Tylenol, for Christ's sake. Take it."

Sarah held out her hand and accepted the pills.

"Come downstairs when you are ready, and we'll talk."

Rodney stood and left the room without glancing back.

Sarah stared at the pills in her hand. She didn't dare take them. She lifted the coffee cup to her lips and took a sip. Her hand trembled. She stopped and considered the pot, wondering if Rodney's coffee had been poured from it. She realized that she couldn't drink the coffee and set the full cup back on the tray.

Crossing the room, Sarah glanced out the window and paused to watch for movement. Everything was silent and white. She went into the bathroom, dumped the coffee in the sink, and flushed the pills away.

As Sarah brushed her damp hair into a high ponytail, she narrowed her eyes in thought. *I need help to get out of here and find Jeremy. If I can get to a phone, I can call Claire.*

***

She left the bedroom and walked down the hall toward the stairs. The boy's door stood open. Maybe he'd have a phone, even though the list said otherwise. Sarah listened carefully. Sounds floated up from downstairs: voices and the clinks of someone eating breakfast.

Creeping quietly, Sarah moved past the stairwell and hurried to the boy's room. She stopped and listened again, hoping to hear the boy's voice mixed with Rodney's deeper tones. She took the last steps and stood in the doorway.

"Good morning, Mother. Did you sleep well?"

Sarah gasped. The boy sat on the edge of the bed. His back was stiff and straight, a book balanced on his knees.

"What are you reading?" she blurted.

The boy smiled and tilted the book so the cover was visible. "It's Percy Jackson. *The Sea of Monsters.*"

"That looks like a chapter book."

The boy looked puzzled. He nodded. "It's really good. I already read the first book, *The Lightning Thief.* This one is even better."

Realizing the book was too advanced for six-year-old Jeremy, Sarah suppressed a shudder and stepped into the bedroom. She held out her hand. "May I see it, please?"

"Sure." He stood and extended the book.

Sarah took it, flipped to the back flap, and read silently: "Prized by readers aged 8–80." She glanced at the boy and continued reading: "Accompany the son of the sea god Poseidon and his other demigod friends as they go on a series of quests that will have them facing monsters, gods, and conniving figures from Greek mythology. Do they have what it takes to save the Olympians from an ancient enemy?"

"Rodney said you were doing very well in school, but I had no idea you could read a book like this."

The boy blushed and snatched the book from her hand.

Sarah's heart softened at the look of fear on his face. *He's just a kid,* she thought. She smiled. "It's all right; I won't mention the book to Rodney."

She watched as his lip trembled and he caught it in his teeth. He blinked back tears.

"Thanks," he mumbled and turned away to tuck the book under his pillow.

"Have you had your breakfast?" Sarah asked.

He nodded.

"Well, walk down with me and have a glass of juice or something," Sarah said. "You can keep me company while I eat. I'd love to hear all about your school."

"Okay." He nodded. "I can do that."

Sarah smiled.

They walked in silence to the stairs and went down together to the landing. The boy paused and looked out the window. "Did you see that?" he asked.

"What?"

"I think the dog is out there." The boy leaned his forehead on the glass.

Sarah's heart skipped. She took a deep breath to control herself and stepped to his side. She, too, pressed her forehead to the window.

They stood silent for a long moment until the boy stepped back and sighed. "I guess not," he said.

Sarah swept her gaze over the woods. She reasoned that anyone hiding out there would be concealed somewhere in the undergrowth.

Her breath was fogging the window. She leaned back from the glass.

Something moved.

Quickly she lifted her hands, cupped them against the glass and pressed her face into them.

The man was there. She was sure of it.

Sarah scanned to the right and saw a fleeting flash of light. She focused on the spot.

"Got ya," she whispered. The camouflaged man lay prone, holding the binoculars steady. He seemed to be focused on the lower windows of the house.

"Is it the dog? Do you see him?"

Sarah jumped and dropped her hands. "No, nothing," she lied. "It was just the wind."

They continued down the stairs and entered the dining room together.

Rodney sat at the head of the table, reading a newspaper. A red coffee mug decorated with a golden fleur-de-lys rested by his right hand.

He looked up. "Jeremy. Please tell Mrs. Hendricks your mother is ready for her breakfast, and then pack your bag. Billy has invited you to a sleepover this weekend. His mother is going to take you into Seattle."

The boy nodded and slipped away.

Rodney turned his gaze on Sarah. "Sit." He gestured to the chair on his right.

Sarah sat, her back to the open doorway. Glancing toward the window, she forced herself not to stare out at the woods and waited for Mrs. Hendricks to appear.

Rodney peered over his paper and studied her.

Sarah slipped her hands off the table and into her lap, twisting her fingers together, determined not to be the first to speak.

"Feeling better?" he asked.

"Yes, thank you."

"Good." He turned a page of the paper and scanned the columns.

Sarah glanced at the window.

"Looking for something?" He turned another page.

"No, just thinking the snow looks pretty. It seems very peaceful out there."

"As opposed to in here?" His voice held a touch of anger and his fingers crumpled the edge of the paper.

Sarah flinched. She clenched her hands tighter as her eyes flicked to the paper.

Rodney lowered it. "Nothing in here you need to see. The doctor doesn't want you upset."

"I was just wondering what day it is."

He folded the paper neatly and placed it on the far side of the table. "Does it matter?"

"No, I was curious because you and Jeremy are both home, and I thought it might be a holiday."

"Saturday, Sarah. It's Saturday."

She nodded. "And the boy—Jeremy is going to his friend's house today."

Rodney took his phone from his pocket and glanced at the time. "Yes. He'll be gone all weekend."

Mrs. Hendricks bustled into the dining room carrying a tray loaded with a plate of toast, half a grapefruit, a coffee decanter, and a mug. She served Sarah, filled the mug, and set it next to Sarah's knife.

Sarah pulled the mug toward her and turned it to see the golden design. "I remember these mugs."

Mrs. Hendricks beamed. "Oh my, that is so exciting! Good for you, dear." She lifted the decanter. "May I give you a warm-up, sir?"

"Just a splash." He raised his mug and the housekeeper filled it. Rodney kept his eyes on Sarah.

Sarah stared at the mug in her hand. *It must be safe. He's drinking it too.* She took a sip of the coffee and waited for the housekeeper to leave them alone.

When Mrs. Hendricks had returned to the kitchen, she lifted her head to meet his gaze. "Rodney, these are my mugs. They were in my cabin. Jeremy picked them because he said they looked like a king's cup."

Rodney's lips twisted, but it wasn't a nice smile. He leaned toward her and said, "No one will believe you."

He crumpled his napkin on the table, drained his coffee, and stood. "I'll be back after I drop Jeremy at Billy's house. Eat your breakfast like a good girl." He picked up the paper and walked away.

Sarah took a few bites of the dry toast and listened as Rodney and the boy left the house together. She kept watch out the dining room window. A light flashed, and she spotted the man again. She watched as his binoculars moved away from the dining room and slid to the driveway.

She finished her coffee. *Is he watching Rodney or that boy? Or me?*

The man stood, slipped deeper into the woods, and disappeared.

Mrs. Hendricks returned, tsked over Sarah's uneaten grapefruit, but refilled her coffee mug.

Sarah thanked her, then excused herself and carried her coffee upstairs, and turned toward her room. The sound of a ringing phone stopped her. She listened carefully. It was coming from the boy's room.

She ran down the hallway, heedless of the spilling coffee. The ringing stopped, but it was definitely coming from the bedroom.

Sarah stepped into the room and looked around. No phone on the desk. No phone on the bedside table. She remembered the book and looked under the pillow. The book was gone. She lifted the bedspread and checked under the bed. "Ring again, damn it!"

She stood still and surveyed the room, looking for places a boy might hide his phone.

The sound of the phone chiming a notification caused Sarah to spin around, trying to determine where the sound had come from. All the drawers had been empty when she was in there yesterday. Scanning the room again, Sarah searched every surface.

"The bed," she said, bending down and patting the taut bedcovers. *Nothing!*

"It has to be here."

Finally, she pulled open the drawer in the bedside table and there it was. She grabbed the phone and scurried down the hall to her room.

Inside, she pressed her back to the door and caught her breath. Her hands trembled, and she fumbled the phone, dropping it on the floor. She squatted and picked it up, pressing the "on" button. The phone lit up with the familiar grid of dots, requesting that she draw the unlock pattern.

Sarah stared at the screen, thinking. She remembered teaching Jeremy how to open her phone in case of an emergency. She'd wanted it to be simple, like "tic-tac-toe." Sarah placed her finger on the upper left-hand dot and moved it down in a diagonal line across the dots. She took a chance and drew up to the middle dot in the last row—an incorrect access code appeared.

She tried again, this time drawing the diagonal and then moving left to the bottom-row middle dot. The phone opened.

"Yes!" Sarah pumped her fist in the air, hit the call button, opened the keypad, and quickly typed Claire's number.

Four rings and the phone answered.

"Hi. This is Claire Hamilton."

"Claire, it's me—"

The voice continued, "I am currently unavailable. Please leave a message or call my office at 425-925-0000 for immediate assistance. Thank you, and have a nice day."

Sarah held the phone to her ear, waiting for the beep.

"Claire. It's me. Sarah. I need your help. Jeremy is gone, and Rodney won't tell me anything. I don't have a phone— wait—yes, I do. I have this phone. But I don't know the number. I stole it. Call me back, please." A long beep sounded, and the robotic voice said, "Your message has been sent."

"Damn it! She's going to think I'm crazy." She pressed the call icon again.

The phone buzzed in her hand. *Warning: Low battery. Less than 6% remaining. Charge or turn off.*

Frantically, Sarah pushed "recent calls," and pressed down on Claire's number.

The phone buzzed again and shut down.

Frustrated, she threw it on the bed. Tears flooded her eyes. Impatiently, Sarah brushed them away. *The charger must be in his room,* she thought. She picked up the phone, rushed to her bedroom door, and flung it open.

Rodney stood, hand raised, ready to knock.

Sarah gave a single short yelp.

"Did I scare you, darling?" Rodney asked.

Sarah slipped her hand behind her back and slid the phone into the pocket of her jeans. She gave him a small smile. "A little. I didn't know anyone was there."

"I told you I'd be back soon so we could talk. Are you ready?"

Sarah nodded and thought quickly. "Of course, but let's go downstairs. I just need to brush my teeth, and I'll be right down."

"I'll meet you in my office. Don't take too long." He turned away.

Sarah closed the door and attempted a deep, calming breath. *I have to hide this phone*, she thought. *Somewhere he won't find it.*

She moved toward the closet and stopped herself. *No good; he's in there all the time. Under the bed? No, Mrs. Hendricks might find it.* "Hurry," she whispered to herself. Stepping into the bathroom, she checked the cabinet under the sink. It contained nothing but rolls of toilet paper and nowhere to conceal the phone. Sarah returned to the bedroom and crossed to the table and slipper chairs arranged by the window. Quickly, she shoved the phone between the seat cushion and the back of one of the chairs. *I'll find a better place later.*

Stepping back, Sarah studied the chair. Nothing appeared out of place. She glanced out the window toward the woods. The yard and tree line stood empty. *Hurry,* she reminded herself and left the bedroom.

The wide French doors at the bottom of the stairs stood open, revealing Rodney's office. He sat at his desk, watching her approach, looking for all the world like a spider in a web.

Sarah forced a calm smile as she pushed her fear away.

"Make yourself comfortable, Sarah." He stood and walked around the desk, waiting for her to sit in a leather chair before taking the matching chair. He settled himself and crossed his right ankle over his left knee.

Sarah sat primly, her feet tucked back, her toes skimming the floor. She kept her hands loose in her lap, determined not to show her anxiety.

Neither spoke for a long minute.

Sarah wanted to scream at the look of amusement she saw on Rodney's face. Instead, her eyes drifted around the room. Finally, she said, "This is a lovely home. Have you lived here long?"

Rodney chuckled. "Still playing games?"

When Sarah didn't respond, he continued, "We have lived here for over two years, Sarah. We moved here from Seattle when Jeremy was almost four. We wanted him to attend a better school. You were quite happy to move to this beautiful location and devote yourself to your home and family."

Sarah shook her head slowly. "That is not true, and you know it."

"Do I?" Rodney mocked. "I'm afraid you are having a tough time recovering from your head injury. I was hoping we could go into Seattle this weekend and have dinner with friends, but I see that your health is still precarious."

Sarah shifted in her chair. She wanted to scream at him and demand answers, but she knew how he'd reacted to confrontation in the past. So instead, she looked around the room and said, "I'm very confused. My memories are so different from what you tell me is true. Mrs. Hendricks seems to believe I tried to kill myself."

"You've been seeing a therapist for over a year now." Rodney shifted slightly in his chair and grasped his ankle as he leaned forward; his crow's-feet deepened as his apparent sincerity darkened his brown eyes. "Your suicide attempt deeply saddened him."

"How do you know it wasn't just an accident?" Sarah pushed her angry disbelief away as she asked, "Did I leave a note?"

Slumping against the back of his chair, Rodney shook his head. "No, but you've threatened to kill yourself many times."

Never! Not ever!

Rodney continued, "Dr. Leavitt is concerned about your refusal to accept that we are married and that Jeremy is your son. He wanted you to be committed to a care facility, but I insisted I could protect you. You should be grateful you are here and not in a locked hospital ward somewhere."

"But—" Sarah interlaced her fingers and held them palm up. Questions flashed through her mind. She chose the simplest one: "Why are all my memories from before wrong?"

"I'm not a doctor, Sarah, but I think it is because you have alcohol-induced dementia."

Sarah gasped and leapt to her feet. "What the hell? Rodney. I'm thirty-five years old!"

"And, you have a serious drinking problem. A problem you have refused to accept or get treatment for."

"You said that at the divorce hearing, but the judge ruled against your claim."

"Only because I—" Rodney caught himself and said instead, "We are not, I repeat *not*, divorced. Your inability to remember something so basic supports my claim, and," he sneered, "I'm sure Dr. Leavitt agrees with me."

Sarah narrowed her eyes and studied him.

He stood, crossed to the window, and pulled the drape aside, gazing out at the snow.

When he didn't speak, Sarah said softly, "So, we did divorce?"

"No!" Rodney kept his back turned another long minute before he returned to his chair. "No. You filed for divorce, and we went to court, but we reconciled. We love each other. We wanted to work things out. You promised to quit drinking, and I gave you another chance."

Twisting her hands together, Sarah frowned and bit her lip. "I know I was drinking during our marriage. I admitted my drinking to the judge. I accept that it contributed to our problems, but," she raised her eyes to look at him, "your abusive behavior was the thing that caused us to divorce. And the reason I have custody of Jeremy."

Rodney slammed his hand on the arm of his chair.

Sarah flinched and looked away.

"God damn it! I have never laid a finger on you. How long are you going to play this stupid game?"

A tap on the office door interrupted.

"Yes," he growled.

"I just wanted to let you know I'm leaving now," Mrs. Hendricks said, "unless you need anything else."

"We're fine. Thank you."

"All right, then. Have a nice weekend."

"Just a moment."

Sarah watched as he rose, composed his face, then stepped to the door and opened it. He smiled at the housekeeper. "Come in. I have your check right here. Let me get it for you." He turned to the desk.

The two women looked at one another.

Mrs. Hendricks raised her eyebrows and silently formed the words, "You okay?"

Sarah nodded.

Turning back with a wide, friendly smile, he handed over the check. "We'll see you first thing Monday morning."

"Yes, sir. I'll be here." She looked toward Sarah. "Get some rest, Mrs. Blake. I'm sure next week will be better."

Sarah nodded, grateful for the kindness.

They sat in silence until Mrs. Hendricks's car passed the window. Then Sarah stood. "I'd like to rest now. If you don't mind, I'll go upstairs."

She thought she saw a movement in the yard. Her eyes flicked toward the window. *I know Ajax is real. And, I know there is someone watching this house.*

She sat back down and took a deep breath.

Rodney caught her quick glance. He turned his head and looked out the window before facing her again. "What's up?" he asked.

"Exactly my question. If anything you say is real, I need to understand. I want to meet with this Dr. Leavitt."

"Hmm!" He leaned back and pursed his lips. "Are you sure?"

"Absolutely." Sarah nodded. "I'd call him myself, but, as you know, I don't have a telephone."

"The police have your phone."

Sarah gasped. "What! Why?"

"My understanding is that they have some questions about your activities leading up to your," he raised his fingers in quote marks, "accident."

Sarah felt her jaw drop. "But—"

"I really am on your side in all this, Sarah. I love you, and I know you love me. As soon as your memory clears, you'll remember all of the hard work we've done to make our marriage a success." He reached out and placed his hand over her trembling fingers.

She allowed his touch.

"I'm doing my best to protect you until your memory clears. However, if you see Dr. Leavitt, he may tell the police you are ready to face their questions."

"What do they think I did?"

Rodney squeezed her hand and smiled gently. "Sorry, I really don't know. They didn't share details with me. I only know that they want to question you as soon as the doctor says you are ready." He studied her face. "Are you ready?"

Sarah shook her head as tears filled her eyes. She rubbed them away. "I need to understand."

"I get it. You are going to have to trust me for just a little while. Let me help you, please?"

She nodded and took in a deep breath. "I thought I saw a man in the woods watching the house. Do you think it's the police?"

"When?" The color drained from his face. He stood quickly and strode to the window.

"This morning. He watched you drive away with that boy."

Rodney studied the woods and then shook his head. "I don't see anything. If you see him again, you need to tell me. I don't like the thought that the police have you under surveillance. Whatever they believe you did, it must be serious."

"I remember our son, our marriage and the divorce, and moving to the cabin with Jeremy." Biting her thumbnail, she continued. "I have a job with the Parks Department. I remember waking up in the cabin on Saturday morning. Jeremy was gone, and it was snowing, snowing hard. I followed Ajax through the snow, and I fell." She lifted her gaze to meet Rodney's. "Then I woke up in the hospital. You brought me here. I didn't do anything wrong."

"Most of that is untrue. I sent Jeremy to his friend's house because I had planned on forcing you to admit the truth today. But now I'm not so sure that's the right idea. Where is this cabin you believe you lived in? Perhaps it would help if we drove there, and you could see that there is no such place, nor any other Jeremy".

"It's on Alta Lake."

"Oh, Sarah." Rodney sighed and shook his head sadly. He returned to his chair and stretched out his hand toward her.

She stiffened and pulled away.

"There was a cabin on Alta Lake. A long time ago. Your grandparents lived there."

"Yes!" Excitement brightened her voice. She sprang to her feet. "I remember that. I used to spend summers there. Then when we divorced, Jeremy and I moved to the cabin."

"The cabin burned down more than six years ago. When you were pregnant with Jeremy." He paused and continued, "Your grandparents died in the fire."

Sarah swayed and grabbed for the back of a chair to keep from falling. The tears she'd been fighting flowed down her cheeks. She sobbed aloud.

Rodney took her hand and moved her toward the open doorway. "I think you're right. You do need to rest. We can talk again later. Let me help you to your room."

Sarah nodded.

CHAPTER NINE

BEFORE: 7 Years Ago

Sarah and Rodney followed the nurse from the reception area to Dr. Greenberg's office. He stood as they entered, greeted Sarah, and briefly shook Rodney's hand. When everyone was seated, the doctor opened a file on his computer screen and took a moment to review the chart. He turned to face the couple. "Mrs. Blake, the results of your fertility tests show no abnormalities. You are a very healthy twenty-eight-year-old woman. Your menstrual cycles are regular, and your hormone levels are normal."

"Then why isn't she pregnant?" Rodney asked.

Dr. Greenberg focused on Rodney. "These things often take time." He glanced back at the chart notes on his screen. "You've been married less than two years, and neither of you has a history of sexually transmitted disease. If you are having relations on a regular basis, it will happen." He paused and looked at Rodney. "Unless you are infertile, Mr. Blake."

Sarah turned to stare at Rodney. Her eyes widened as she watched him stiffen and saw the rage building in his clenched jaw. Reaching out, she placed her hand on his thigh and squeezed lightly.

Rodney brushed her hand aside. "There is nothing wrong with me!" he declared. "I had a physical just last month. My testosterone levels were through the roof!"

"A normal physical does not include looking at fertility issues. We could begin with a urology exam and a simple sperm analysis."

"I'll have you know my boys are fine and healthy." Rodney stood and pulled Sarah to her feet. "We don't need to consult with a quack like you." He grasped Sarah's upper arm and propelled her out of the office.

Sarah glanced back and saw the sympathy in Dr. Greenberg's eyes.

Rodney marched her down the hall to the elevator. He punched the button with an impatient finger. When the doors opened, he thrust her inside. As the doors closed, his hand dropped from Sarah's arm. She rubbed away the pain, sure that she'd find a bruise later.

Rodney stared straight ahead as he muttered, "The man's an idiot."

"He's considered the best in Seattle." Sarah stopped herself, aware that his anger was growing.

"I highly doubt that. Who told you that? Know-it-all Claire?"

Sarah shook her head. *You did.* Aloud, she demurred, "I don't remember."

***

Rodney drove home in glacial silence.

Sarah rubbed at her arm and then twisted her hands in her lap, unsure of what she could say to make things better.

When they pulled into the garage, Rodney didn't turn off the engine; instead he said, "I'm going back to work."

Sarah kissed his cheek, pushed her door open, and said, "Okay. I'll have dinner ready at seven."

"Don't bother. I'll be late."

She stepped back from the car and watched as Rodney backed out and roared away.

The empty house was too large and too quiet.

Sarah thought about calling Claire, but she'd be at work. So instead, she called her mother.

"Hi, darling," Lydia Ross answered on the first ring. "Do you have good news from the doctor?"

"I guess so. He says there's nothing wrong with me, and we should keep trying."

"*I* certainly never had a problem. I'm sure you won't either. You just need to relax." Lydia hurried on. "You should fix yourself up, make a nice dinner, and share a bottle of wine. You worry too much, Sarah. You always have."

"Thanks, Mom. Maybe we'll do that."

"I have to run. Your dad and I are going to the club for dinner."

"Okay, 'bye." Sarah ended the call. *Right, Mom. A nice home-cooked meal would solve everything if my husband were coming home for dinner.*

In the bedroom, Sarah removed her dress and slipped into a pair of leggings. She grabbed an old, oversized University of Washington sweatshirt and pulled it over her head. Her arm ached. She examined it in the closet mirror. A hand-shaped bruise was forming, four fingers and a thumb. Leaving her arm out of the sweatshirt, she went to the bathroom and found the tube of arnica gel. It might help minimize the discoloration, and it certainly wouldn't make it worse. Gently she rubbed the gel into the bruised area, pulled her arm through the sweatshirt, and went to the kitchen.

The oven clock showed 4:01. Sarah took a bottle of sauvignon blanc from the refrigerator, grabbed a glass from the cupboard, and settled herself in front of the television. She turned on Netflix and found a movie. *If I'm not going to be a mother, I need to do something.* She filled her glass and tried not to think anymore.

At 5:30, Sarah opened a second bottle of wine, made herself a peanut butter sandwich, and called Claire. She didn't answer. Sarah hung up without leaving a message. She flipped through the channels and settled on an old *Love It or List It* episode.

By 7 p.m., Sarah was asleep, the empty second bottle on the table beside the sofa.

The vibrating phone woke her. The room was lit only by the light from the television, but the phone glowed, and Sarah picked it up. Rodney's face smiled at her from the screen. She pulled herself to a sitting position and answered the call.

Her tongue felt thick, and she stumbled over her greeting. "Mmm, hi."

"Hey. How's it going there?"

Sarah could hear noise and the sound of voices and laughter. "Where are you?" she asked.

"Just getting a bite with some of the people from the office."

"What time is it?"

"About nine-thirty, I think. You sound tired."

"I fell asleep watching a movie."

Rodney chuckled. "I guess you didn't miss me, then." He paused. "Or have you been drinking?"

Someone called his name, and Rodney responded, "I'll be right there." Then he said, "I have to go, Sarah. Don't wait up."

The phone disconnected.

Sarah walked to the kitchen, cut herself a piece of cheese, and opened another bottle of wine.

***

Alone in the house all day, Sarah tried to keep herself busy, but the days passed slowly, and she found herself brooding about her marriage and watching movies that featured infertility. She knew they needed to discuss what to do and make some decisions, but Rodney hadn't mentioned the doctor's visit and Sarah was afraid to bring it up.

After a week, she couldn't stay silent any longer. Sarah screwed up her courage and made a plan. She tidied the house to be sure everything was in place and prepared Rodney's favorite dinner.

At 5:30, she changed into trim black slacks and a silk shirt that she hated, but Rodney loved, and brushed her hair into loose, shiny waves. At 6:00, she slid the salmon into the oven to slow bake and poured herself a large glass of chardonnay for courage. Rodney's car pulled into the garage at 6:15. Sarah tipped her glass up and quickly drained the contents. She poured a second glass for herself and pasted on a brilliant smile as Rodney entered the kitchen.

"Hi, darling." She stepped close and kissed him. "I've just poured a glass of wine. Would you like one?"

Rodney picked up the bottle and read the label. "Not bad. Your taste is improving." He set the bottle down. "But make me a scotch instead."

Sarah complied. "How was your day?" she asked, handing him a Glencairn glass filled with one ice cube and two fingers of scotch.

Rodney leaned against the counter as he took the first sip. "Good. Nothing exciting. Something smells great in here."

Sarah felt herself relax. "Baked salmon with capers and lemon."

He took another sip and smiled at her. "What's the occasion?"

"No occasion. I went to the grocery today, and the salmon looked especially good." She sat on a bar stool and twirled her glass in a lazy circle. "Dinner will be ready in about thirty minutes."

Rodney added a little scotch to his glass and raised the wine bottle in her direction. Sarah nodded, and he refilled her glass.

"I'll go catch the local news on TV. Okay?"

"Sure." Sarah stood. The room wobbled.

"You okay?"

"Just a little light-headed." She laughed. "You go relax, and I'll call you when it's time to eat." After Rodney left the kitchen, she cautioned herself to slow down and set her glass, out of reach, on the windowsill.

Then she busied herself making a salad and double-checking the table. When the rice cooker beeped and the broccoli was steaming, she turned off the oven and carried the salad to the table. She lit the candles, turned down the dining room light, and went to tell Rodney dinner was ready.

He was talking to someone on the phone, but he smiled and said, "I gotta go. Talk tomorrow," and ended the call. As he rose from his chair, he took Sarah's hand and kissed her palm. They entered the dining room together. Rodney paused at the doorway and looked around.

Sarah held her breath.

"Everything looks lovely, darling."

"Thank you." Sarah smiled and allowed Rodney to hold her chair as she sat.

He moved to the wine bucket Sarah had positioned on the table, lifted the wine bottle, and studied the label. "Nice! Gérard Boulay Clos de Beaujeu Sancerre 2019." He poured a bit into his glass and tasted the wine. Then, he smiled again and saluted Sarah before filling their glasses.

As Sarah watched her husband eat his salad, she nibbled at her own and considered how to broach the subject of fertility.

Rodney glanced up and, noticing her pensive gaze, asked, "What are you thinking about?"

She blushed and quickly sipped at her wine. "Nothing important. Just something my mother said."

He waited for her to continue.

"She suggested that I need to relax and stop thinking about having a child and it would happen. She thinks I need to keep busy."

"I'd say Lydia is right. I did a little research today and the stats indicate that a woman's level of stress is a major factor."

"Not the man's?"

"Nope. A woman who is stressed takes twenty-nine percent longer to get pregnant and when a woman drinks alcohol it takes even longer. It seems to be all on you."

Sarah flinched. "So," she forced herself to stay calm, "you aren't going to be tested?"

"No need." He ate the last of his salmon and refilled his glass. "Would you like more wine?"

Sarah shook her head no.

"Good girl. Lay off the booze for a month, and you'll be carrying my son before you know it."

Pompous ass, Sarah thought, as she smiled and said, "I think I need to fill up my time, not drink less. Maybe I'll go back to work."

"Don't be ridiculous! My mother never worked, and neither did yours. That little job you had didn't bring in enough money to do anything but push us into a higher tax bracket."

Sarah started to protest, but Rodney kept talking. "Your job is to be my wife." He raised his glass in a mock toast and winked, adding, "And you are getting better at it every day."

Sarah felt her stomach clench. She pushed her chair back and stood. "I'll clear the table, and then let's have an after-dinner drink in the den."

"Can't. I'll just finish my wine in the office. I need to make some phone calls." Rodney stood and picked up his glass. "Why don't you find a movie to watch." He walked a few steps and then came back to kiss her cheek. "Dinner was good tonight. I think you're almost ready to entertain my business associates."

She glared at his back as he walked away and flipped him off.

Sarah reached for the wine bottle and emptied it into her glass.

CHAPTER TEN

NOW DAY 5: Monday 01/29 MORNING

When Sarah woke, the room had the soft gray look of dusk. *Wow, I must have slept all day,* she thought. Stretching her arms over her head, she arched her back and groaned. Rolling to her side, she spied a glass of water on the nightstand and realized that her lips felt gummy and her mouth seemed full of cotton. *I must have slept with my mouth open.* She stretched as she pulled herself up to a sitting position.

She emptied the glass in rapid gulps and stood. Her stomach growled loudly. Glancing down, Sarah realized she was wearing a nightgown. Her breath quickened as she processed the information. No bra. No panties. She bit her lip. *I'm sure I was wearing regular clothes when Rodney and I were talking. I only came up here to rest and think. When did I change?*

"Focus!" she commanded herself. "Think!"

The memory of Rodney telling her that the man she'd seen in the woods was a policeman overwhelmed her. He'd been so patient, so caring and concerned. He'd calmed her down and they'd walked upstairs.

Sarah sank onto the bed, closed her eyes, and tried to picture what had happened next.

How did this happen? He must have removed my clothes. She ran her hands over her arms and down her legs, shivering at the thought of his touch.

Maybe I really am losing my mind. Sarah struggled to remember the previous night. She knew he had told her the police wanted to question her and she'd become very afraid. Rodney had been kind and they'd walked upstairs together. *We came in here and I went to the window and looked out. Rodney came up behind me and stood there, but nothing moved in the woods. I sat down by the window and Rodney said I looked pale, and he thought I should lie down.*

Sarah grabbed her elbows and pulled her arms tight across her stomach. *I was shaking, and I needed time to think. He went into the bathroom and got a glass of water for me. I drank it and lay down, and then I must have fallen asleep. Did I sleep all day? But I never changed clothes, I know I didn't.*

Anger pulled at Sarah's confusion. *What game is he playing? I let him trick me again. What the fuck is wrong with me? I have to find Jeremy! I have to concentrate!*

The sound of a car drew her to the window. She pulled the drape aside and watched as Mrs. Hendricks parked her car and walked toward the house. *Why is she here tonight? I'm sure Rodney said he'd see her on Monday when she left on Saturday.*

Mrs. Hendricks disappeared from view.

Sarah dropped the drape and turned away, then she spun back and pulled the drape aside again to scan the woods. Slowly she searched the tree line, moving her eyes from left to right, looking for any sign of a man. The snow lay smooth, unbroken by footsteps. No wind disturbed the tree branches. A bird burst from the woods, the flash of its bright red feathers catching her eye and causing Sarah to sweep her gaze back to the left.

What was that? Is someone there?

She froze and forced her breathing to slow, never moving her eyes from the spot where something looked wrong.

The snow was different under that large cedar tree. She was sure of it. Not blown smooth by the wind but piled in a lump. Slowly, she allowed the drape to drop back into place, leaving just a narrow opening. She removed her hand but kept her eyes on the pile of snow. A long minute passed and then Sarah saw movement.

A large man in winter camouflage shifted his position. She was sure of it—someone was in the woods. As Sarah watched, he lifted his binoculars and focused on the house. *I don't think those are pointed at me. I think he's looking in the kitchen.* Sarah stepped back and hurried to the bedroom door. *I need to find out what's going on!*

She twisted the doorknob. *Locked! God damn it!*

Sarah sank to the floor and rested her head against the door.

Think! Pull it together. Deep breaths. In through your nose. Out through your mouth. Now get up off the floor and get dressed.

Sarah rose and crossed the room to the closet. Once again, only one set of clothing hung in the vast, empty space. Pale beige wool slacks and another creamy sweater, this one with a deep V-neck. "Fucking Rodney," she muttered. "I hate these clothes and he knows it. I want my own clothes."

Grabbing the clothing, she threw the items on the unmade bed and moved to the bathroom. She turned the shower to hot and stripped off the nightgown. A large bruise in the bend of her arm caught her attention. She examined it carefully. Her arm was tender. "What the hell happened last night?" she asked her reflection in the mirror.

Sarah stepped into the shower and allowed the hot spray to cascade over her body. She scrubbed herself and shampooed her hair with the rose-scented product and then rinsed, over and over, until she was sure the scent was gone. She cranked off the shower and grabbed a towel from the hook outside the stall.

The bathroom door moved.

Sarah froze.

"Who's there?"

No one answered, but she thought she heard the bedroom door close. "Rodney?" There was no answer. *The bastard is spying on me. I know it. He unlocks the door when I take a shower.*

Sarah wrapped the towel around her body, stepped out of the shower, and entered the bedroom. Nothing looked disturbed. Crossing the room, she tried the door.

The knob turned.

She jerked the door open.

The hallway was empty.

Sarah slammed the door shut. "What the hell?"

It only took a minute to pull the unfamiliar clothes on over her damp body and to wrap her wet hair in a towel. Her anger surged and she forced herself to slow down, remembering that without Rodney she might never find Jeremy. *Just for now,* she told herself. *I have to pretend that he's telling me the truth. But I'm going to find a charger and call Claire. And, I'm not going to eat or drink anything he gives me.*

Sarah pulled the towel off her hair, brushed it back into a ponytail, and went downstairs. As she approached the dining room, she could hear Rodney talking.

"I'm giving you another chance, but if there is a repeat of Friday's breach of safety, I will have to find someone else. Do you understand?"

Sarah stopped in the hallway and listened.

Mrs. Hendricks's reply came quickly. "Yes, Mr. Blake. It was just that Mrs. Blake seems so sad. She wanted to go outside, and I thought a little fresh air would cheer her up. And—"

Sarah heard the woman take in a quick breath.

"That dog did seem to know her."

"No matter what she looks or sounds like, Sarah is not well. I told you that. She has a way with animals. God knows why all dogs like her."

Rodney's coffee cup clinked against the saucer.

Sarah waited.

"She became very hysterical Saturday afternoon. I had to call Dr. Leavitt and he sedated her. Our Sunday was quite pleasant."

Sarah lifted her fist to her mouth and bit her finger to force herself to stay quiet. *It must be Monday. This must be the fifth day but how could I sleep all day Sunday?*

"I love my wife and I don't want to see her hospitalized or worse. I want to keep her safe, and I need you to help me do that." The cup clinked again. "Can you do that?"

"Yes, Mr. Blake."

"Good. Don't forget and don't let her fool you. She's very good at lying."

A chair scratched across the floor.

Sarah thought about hiding or running back upstairs. She hesitated.

"I need to get to my office. Mrs. Blake should be down soon. If you have any concerns, call me. Immediately."

Sarah took the last few steps and appeared in the dining room doorway.

"Good morning, Rodney." She smiled. "Good morning, Mrs. Hendricks. Did you have a nice weekend?"

Rodney's face flushed, as Mrs. Hendricks smiled at Sarah and said, "I did. Thank you."

Sarah walked to the table and pulled out a chair. She smiled at Rodney and made eye contact as she said defiantly, "I'd like to have an omelet with sausage and cheese, please. I feel like I haven't eaten in days."

"Excellent!" Mrs. Hendricks said. "I'm glad your appetite is back." She picked up the coffee carafe and bustled from the room.

Rodney broke eye contact and shifted slightly in his chair.

"Would you like to explain yourself, Rodney? I heard you lying to your housekeeper." Sarah reached for the coffee carafe, poured herself a cup, added a large dollop of cream, and stirred slowly. "I don't believe you called the doctor, nor do I believe that the men watching this house are with the police."

Rising from his chair, Rodney cocked his head and looked her up and down.

Sarah felt herself quiver with a quick burst of fear. *Is he going to hit me?* She stared at him, refusing to allow herself to look away.

"I really don't care what you believe, darling. You are a broken wreck. A chubby drunk with memory loss. If, in fact, you had anyone to tell, exactly who do you think would believe anything you say?" He smirked at her. "You seem to forget that there is no one here but you and me."

And Mrs. Hendricks, she reminded herself.

Sarah dropped her hands to her lap and held them tight to still her tremble.

"I'm going to pick up our son at his friend's house and take him to school. Then go to work. You be a good girl and do as you're told today and maybe tomorrow, if you recognize Jeremy tonight, I'll tell Mrs. Hendricks you seem a little better and are ready to fill your time with those love stories you like to watch on TV."

He took a few steps and turned back at the door. "I'll tell Mrs. Hendricks to unlock the door to my workout room. You don't want to gain any more weight, do you, darling? A jog on the treadmill would do you good."

Sarah glared at him. "If you bring home my real son, I'll call him Jeremy, but not until then."

"Now, now, you should stop saying things like that. People will call you crazy."

Gritting her teeth, Sarah turned away.

Rodney chuckled and left the room.

Sarah listened as he moved through the house. He spoke to Mrs. Hendricks, but she couldn't make out their words. Keys jangled. A door opened and shut. She stood, glanced back to the dining room entry, and, seeing no one, crossed to the window. Rodney's Mercedes sedan emerged from the garage and sped away.

Sarah scanned the woods. The man was there, half hidden in the trees.

She watched as Rodney's car turned right at the end of the drive. The man turned away, walked into the woods, and disappeared. *He's not watching me. He's watching Rodney. I'm sure of it, and I need to know why.*

Sarah picked up her coffee and moved to the kitchen.

Mrs. Hendricks looked at her and smiled.

Sarah forced her attention away from Rodney and the man as she asked, "Do you mind if I eat in here? It's lonely in that dining room."

"Of course. Your omelet is almost ready." She gestured toward the coffeepot. "I just made a fresh batch. Freshen your cup and I'll pop the toast in the toaster. Raspberry jam or orange marmalade?"

"Raspberry, please. That sounds lovely."

Sarah helped herself to the coffee and then took a seat at the table in the breakfast nook as Mrs. Hendricks laid out a placemat and napkin. "Thank you. You're very kind. I'm not used to having someone do so much for me. Usually, Jeremy and I eat instant oatmeal for breakfast."

"When I was about your Jeremy's age, I refused to eat anything but peanut butter sandwiches," Mrs. Hendricks said. She chuckled, and Sarah joined her. "He'll grow up fast enough. Enjoy your boy while you can."

Tears filled Sarah's eyes. *I wish I could, but I don't know where he is.* She blinked hard, forcing her tears away.

Mrs. Hendricks patted her hand. "Don't worry. Your appetite is back. You'll be feeling better in no time." She turned to the stove and plated Sarah's omelet and toast.

"Sit down with me and have a cup of coffee and some of this toast," Sarah offered. "I really don't like to eat alone."

"I know what you mean. After my Albert died, I missed him most at breakfast."

Sarah watched as Mrs. Hendricks filled her mug and sat across from her.

"Were you and Albert married a long time?"

Mrs. Hendricks's laugh rang out. "Goodness, no! Albert was my beagle. I had him for twelve years. The best friend a girl could have. Eat up now, before your eggs get cold."

Still smiling, Sarah pushed up her sweater sleeve and reached for her fork.

"What happened there?"

The sharpness of her tone caused Sarah to look up and then follow the housekeeper's eyes to her arm, where the bruise now looked angry and dark against the pale silk of her sweater. "I'm not sure. It was there when I woke up this morning."

She pulled at the sleeve, but Mrs. Hendricks stopped her by reaching out and picking up her arm.

"It looks like a bad IV stick." She pushed the sleeve higher and examined it closely. Then she looked at Sarah, her concern evident. "I thought Mr. Blake said the doctor gave you an injection."

Pulling her arm away, Sarah rubbed the bruise and covered it with the sleeve. "Someone did something," she murmured. She pasted on a bright smile and said, "I do have something you could help me with. Rodney found my phone and gave it to me, but I need to charge it. Do you know where I can find a charger?"

"Absolutely! There's one of those wireless charger pad things in the drawer. Is your phone in your pocket?"

Sarah shook her head. "It's in my room." She placed her hands on the table to rise.

"Sit, sit. Finish your breakfast, and then you can get it. Do you have someone you want to call?"

Sarah nodded. "My best friend, Claire. I think if I talk to her, she can help me understand what's happened."

"I'm sure she can. That's what best friends are for."

Sarah raised her cup in a salute.

"Exactly." She picked up her fork and quickly finished her omelet. "I'm going to run upstairs and get my phone and then I'll have another cup of coffee while it charges, or I can take the charger upstairs and stay out of your way."

"Go get it. It's just us in the house and I'd enjoy the company."

When Sarah returned to the kitchen with the phone, she brought the pencil and yellow legal pad down as well. Mrs. Hendricks had the phone charger plugged in and waiting on the breakfast nook table. Sarah placed the boy's phone on the charger's flat surface and was relieved to see the charging circle appear on its screen. She felt her tension ease and smiled gratefully. "Thank you," she said. "I'm trying to make a list of things I remember. Do you think you could help me?"

"I don't know how much help I can be."

"I thought if Rodney has told you something about me you could share it with me."

The housekeeper frowned. "I'm not sure Mr. Blake would like that."

"I just mean if I don't understand something, maybe you could help me figure it out."

Mrs. Hendricks hesitated and then nodded. "I guess that would be okay."

"Good." Sarah pulled the pad closer and thought a moment before saying, "Let's start simple." She tapped the pencil against the pad and then wrote: *Name*. "I know my name is Sarah Ann Blake. And I know my ex—my husband is Rodney Aaron Blake." She wrote the names on her pad.

Mrs. Hendricks smiled approvingly.

"Our son's name is Jeremy Scott Blake. He is six years old."

"Only six? I would have guessed eight or nine, maybe even ten. He's going to be tall, I suppose."

Sarah hesitated. Trying not to sound accusatory, she said, "That's one of the things that I can't figure out. Jeremy has always been a bit small for his age. He seems to have grown so much during the time I was in the hospital. It's," she paused and then continued, "it's almost like he's a different boy. Even if I was in the hospital a couple of weeks, I should be able to recognize my own son."

Sitting down across from Sarah, Mrs. Hendricks said thoughtfully, "Tell me what you see that makes you doubt that this boy is your son."

CHAPTER ELEVEN

BEFORE: 7 Years Ago

The morning following Rodney's refusal to be tested, Sarah called Claire and suggested they meet for lunch. Claire was surprised but accepted, provided they could make it a late lunch, and they agreed to meet at a small bistro near Claire's office. Sarah arrived first and ordered a glass of wine.

"What's up, buttercup?" Claire asked as she swept into the restaurant and seated herself across from Sarah. "Does your jailer know you are out on the town?"

"He's not that bad," Sarah protested. "I can have lunch with a friend anytime I want."

"Ah, so you just haven't *wanted* to have lunch with me in the last six months."

"Actually, that's one of the things I need to talk to you about. A few days ago, Rodney said you called his office to see why I hadn't shown up for lunch."

"Huh? What lunch? You and I have barely spoken lately." Claire narrowed her eyes and scanned Sarah's face. "When you first married Rodney we had lunch a few times and called each other, but since you moved to that house we haven't had lunch a single time. What's going on? Why did you call today?"

Sarah's hands played with her fork, flipping it over and over.

"I guess you didn't call to tell me all your dreams have come true, and you're going to have a baby. It's almost happy hour and you sound like you need to talk." Claire signaled the waiter. "Let me order my wine and then we can talk."

Claire watched closely as Sarah fiddled with her wineglass, turning it in her fingers and avoiding eye contact. Claire stretched out a hand and placed it on Sarah's arm. "Hey, whatever it is, just tell me. We're friends, remember?"

Tears flooded Sarah's eyes and she blinked rapidly to clear her vision. She lifted her glass and drained the contents. Before speaking, Sarah raised her glass toward the waiter to signal for a refill. "I don't know what's wrong. Maybe nothing. Maybe everything."

Claire waited.

"Rodney really wants a baby."

Claire nodded encouragement.

"We went to the doctor." Sarah's lower lip trembled.

"Are you okay? Are you sick?"

Sarah shook her head, unable to speak.

"Now you're scaring me." Claire laid her hand over Sarah's. "Talk," she ordered.

Sarah blurted out, "He didn't find anything wrong with me but he said Rodney might be infertile."

Claire giggled.

"It's not funny!"

Helplessly, Claire's giggle turned to a full-on laugh.

Stunned by her reaction, Sarah glared indignantly. "Stop that!"

"Oh my god! Rodney?" Claire's laugh exploded again. She sputtered, "Of all people. I bet he didn't like hearing that."

Sarah's lips twitched and a snicker escaped.

Claire snorted.

The waiter approached their table and asked for their order. Claire took a deep breath and calmed herself enough to say, "We need more wine. Actually, bring the bottle. This is going to be one of those conversations."

By the time the waiter returned with the wine, they were under control enough to order their sandwiches.

With that task complete, Claire asked, "How did he take the news?"

"He still thinks it's my fault I'm not pregnant. He thinks if I drank less and spent more time with my mother, I'd already be pregnant."

"Your mother? How is that supposed to help? Doesn't he know how babies are made?"

Sarah's giggles erupted again as Claire sat back and grinned at her. "Okay, seriously, what did the doctor suggest?"

"That Rodney be tested."

"And?"

"He won't. He really believes it's me, that there has to me something wrong with me."

"Hmm." Claire paused to consider her next question carefully. Then she asked, "How is your marriage, Sarah? Are you happy?"

"Of course I am. We have a beautiful house. Rodney has a great job. If I could just have a baby, everything would be perfect." She lifted her glass and took a large gulp. "But it's kind of lonely."

"Why not go back to work while you are waiting for this miracle baby?"

"I suggested that, but Rodney says everything I earn would just go to taxes and commuter expenses."

Claire pursed her lips and shook her head. "I doubt that that would be true."

"He likes me to be home every day."

"But what do *you* like? How do you fill up your day?"

"I take online cooking classes to learn to cook the food Rodney likes. I run a few errands. You know, stuff like that." Sarah spun her glass and watched the wine form legs and then subside. "First, I was really busy helping the decorator to furnish the house. 'Helping' isn't exactly right. Rodney chose everything, but I had to be home for deliveries. Now—now I just wait."

"Wait?"

"Yeah, wait." Sarah leaned forward and spit out the list. "Wait to get pregnant. Wait for the mail to be delivered. Wait for Rodney to come home. Wait for dinner to cook, wait, wait, wait."

"Wow! That doesn't sound like much of a life. What about fun?"

"We go out quite often. Rodney has to entertain for his job, but I'm not a good enough cook to cook for others yet. So we go to fancy places instead of inviting people to our house."

Claire protested, "You're a great cook. You always used to have the best parties."

"I can cook regular food like meat loaf and steak, but not the fancy gourmet meals Rodney wants."

"Got it." Claire frowned. "What else?" She studied Sarah, waiting for her to continue.

"It seems like a petty thing to even mention, but Rodney buys everything. I only buy the groceries he puts on the list." Sarah smiled. "Remember when I used to buy my clothes at thrift stores?"

Claire nodded. "You always put together great outfits."

"I liked shopping, but Rodney thought that my wardrobe needed an upgrade." Sarah sighed, picked up her sandwich, and then placed it back on the plate without taking a bite.

Looking directly at Claire, she continued. "He threw away all my clothes and bought me an entire new everything."

"He *what*? What do you mean, 'everything'!"

"Everything. Underwear, slacks, tops, dresses, shoes, jewelry, coats, nightgowns, everything. The only thing I still have from before is this locket." She tapped the gold heart hanging tucked into her blouse. "I lied and told him it was my grandmother's."

"When was all this? That's not okay, Sarah."

"For my birthday. Right before we moved to the house. He thought it would be a nice surprise. My mom told me she thought it was a grand romantic gesture and that I should be appreciative, but—I miss looking like me. I miss being me."

"Then you need to tell him how you feel."

"I tried, but he got so upset. He has a lot of stress at work and I don't want to make it worse."

"Why not go shopping for yourself anyway?"

"I can't. I don't have any cash except what he gives me. He pays the credit card bills, so he knows where I shop and what I buy. I tried to add cash to the grocery bill once, but he saw it and was hurt that I didn't tell him I needed money. When I ask, he says he'll stop at the bank and get cash, but he never does. He checks on me all the time.

He knows how long it should take me to do the errands and groceries and how many miles I'll put on my car."

Claire's pale skin flushed as she clenched her teeth and then blew out a deep breath. "Sarah," she said sternly, "that's abuse."

Sarah shook her head. "He doesn't hurt me. He doesn't hit me." She placed her hand on her bicep, rubbing the bruise that had formed there in the shape of Rodney's fingers.

"Did he hit you, Sarah?"

"No, never!"

"Then what's wrong with your arm? Why are you rubbing it?"

"He grabbed me last night, but it doesn't mean anything. He didn't realize how easily I bruise. He just wanted me to listen."

"Abuse comes in many forms, Sarah." Claire stopped, unsure of how much to say.

"You don't need to worry about me, Claire. I was just venting. Life is fine. You're right: I need to tell Rodney I want to buy my own things; he'll understand. And, maybe I will insist on going back to work until I'm pregnant."

"Got it," Claire said. "Promise me you will take care of yourself. The way you're living isn't normal."

"Everybody's normal is different. Rodney loves me. He's really very good to me."

"I'm not sure being good to you is the same as being good *for* you. It's not right to give up yourself in order to make your husband happy."

Sarah looked away and shifted uncomfortably in her chair.

Claire considered her friend. "Is there something else?"

Sarah bit her lip. "Well, things are different."

Claire waited, but when Sarah didn't continue, she prompted, "Different how? What things?"

She refilled Sarah's glass and then her own, giving Sarah space to find the courage to explain.

"We've been married over two years."

Claire nodded, staying quiet.

"Relationships change."

Claire nodded again.

Sarah kept her eyes glued to the tabletop. "No one has great sex all the time."

"Probably not." Claire tried to sound nonchalant. "The honeymoon doesn't last forever."

Sarah lifted her eyes and looked directly at Claire. "I know, but— six months ago he started charting my basal temperature."

"He what?"

"You know, taking my temperature as soon as I wake up. If it goes up a little, you know it's a fertile day."

Claire nodded. "Okay. So, how do you feel about that?"

"It's okay, we are trying to have a baby, but…" She took a sip of wine for courage. "We only have sex if it's a fertile day, and then sometimes he can't—you know." Sarah blushed and looked away. "Can't—like, do it."

Unsure how to respond, Claire sipped her wine and waited. When Sarah didn't continue, she said, "It's hard to get pregnant without sex."

Sarah's lips lifted in a wry smile. "I know. I tried to talk to him, but he just gets mad and storms off. I suggested that we go to counseling."

"And?"

"He got really mad. He said we didn't need it and begged me not to leave him. He promised that as soon as things settle down at work it will be better. He swears he just wants to make my life perfect."

"Maybe you should talk to someone on your own."

"Maybe so, but how would I pay?"

"It's seeing a doctor, Sarah. He'd pay your medical bills. You need to take care of yourself, and that means physically and mentally."

"I'm not crazy, Claire. I'm just tired of waiting."

"I don't think you're crazy." Claire reached across the table and squeezed Sarah's hand. "I want you to be happy, and maybe talking to a therapist would help you figure out what to do."

Sarah pulled her hand away. "I know what I want to do. I want to have a baby, and that means I need to have sex with my husband." She gulped her wine and set the empty glass down with a thump. "He says that if I took better care of myself, he'd be fine."

Claire sighed. "You haven't gained an ounce."

"Maybe, but—" Her phone vibrated on the table and she flipped it over. "Oh shit! He wants to know where I am."

"Didn't you tell him we were going to have lunch?"

Sarah nodded. "I did, but I promised it would be quick and it's almost five. I've got to go." She jumped to her feet and pulled some bills from her pocket.

Claire waved them away. "I've got this. Don't worry."

"Thank you." Sarah took a few steps and glanced back. "Don't tell him I told you any of this stuff. I'm just being silly."

Claire shook her head. "I won't. I'm your friend, Sarah. Don't forget that. Call me soon so we can do this again. I miss you."

Sarah gave a half wave and rushed away.

Claire signaled the waiter and checked her messages while she waited to pay the bill. She thought for a long moment and then sent a text to Sarah.

Gr8 seeing you. Good luck. Call me when you can.

CHAPTER TWELVE

NOW DAY 5: Monday 01/29 AFTERNOON

Sarah blinked back the tears that flooded her eyes as she pictured her son. She tapped her pencil on the notepad, then flipped to a new page and titled it *Jeremy Scott Blake.* "Some of this stuff is going to sound crazy," she said and drew a line down the middle of the page.

Mrs. Hendricks nodded her encouragement and remained silent.

"Jeremy never calls me Mother, always Mommy, unless he's mad, and then he calls me Mom."

Mrs. Hendricks nodded again. "Write it down."

Sarah titled the columns **For Sure** and **????**, and began her list.

1. **Mommy/Mom – Mother**
2. **Just learning to read – reads chapter books**
3. **Loves to cuddle – stiff hug**
4. **Smells like my kid – smells wrong**
5. **Very active – too polite, stiff**
6. **Can't sleep without Gaffy – Missing**

Sarah stopped and stared out the kitchen window. "None of this is anything that I can prove."

"May I?" Mrs. Hendricks reached across the table and spun the pad to read the short list. "What's a Gaffy?"

"Stuffed giraffe." Sarah's lips curled in a smile. "He's had it since he was a baby. I have to wash it when he's asleep."

"How do you know it's missing?"

Sarah froze, her eyes wide. Not sure what to say.

The phone on the charger chimed. Sarah grabbed it and glanced at the screen:

You have one new message.

Mrs. Hendricks kept her eyes on Sarah and tapped her fingers against her coffee mug. Waiting for an answer.

Afraid to admit that she'd searched the boy's room, Sarah mumbled, "Umm, I guess I don't know, but I haven't seen it."

"Maybe he's just outgrown it," the housekeeper suggested. "Kids do that. One day it's all about a particular toy and the next day they've forgotten about it."

Sarah shrugged and glanced down at the boy's phone again. She drew the pattern for his security code and watched the screen as the message appeared:

J U 4got your history book. Call me if U need it. M

"Is it from your friend?" Mrs. Hendricks asked.

Sarah didn't answer. *If J stands for Jeremy, maybe I'm wrong; maybe this phone does belong to my son,* she thought. *That's crazy. Jeremy doesn't have a phone or a history book.* She slipped the phone into her pocket and stood up. "I'll be right back." She hurried from the kitchen, up the stairs, and into her bedroom.

Shutting the door behind herself, Sarah pulled the phone from her pocket and called Claire. Her face fell as the same answer message played. "Damn!" she muttered, then punched in the office number.

This time her call was answered on the first ring. "Magnolia Northwest Realty. How may I help you today?"

"I need to speak to Claire Hamilton." Sarah heard the quiver in her voice and forced herself to calm down.

"Ms. Hamilton is unavailable, but I'm sure someone else will be happy to assist you. May I connect you to another agent?"

"No. I need to talk to Claire! Where is she?"

"Ma'am, I can't give you that information."

"This is an emergency. I have to talk to Claire."

"One moment, please." The voice on the phone was replaced with a muffled whisper and then returned. "I'll connect you to Mr. Phelps now."

"Ra—"

Sarah interrupted the new voice, "Randy! This is Sarah Ross. Claire's friend."

"Hey, Sarah. Long time no see. What's up?"

"I need to talk to Claire and she's not answering her phone."

"Didn't she tell you she was going out of the country?" Randy sounded surprised.

"Without her phone?"

Randy chuckled. "That's what I said, but you know Claire. She wanted a break from all the email and social media."

"But you have a way to contact her, don't you? I really have to talk to her."

"Sorry, Sarah. No can do. She took a prepaid phone with her, but even I don't have the number. She didn't want to be in touch. If she calls in, I'll tell her you want to speak to her. Or tell me what you need, and I'll help you if I can."

Sarah clenched the phone and struggled to control her breathing as she asked, "When will she be back?"

"Back in the country, or in the office?"

Sarah resisted the urge to scream an obscenity. "When will she be home?"

"Couple of weeks, I think."

Sarah thanked him and hung up. She slumped down on the bed and composed a text message to Claire; maybe it would reach her somehow.

I need your help. Jeremy is missing and Rodney is holding me captive.

I think he has been drugging me. Please call me at this number.

She pressed "send" and fell back on the bed. Her mind raced. She needed help. Who else could she call? Would the police believe her? Maybe Mrs. Hendricks? Or her parents?

Sitting up straight, Sarah called her mother's number and waited for her to answer.

"Hello."

"Mom." Tears overflowed and Sarah began to sob.

"Who is this?"

"It's me, Mom. Sarah. I need—"

"What have you done now? Are you drinking?"

"No. I'm not drinking. Jeremy is missing and Rodney won't tell me anything."

"Stop it, Sarah." Disgust filled her mother's voice as she continued, "I won't listen to any more of your crazy lies. I told you at Thanksgiving not to call me until you got your act together and I meant it. Neither your father nor I will help you until you do."

The phone beeped and went silent in Sarah's ear. Her mother had hung up on her again.

Sarah clenched the phone and quaked with anger. Finally, taking a deep breath, she forced herself to calm down and think.

I should have known better than to call my mother. She still believes everything Rodney tells her. How could I be so stupid? What if she calls Rodney and tells him I called? He'll find out I have a phone.

Sarah stood and strode to the window. Pulling the drape aside, she looked down at the snowy yard, searching for the man and the dog. She considered her options. There had to be someone who would believe that Jeremy had disappeared, someone who would help find him.

"The police have to help," she said aloud.

She dialed 911.

The operator answered immediately. "911. What is your emergency?"

"My son is missing, and my husband is holding me captive."

"Can you tell me your name?"

"Sarah Blake. My son is Jeremy Blake. The police need to find him."

"Where are you now, Sarah? Are you safe?"

"I'm okay, but Jeremy is missing."

"Is your husband with you, Sarah?"

"No. He's at work."

"Did your husband hurt you or your son?"

"No. I told you, Jeremy is missing. I'm not sure how long he's been gone. Rodney gives me drugs. There's another boy here that Rodney says is Jeremy, but it's not. I know it's not!" Her voice rose hysterically. "You need to help me!"

"Where are you now, Sarah? Are you at home?"

"No. I'm in Rodney's house. It's in the woods somewhere."

"We are tracing your location now, and I'll dispatch the police, but I need you to stay calm. Is anyone in the house with you?"

"Mrs. Hendricks is here, and there's a man in the woods." Sarah searched the woods, trying to find the faceless man among the trees.

The call-taker's voice displayed no emotion as he said, "Tell me about the man in the woods."

"I can't see the man now, but he was there this morning."

"Do you think he has a gun?"

Sarah's voice rose. "How would I know? He's just out there watching."

"Sarah, I need you to stay calm. I'm here to help. Who is Mrs. Hendricks?"

"Rodney's housekeeper. She watches me, too."

"Your telephone number is registered to Jeremiah Johanson. Is that your son?"

"No, I told you, Jeremy is missing. He doesn't have a phone."

"I understand. Just wait one second while I ensure the police are on the way."

Sarah held her breath and waited, listening to the recorded voice saying, "You have reached 911. Please do not hang up." Her hands trembled. She bit her lip and struggled to stay in control.

"Sarah, are you still there?" The voice came back on the line.

"Yes." Sarah nodded as if the voice could see her.

"We've identified your location, and a car is on the way. I need you to stay on the line until they arrive. Okay?"

Sarah nodded.

"Sarah, can you hear me?"

"Yes, please hurry."

"Tell me about Jeremiah. How old is he?"

"We call him Jeremy. He's six."

"When did you last see your son?"

"I don't know. What day is this?"

"This is Monday."

"I was in the hospital, and then Rodney brought me here." Sarah paused and tried to figure it out. "I think he brought me here on Thursday, and Jeremy wasn't here. So, maybe a week."

The sound of a vehicle caused Sarah to look out the window. A black and white police vehicle swung around the curved drive and stopped at the front door.

Sarah sucked in an audible breath. "They're here."

The doorbell chimed from downstairs.

"Don't hang up, Sarah. Are you able to answer the door?"

Sarah didn't answer. Still clutching the phone, she ran from the bedroom and dashed down the stairs, arriving at the entry hall as Mrs. Hendricks opened the door. A uniformed man and woman stood on the porch.

The man said, "Good afternoon, ma'am. We've received a report of a missing child."

Mrs. Hendricks looked over her shoulder at Sarah and then back to the police officers. "There must be some mistake," she said.

The woman glanced down at her iPad. "911 received a call from a Sarah Blake stating that her son Jeremy is missing. We traced the call to this address."

"Jeremy isn't missing. He's in school."

Sarah rushed forward.

Rodney's car whipped up the drive and pulled to a stop next to the police car. The police turned at the sound. Sarah stepped back and cowered behind Mrs. Hendricks.

"Is there a problem, Officers?" Rodney asked as he stepped from his Mercedes, slamming the door behind himself. "Is my wife okay?" He frowned, his forehead creasing in concern as he met the policeman's eyes.

The male officer gestured to his partner to stay with the women and stepped down the stairs to meet Rodney.

"Mr. Blake?" he asked.

"Yes, Rodney Blake. What's the problem?"

"We received a 911 call from this address."

Rodney looked up at Mrs. Hendricks. "What happened?" he demanded. "Is Sarah okay?" He dodged around the policeman and stepped toward the porch.

"Your wife is fine, Mr. Blake." The officer's voice stopped Rodney's movement. Keeping his eyes on Rodney, he continued, "Officer Merrill, go into the house with the ladies." He motioned

Rodney back toward the car. "Please step over here a moment. I need to ask you a few questions."

Rodney looked toward the doorway again and watched it close behind Sarah, Mrs. Hendricks, and the female officer. He smiled at the policeman and shook his head in a weary manner as he tsked. "My wife has been quite ill," he said. "Why did our housekeeper call 911?"

"Your wife made the call, Mr. Blake."

Rodney's eyes opened wide, and he stumbled slightly, catching himself on the roof of the car. "Sarah? How in the world did she do that? What did she say?"

"You look a little pale, sir. Are you okay?"

Rodney forced a smile that didn't reach his eyes. "Yes, yes. Just a little cold. The wind seems to be picking up." He pulled his coat together and buttoned it. "Can we go inside to talk?"

"This will only take a minute. Your wife said that your son," he glanced down at his notes, "your son Jeremy is missing and that she is being held captive."

"Oh, for God's sake!" Rodney spat out the words. "She's fine and free. You saw that for yourself, and as for Jeremy, he's in school where he belongs." He pulled his phone from his pocket and checked the time. "In fact, I need to leave in a moment to pick him up."

"Why would your wife make such a call?"

Rodney sighed and brushed his hand over his face. "She's been ill. She took a bad fall and ended up in the hospital with a brain injury. Since then, her memories have been scrambled. The doctor wanted to have her placed in a psychiatric care facility, but I thought being at home where things are familiar would help her remember." He frowned, causing vertical lines to appear between his eyebrows.

"Sarah's been home five days, and she still insists that Jeremy isn't our son. She thinks he's a stranger. I feel so bad for the little guy. I've been trying to protect him from her craziness, but she's his mom."

"Must be tough." The policeman tsked in sympathy. "Who's the other woman?"

"Our housekeeper, Judy Hendricks. She's been working extra hours to keep an eye on Sarah while I'm at work. I don't want her to be alone."

"Got it." The officer nodded. "I don't think the housekeeper had any idea about the phone call. She certainly didn't think your kid is missing. Just believed that he was in school."

"He's not missing, Officer. But maybe the doctor was right, and I do need to choose a facility."

"Maybe you should. It's always a good idea to follow the doctor's advice."

Rodney looked toward the house. "I need to check on Sarah."

"No need. You go ahead and pick up the kid. I'll just gather my partner and give your wife a little warning about not calling 911 again."

Rodney extended his hand. "Thank you. I'm sorry for the trouble."

They shook hands.

"No problem, Mr. Blake. It's all part of the job. I'm just glad the kid is okay. I've got three of my own. It breaks my heart when a kid is missing."

He turned toward the house as Rodney opened the car door and slid behind the wheel.

Rodney watched the front door close. He pounded his fist against the steering wheel and pushed the ignition to start the car. "Damn it," he muttered.

After the terse warning from the police, Sarah stood with her arms wrapped around her shaking body, tears running down her face. Mrs. Hendricks thanked them and closed the door.

She turned to face Sarah. "I think we need to talk before Mr. Blake gets back. He's going to be very upset."

Sarah nodded.

"That isn't your phone, is it?"

Sarah shook her head and clutched the phone tighter, her fingertips turning white.

"Where did you get it?"

Sarah stayed mute.

"Listen, I know you don't trust me, but we don't have much time, and I can't help you if you don't tell me the truth."

Sarah lifted her eyes and studied the housekeeper's face. "Why would you help me?"

Mrs. Hendricks narrowed her eyes and considered her answer. "Actually, I'm not sure. But something is going on here that doesn't make sense, and right now, I guess I feel like you need protection from your husband. That isn't your phone, and he didn't give it to you, did he?"

Sarah shook her head. "It's the boy's. I found it in his bedroom."

"That's not good." She thought for a moment. "I think we'd better say it was mine and you called while I was in the bathroom."

Sarah looked puzzled.

"We don't want to get the kid in trouble."

"Rodney will fire you if you let me use your phone," Sarah protested.

"Well, we're not going to tell him that. We are going to say you did it without my knowledge. Did you call anyone else?"

Sarah stammered, "Claire and my mother."

"And they wouldn't help you?"

"Claire didn't answer, and her office said she is out of the country. My mother hung up on me."

Mrs. Hendricks extended her hand. "So three calls plus 911, right? Give me the phone and I'll delete the call record. When he asks how you got the phone, say it was on the floor under the table. I'll say it must have fallen out of my pocket. We don't want him to think I'm helping you."

Sarah handed her the phone and protested, "But the police know whose phone it is. They said so."

"Are you sure? I didn't hear them say anything." Mrs. Hendricks pressed the power button. "What code did you use to get in?"

Sarah reached out and swiped the pattern as Mrs. Hendricks waited.

Then Sarah watched as the recent call to Claire was wiped from the phone, leaving only the call to her mother and the 911 call.

"Didn't you get a message on this phone?"

Sarah nodded. "I think it was for the boy."

Opening the message log, Mrs. Hendricks found only one text. She scanned it.

J U 4got your history book. Call me if U need it. M

"What do you think this means?" she asked Sarah.

Sarah stood mute and shook her head.

"J is probably the name of the person who receives messages on this phone. When did the police tell you they knew the registered owner?"

"The 911 man said that they'd traced the phone, and it was registered to Jeremiah something. 'J' could mean Jeremiah." Hope lifted Sarah's voice. "Maybe the boy's name is really Jeremiah."

"Listen to me, Sarah. Your husband is going to return very soon with your son. I'm going to take a screenshot of this message and send it to myself. Then I'll erase it. We don't have time to figure out what it means, but until we do, I'll try to help you. You will have to play along. Can you do that?"

Sarah clenched her fists and took a deep breath. She managed a nod.

"One more thing. Is Jeremy's real name Jeremiah?"

"No. He's just Jeremy."

Mrs. Hendricks quickly typed on the phone and then put it in her pocket. She caught Sarah's eye and smiled. "I could use a stiff drink, but I think we'd better stick to tea. Come to the kitchen with me, and we'll wait for Mr. Blake. You don't want to face him alone."

CHAPTER THIRTEEN

BEFORE: 7 Years Ago

Sarah's heart raced as she drove home in a panic. She knew how angry Rodney would be if he found out she'd talked to Claire about their sex life. Pulling her Honda Accord into the driveway, she pressed the lift for the garage door. The wine she'd shared with Claire roiled in her stomach when she saw Rodney's Porsche Carrera already parked in its space.

Glancing in the rearview mirror to ensure that her hair and makeup were still in place, she took a steadying breath, picked up her purse from the passenger seat, and stepped out of her car. Pasting a smile on her lips, Sarah entered the house from the garage and called out, "I'm home."

Silence answered her.

"Rodney?" She raised her voice slightly and waited. Again there was no response.

Sarah crossed the laundry room and entered the kitchen. She glanced about. Everything was exactly as she'd left it. Sunlight bounced off the chrome faucet and formed a prism in the polished stainless steel of the refrigerator door.

Sarah placed her handbag on the counter and called again. "Rodney."

The living room and dining room both were empty. Sarah shook off her apprehension. She climbed the stairs to the second floor and glanced at the room Rodney used for a home office. The door was open. He always shut it when he was working. *Maybe he went for a run*, she thought and entered the master bedroom.

The sound of the grandfather clock in the entry chiming six times echoed throughout the house.

Sarah unzipped her skirt, stepped out of it, and tossed it onto the bed. She pulled her sweater over her head and felt a hand drop on her shoulder.

She jumped. A scream escaped her lips.

"It's only me," Rodney said.

The sweater snagged on her hair clip and she struggled to free herself from the cashmere. "You scared me," she stammered. "I didn't think you were home. Why didn't you answer me?" The sweater pulled free and she dropped it on the bed next to her skirt.

Rodney ignored her question. He studied her carefully. "Did you have a good time with your little friend?"

Defiance surged through Sarah and she felt her face flush. "Yes, I did." Sarah turned away and crossed to the closet.

Rodney took two long strides and grabbed her arm. "Aren't you forgetting something?" he snarled.

Sarah winced at his tone.

His hand tightened on her arm.

"Let go, Rodney. You're hurting me."

Rodney twisted the skin on Sarah's arm. She gasped and tried to pull away. He tightened the twist. "I give you everything and you appreciate nothing!"

"Please stop." Sarah's voice broke as she held back a sob.

Rodney flung her arm away. "That sweater," he gestured toward the bed, "is a Loro Piana and the skirt is a perfect match. I chose them especially for you, and yet you throw them on the floor as if they mean nothing."

"They aren't on the floor," Sarah protested.

Rodney glared at her and Sarah stepped back.

"Pick up your clothes and put them away, now!" he said, enunciating each word.

Sarah kept her eyes on her husband as she stepped sideways to the bed and carefully picked up her sweater. She searched for something to say that would calm him down as she moved to the armoire and pulled out the folding shelf. Carefully, she smoothed the delicate sweater flat and crossed its sleeves over the front. Her hands trembled. She folded the bottom of the garment up to the top.

Rodney grabbed her arm again.

Sarah flinched and tried to pull away.

"For God's sake, Sarah. You know you need to fold tissue paper between the layers. What is wrong with you?"

"I'm sorry, I wasn't thinking."

Rodney dropped her arm and turned away. "You're completely selfish and thoughtless," disgust filled his voice, "and lazy. Do it right, then hang up your skirt and get dressed. I'll be downstairs." He strode out of the room without looking back.

Hurriedly, Sarah placed acid-free tissue between the folds of her sweater and placed it on the stack of pastel cashmere sweaters in her drawer. "I hate these dumb sweaters," she said, slamming the drawer shut.

She grabbed the skirt from the bed and hung it in its proper place in the closet. For a second she remembered the happy, colorful jumble that used to hang in her closet. Claire was right: she used to put together great outfits.

Sarah pulled on heavy, black linen slacks and a matching tunic. She considered her reflection in the full-length mirror. *I look like my mother, but Rodney likes it.* After glancing around the room to be sure she'd left nothing out of place, Sarah went downstairs to join her husband.

Rodney was in the kitchen, chopping vegetables on the island. Catching sight of his wife, he smiled at her and gestured with the knife. "Since you've been out all day, I thought I'd better figure out dinner. Why don't you keep me company while I get this started and you can tell me all of Claire's gossip."

Relief lifted the cloud of angst from Sarah's thoughts. She smiled and slipped onto one of the tall stools. "No gossip. Just girl talk."

"I expected you home before four. Did you forget I had an early day today?"

Sarah frowned slightly. She remembered telling him about her plans for a late lunch and promising to keep it short, but she was certain he hadn't mentioned that he planned to be home early. "Time just flew by. It's been months since we had lunch together."

The knife flashed, up and down. Vegetables accumulated in thin, even slices.

"Well, you must have talked about something. You were gone for hours."

"Not that long," she protested. "We had sandwiches at that little bistro by Claire's office."

"And wine?"

"Just a glass."

Rodney cocked his eyebrow and gazed at Sarah. "One?" he asked.

"I don't know, Rodney. We were having a good time. Might have had two—does it matter?"

"It matters that you prefer to have drinks with Claire instead of spending my afternoon off with me."

"I had no idea you had the afternoon off. You never mentioned it. If you had, I wouldn't have gone to lunch with Claire."

The knife slammed down on the cutting board. "Are you calling me a liar?"

Sarah jumped. "No! Of course not. I must not have been listening," she stammered.

Rodney gestured toward Sarah's handbag on the counter by the door. "Claire left you a message."

He kept his eyes on Sarah as the color drained from her face. She saw his lips form a smile, but his eyes remained cold and calculating.

Sarah stopped breathing, bile slipped up her throat, and for a moment she thought she'd throw up. She avoided making eye contact with her husband, afraid that he would sense her fear.

Rodney resumed chopping vegetables, the slices no longer thin and even, as he said, "First you weren't thinking and now you're not listening." He pointed the knife at Sarah. "Seeing Claire is never good for you. She's a bad influence."

Anger ignited Sarah's indignation. "That's ridiculous. What makes you even think such a thing?"

"It's obvious Claire thinks something is wrong in our marriage." He reached across the counter and pulled Sarah's phone from under her handbag. "Why else would she need to wish you good luck?"

"You read my messages? What's wrong with you?" Sarah grabbed the phone and swiped open her message app. "Messages are private."

"If you didn't have anything to hide, you wouldn't mind." Rodney bounced the knife on the cutting board. "I think you've been oversharing again."

"She's my best friend, Rodney."

"I'm your husband."

"Of course, I know that."

"And do you know that what happens between a man and his wife is private?"

Sarah nodded. "I just told her we'd been to the doctor."

"Then," Rodney stabbed the point of the chopping knife into the cutting board, "why did she text 'call me when you can'?"

"Ummm, I don't know."

"I believe you know exactly why."

Sarah flinched and tried to think of something to say. Anything but the truth.

"You told her there is something wrong with me, didn't you."

"Of course not." Sarah stood and backed away from the stool. "I told her I was thinking about going back to work until I have a baby."

Rodney's eyes narrowed.

Sarah felt herself flush.

In a flash, he rounded the counter and grabbed her arm, pinning it behind her back, holding her too tight.

"Stop it, you're hurting me!"

He tore at the collar of her tunic, but the linen refused to tear.

Sarah struggled against him and managed to twist out of his grip. She took a step away, but it was too late.

He swung. His open palm connected with her cheek.

She screamed. Pain flared, and she stumbled and fell.

Rodney was on her, ripping at her clothes and shoving his knee between her legs.

"Stop," she tried to scream, but it was only a whimper.

***

Sarah lay on the floor, too frightened to move or cry. The cold tile pressed against her naked legs. Her heart raced. Cramps seized her thighs and her legs quivered. She struggled, trying to take a deep breath and force the shaking to stop. She wanted to scream but knew she should stay quiet.

She opened her eyes. Rodney was gone. The kitchen was silent, filled with the glow of the setting sun. Sarah rolled to her side and managed to sit up. Her head throbbed as the kitchen seemed to spin. Closing her eyes, she waited for the dizziness to pass.

"He raped me," she murmured. The memory crashed her defenses. She covered her mouth with her hand, forcing back a scream as spasm after spasm of loathing quaked through her body.

A soft, warm blanket settled over her shoulders. Sarah grabbed it and pulled it close.

"Oh, baby," Rodney whispered, "I'm so sorry. I didn't mean to hurt you."

Sarah pulled her knees close to her chest and dropped her head.

He caressed her hair.

She pulled her head away.

Rodney placed his hand on her cheek and tipped her head up.

She closed her eyes.

"Look at me, baby. You know I love you."

Sarah shook her head.

"Don't do that, Sarah. I just need you to listen to me."

"You raped me!"

Rodney drew back and dropped his hand. "What?" His mouth dropped open in shock. "Rape? Why would you say such a thing? What's wrong with you?"

Outrage filled Sarah. Her eyes narrowed and she spit out, "You forced yourself on me! That's rape!"

"I was mad and I admit I was a little rough, but," he shook his head and frowned, "that wasn't rape. I apologized."

Sarah picked at the blanket and stared at him.

"Come on, baby. You know I didn't mean to hurt you." He knelt next to her and wrapped his arms tightly around her quaking body.

Sarah froze.

"You need to relax." Rodney rocked her and spoke softly. "When you spend time with Claire you always come home a little drunk and a little crazy. I don't understand why you'd tell her you wanted to go back to work. You know we decided that we'd start our family instead of you working."

"But—"

"Hush now." He stopped rocking.

She felt captive, not comforted. Her body tensed as his embrace tightened. "You knocked me down," she said in a whisper.

"I am sorry, I don't like to hurt you. But you insist on making me mad." He dropped a kiss on her head. "Please, say you forgive me and let's have a nice evening. I promise I won't ask any more questions about Claire or your afternoon."

Slowly, she nodded.

His arms dropped from around her and he stood, holding out his hand to help her to her feet.

Sarah accepted his hand and allowed his embrace.

CHAPTER FOURTEEN

NOW DAY 5: Monday 01/29 EVENING

At the sound of Rodney's car tires crunching on the snow in the driveway, Mrs. Hendricks stretched her hand across the kitchen table. Sarah grasped it so tightly her knuckles turned white. They listened as Rodney and the boy entered through the front door.

"I need to speak to your mother and Mrs. Hendricks, Jeremy. Go upstairs and start your homework."

"May I get a snack first?"

"Not now. It won't take long. I'll call you in a bit."

The women heard the boy on the stairs and then Rodney's approaching footsteps. Sarah dropped Mrs. Hendricks's hand. They straightened and watched as he stepped through the doorway.

He glowered at them, narrowing his eyes and shaking his head. "Now," he began, "what the hell is going on around here?"

Mrs. Hendricks said, "I—"

"Not you." Rodney dismissed her and pointed at Sarah. "I know you called your mother, and, as if that wasn't embarrassing enough, you called 911. What kind of crazy allegations did you make this time?"

Sarah looked down at the table. She steeled herself and raised her eyes to look directly at Rodney. "I told them the truth. Jeremy is missing, and I want him found."

"You're bonkers, Sarah. The kid is not missing. Your mother hung up on you because she assumed you were drunk, and the police will file a report about your crank call. They think I should follow the doctor's advice and send you to rehab." He moved his glare to the housekeeper and asked, "Where'd she get that phone?"

"It was mine. I apologize, sir. I didn't realize I'd dropped it. I checked the recent calls while you were gone, and there are only those two."

"Show me."

Mrs. Hendricks pulled the boy's phone from her pocket and opened the call log. Rodney scanned it and handed the phone back. He turned to Sarah. "I'm trying to be patient, but if you won't cooperate—"

"Cooperate! Cooperate with what? Why are you doing this, Rodney? What do you want?"

"I want you to remember who you are." Rodney frowned and tapped his finger against his lips. He shook his head. "I want to help you."

"But," Sarah said, "I know who I am."

"You think you do. I get that. But we are married. Jeremy is our son. This is our home."

"No!" Sarah's eyes darted to Mrs. Hendricks. "You have to believe me. That boy is not Jeremy."

Mrs. Hendricks looked back and forth between the two, unsure what to think.

Rodney folded his arms across his chest and leaned against the kitchen counter. His cheeks puffed as he blew out his exasperation. "Sarah, how long are you going to fight me on this? Have you been taking the medication?"

"She takes it every time I give it to her," Mrs. Hendricks interjected.

Rodney narrowed his eyes and focused on Sarah.

She dropped her gaze to the floor and shifted in her chair.

"Sarah?"

"What?"

"I asked you a question. Are you taking your medication?"

Sarah avoided answering. "You give it to me at night, and Mrs. Hendricks gives it to me when you are gone. Are you drugging me with something? Did I even have an accident?"

Rodney's arms dropped to his sides. "Those are prescription drugs. Dr. Leavitt says they will help your memory and relieve your headache. He wants you to take them until he sees you again."

"If," Sarah spoke slowly, considering each word, "I had a bad accident, why don't I have an injury?"

"Can't you see that bruise on your forehead? You have a brain injury." His face hardened as he clenched his jaw. He shook his head and glared at Sarah.

Mrs. Hendricks stayed silent, focusing on their argument.

"It's just a fading bruise; it's almost gone. I don't even have a lump on my head. It doesn't make sense that I can remember falling in the woods but I can't remember having an accident. There doesn't seem to be anything wrong with me."

Rodney's hands turned into fists. He stood up straighter and took a step toward Sarah.

Mrs. Hendricks stood up.

Rodney glanced at the housekeeper and then focused on Sarah. "If you'd like, I can call Dr. Leavitt, and he will explain it to you again, but he may insist that you go back into the hospital."

Sarah's voice broke as she asked, "Are you threatening me?"

"Don't be stupid. I'm just telling you what might happen if you continue to act crazy."

Sarah glared at him. Behind his back, she saw Mrs. Hendricks press her finger to her lips in a shushing motion. "I'm sorry," Sarah said. "I'm just trying to understand."

Mrs. Hendricks folded her hands next to her cheek, tilted her head to the side, and closed her eyes for a brief moment.

Sarah frowned, uncertain of what the housekeeper was trying to communicate.

Rodney glanced over his shoulder.

Mrs. Hendricks raised an eyebrow and said, "Perhaps Mrs. Blake needs to rest before dinner. This has been a difficult day."

Shifting his eyes between the two, Rodney sighed. "It certainly has."

"Why don't you go upstairs, Sarah, and I'll bring you a cup of tea." Mrs. Hendricks turned away and reached for the tea kettle.

"Good idea." Rodney held out his hand. "I'll walk you up."

Sarah cringed and ignored his hand. Her knees felt weak, and she shivered as she stood. She kept her voice level. "It's fine, Rodney. You don't need to help me."

"I think it's best." His lips twisted in a smile that didn't reach his eyes. "You seem a little unsteady." He placed his hand on her back. "Come on. Let's give Mrs. Hendricks some space to finish dinner."

Sarah allowed him to propel her out of the room. She glanced back once, but Mrs. Hendricks had her back turned and was busy with something in the cupboard.

Rodney kept a loose grip on her arm as they walked through the house and up the stairs. Sarah didn't struggle. She needed time to think. Stopping at the open bedroom door, she said, "Thank you, Rodney. I'll rest and come down for dinner."

His hand tightened on her wrist. "You'll do more than that," he hissed. "You'll think about what's best for you and Jeremy."

Sarah glanced toward the boy's slightly open bedroom door. She thought she saw a movement through the crack and brought her eyes up to look straight at Rodney. "I've done nothing but think about what's best for Jeremy since the day he was born. I don't know why you are lying, but I know you are, and I'll prove it."

Rodney twisted her arm, drawing it up high and tight behind her back. "You'll do as I say," he snarled and thrust her toward the bedroom door.

Sarah stumbled and saw the boy's door close as Rodney pushed her into the room.

Rodney pulled her door shut.

She leaned her head on the door, too angry to cry.

***

Sarah paced the room; her thoughts flew between fear for Jeremy and anger at Rodney. Her hands flexed, making a fist and then her fingers spreading wide. She paused at the window and looked toward the woods. Ajax sat, half concealed, watching the house. "Find Jeremy," she whispered.

Ajax's head lifted and seemed to peer straight into her window.

"Please," she pleaded, "find Jeremy."

The dog stood and took a tentative step toward the house. He looked away, his attention caught by something. Sarah watched as Ajax wheeled and ran deeper into the woods. She blew out her breath in a long exhale. "I'm smarter than this," she said. "I got away from him once. I can do it again." She resumed pacing, her thoughts racing.

A quiet tap on the door sounded. She paused, unsure if she'd heard anything. The tap sounded again. Sarah scurried to the door. "Who's there?"

"It's me," the boy said quietly. "Are you okay? I saw him push you."

Can I trust this kid? she wondered and made a decision. *I'll ask him to help me. No one else seems to care.*

A second voice said something. Sarah leaned on the door, straining to hear. Was Rodney back? What if he found the boy talking to her?

The boy's voice sounded clear. "No, ma'am. I was just going to knock and ask Mother if she wanted to come downstairs with me."

Sarah pressed her ear even harder against the door.

"That's very nice of you, Jeremy," Mrs. Hendricks said. "I'm sure your mother needs a rest. I've brought her a cup of tea. You run along and get your snack, and I'll check on her."

Sarah listened but heard only silence for a long moment. Then Mrs. Hendricks opened the door and stepped inside, closing the door behind her.

"We only have a minute," she said. "I told Mr. Blake I was bringing you a cup of chamomile tea to calm you down. He allowed it, but if I stay too long, he'll become suspicious." She held out the cup.

Sarah backed away, shaking her head and not reaching for the cup.

Mrs. Hendricks nodded and crossed the room to the adjoining bath. She dumped the tea in the toilet, flushed, and turned to face Sarah. Her lips lifted in a half smile. She shrugged.

Sarah stared at her wide-eyed.

Mrs. Hendricks said, "I don't know if you are telling the truth, but there is something wrong here."

"Did he put something in the tea?"

"Maybe. He said it was sugar."

Sarah clasped her elbows as she pulled her arms tight and bent forward. She rocked herself and managed to say, "Thank you."

Mrs. Hendricks turned and crossed the bedroom to the door. She placed her hand on the knob and then looked back. "Collect yourself," Mrs. Hendricks cautioned. "You need your wits about you." She opened the door, stepped through, and closed it.

CHAPTER FIFTEEN

BEFORE: 7 Years Ago

For the next week, Rodney courted Sarah, kissing her goodbye each morning and bringing home flowers at night. He gently traced the bruise that bloomed on the side of her face and apologized over and over for frightening her. Sarah stayed inside, and every day she resolved that as soon as her bruise disappeared, she would find a job and leave him. She thought about calling Claire but was too embarrassed to admit how right her best friend had been about Rodney.

By the end of week three, Rodney's tender concern waned. The bruise had faded to a greenish-yellow smudge. When she touched it, only a brief sensation of pain remained. Claire sent a message inviting her to meet for lunch, but Sarah made an excuse about being too busy and added she'd let Claire know when she had a free day. Claire sent back a thumbs-up emoji.

Using her phone, Sarah opened the INDEED app and searched for administrative assistant positions in the Seattle area. Multiple listings popped up and a quick scan assured her that she was qualified for several. Pressing the "more information" link led to the need to sign up and upload a resumé. Sarah shut her eyes and blew out an exasperated breath. She closed the app and erased her search history. Rodney would be furious if he knew she was looking for a job without his permission.

Am I really afraid of my own husband? she asked herself.

She glanced at the time and hurried to the kitchen to begin dinner.

***

"You're very quiet tonight, darling," Rodney said, pushing his chair back from the table. "Did you have a busy day?"

Sarah lifted her eyes from her plate and attempted a smile. "No."

"Did you go out?"

Sarah shook her head.

"Talk on the phone to anyone?"

Sarah shook her head again. "Claire sent a text asking me to have lunch." She touched her fading bruise.

Rodney's eyes narrowed. He examined her as he lifted his glass, drank the last of the wine, and reached for the open bottle.

He looks like a snake, Sarah thought. She dropped her eyes, afraid he would see her fear.

"I just answered that I didn't have time and I'd let her know when I did." She forced herself to make eye contact.

"I don't understand what you see in that woman. She's nothing but a troublemaker."

Sarah stayed quiet, watching as he refilled their wineglasses and set the bottle back on the crystal coaster. She saw his look harden and reached for her glass. Her hand trembled, so she pulled it back and placed it in her lap, pressing her hands together.

"Seriously, Sarah. I asked you to stay away from Claire."

Sarah knew she should stay silent but instead heard herself say, "She's my best friend. I like spending time with her."

Rodney's chair scraped across the flooring as he pushed it back and stood. His jaw tightened. He spoke through clenched teeth. "You don't need a friend like that. You need to trust me and stop arguing with me, Sarah. You know I only want what's best for you."

Sarah dropped her eyes and nodded.

He moved behind her chair, and she felt his hand caress the bruise. His voice changed as he said, "Why don't you take your wine and go up and run a nice bubble bath? I'll clean up the kitchen." He slid her chair back. She rose slowly, one hand on the table. Rodney picked up her glass and held it toward her.

Sarah froze.

Rodney grinned. "Goodness, you really are a mess tonight." He moved the glass closer. "Take it and run along. You need to relax. I'll check on you in a bit."

Sarah accepted the glass and felt her eyes fill with tears. She stumbled from the room. Glancing back, she saw Rodney move into the kitchen and pick up her phone from the counter. *Thank God, I didn't lie about Claire's text*, she thought.

Instead of a bath, Sarah changed into white silk pajamas and carried her wine into the bedroom, where she settled on a lounge with a novel and listened for Rodney's movements. She heard the sound of ice clink against a glass and knew he was mixing an after-dinner drink. The click of his study door closing satisfied her concern. She was sure that he wasn't angry anymore. He must have read the text. With any luck, he'd stay in his study until she was sound asleep. It couldn't be more than 8 p.m., too early to take a sleeping pill.

Sarah opened her book and tried to concentrate on the words.

***

The sound of the shower caused Sarah to stir and open her eyes. Morning light filled the bedroom. Rodney's side of the bed hadn't been disturbed. Sarah sat up. The room tilted a bit. Her stomach rolled. She lay back down and took a few deep breaths, hoping to control the rising nausea.

Throwing off the blankets, she struggled to her feet, rushed to the guest room bath, and fell to her knees. She coughed and retched as nothing but yellow bile spilled into the toilet.

"Shit," she muttered and wiped her mouth with toilet paper. Dropping her forehead into her hands, Sarah breathed in through her nose and puffed her cheeks as she exhaled. Another wave of nausea caused her to expel more bile.

She heard Rodney clear his throat.

A damp washcloth pressed against her hand, and she seized it, grateful to feel the cool relief as she wiped her face and neck.

"Are you okay?" Rodney asked.

Sarah blew out another breath and managed a nod. "Something must not have agreed with me. I only had two glasses of wine last night." She turned her eyes up to look at her husband.

He held out a hand and helped her to her feet without commenting. Studying her carefully, he said, "Go brush your teeth. I need to get to work." He left the bathroom.

Sarah stayed where she was until she heard him leave. Then she rose, went into the master bath, brushed her teeth, and took a long, hot shower before going downstairs to find her phone and call Claire.

Claire answered her phone with a cheerful, "Good morning."

"I need to talk," Sarah blurted out.

"Okay, now or do you want to meet for coffee?"

Sarah touched her face. She could hear the quiet sound of Claire typing on her keyboard. She forced herself to admit, "I can't meet you. Are you busy now?"

"Never too busy for you. Go ahead."

"You're right. I need to go to work. I looked at jobs yesterday, but..." She took in a jagged breath. "I can't let Rodney know until I get one."

Claire jumped in. "Got it. You need an email and a phone number that he doesn't know about."

The sound of her keystrokes sped up.

"Exactly, but how?" Sarah's stomach roiled again, and she swallowed rapidly.

"I just googled, and it looks pretty easy to do what you want. Give me a bit to check with our IT people and I'll call you back. Okay?"

"Okay, but don't tell anyone."

"Of course not. What made you change your mind about working? He didn't hurt you, did he?"

Sarah touched the fading bruise again and shook her head. Then, realizing Claire couldn't see her, she said, "No. I'm fine. I've been thinking, is all. I need to get my life back on track." She hesitated before adding, "Can you call me when Rodney isn't home?"

"Yes, but..." Claire paused. "Are you sure you want to do this behind his back?"

Tears filled Sarah's eyes and threatened to spill over. "It's the only way," she mumbled.

"You be careful, Sarah. I'll get back to you before five." Then, keeping her voice light, she offered, "If you want me to kick his ass, you only need to give me the word."

Sarah managed a tiny laugh as she said goodbye.

***

True to her word, Claire called back at 4:45. She spoke quickly. "I've got a client in a minute, but I talked to one of the IT guys."

Sarah asked, "What did you tell him?"

"Don't worry. He doesn't know who you are. I told him I had a friend who wants to search for a job without her boss finding out. I think he thinks it's me that's looking." Claire laughed. "If a rumor about me leaving the firm gets started, I'll know where it came from." She tapped her pen on the desk as she continued. "He says you need an anonymous VPN and an untraceable email, along with a phone and number that is not connected to you."

"I have no idea what that means."

"I wrote everything down. I'll buy you a burner phone using my information and then you can meet me at my condo, and I'll help you set everything up. When do you want to do it?"

"As soon as possible, but it's Friday, so Rodney will be home all weekend." Sarah's voice trembled as she asked, "Maybe Monday?"

"I'll clear my schedule for Monday. How early can you get away? It might take a little while to figure everything out."

Sarah hesitated, her thoughts racing in circles. Her stomach heaved and she forced down the bile that rose in her throat. "I can be at your house by ten, but I'll need to be home by two thirty."

"We can make that work. Are you going to be alright this weekend?"

"I think so." She swallowed hard. "Yes, I'll be fine. Thank you for helping me."

***

That night, Sarah pleaded a headache and went to bed early. On Saturday, Rodney had an 8 a.m. tee time. He left without waking Sarah and then called at 3 p.m. to ask how she was feeling. When she said the headache was gone and asked what he'd like for dinner, he said, "If you feel fine, put on a pretty dress—maybe that green silky one—and come meet Carolyn and Mel at the club. We're celebrating."

Sarah watched her reflection in the microwave window. She looked tired but forced herself to smile, hoping it would be echoed in her voice. "Celebrating what?"

"Mel got a hole-in-one. Drinks are on him."

She heard the slight slur in his words and knew he'd already been drinking. She didn't want to go anywhere except back to bed. She tried to think of an acceptable excuse. "Don't you need to come home to change?"

"I'll shower here." The sound of loud voices and clinking glasses filled the gap before he continued. "Get an Uber so we only have one car. And get here fast," he ordered and then paused before adding, "Be careful with your makeup. I want everyone to admire my pretty, little wife."

She didn't argue, just agreed to hurry, and hung up the phone. But she touched the pale yellowish bruise on her cheekbone and said angrily, "Asshole, I should leave it uncovered."

***

Sunday morning, Sarah felt Rodney's irritation when he entered the kitchen, but she kept her eyes on the magazine she was leafing through as she sipped at a cup of ginger tea. She greeted him without looking. "Good morning."

Rodney gave no response as he crossed to the Keurig, flipped it open, and inserted a pod. He jerked open the cupboard over the coffeepot, took out a mug, and slammed the door shut.

Sarah turned a page and stayed silent.

The coffee gurgled into his mug.

She glanced up and found him, back pressed against the countertop, eyes narrowed, glaring at her.

"What was wrong with you last night?"

Sarah shrugged.

"Everyone noticed. You moped around like some kind of loser."

"You know that I don't know anything about golf. I just didn't have much to contribute."

"You could have smiled and laughed. You didn't even eat your lobster."

"I'm sorry. I guess I was a little tired, and then the smell made me feel sick."

Rodney studied her, his eyes sweeping from her face to her breasts and down over her belly. He chuckled. "I bet you're pregnant. I told you that doctor didn't know what he was talking about."

Sarah's hands flew to cover her stomach. Her lips parted in shock. She shook her head in denial.

He chuckled again. "Go upstairs and pee on one of those sticks. You'll see I'm right."

Sarah stood.

Rodney stretched out his hand to pull her in for a hug.

Sarah ignored it and fled, her eyes filling with tears. *Oh please, not now?* she thought.

CHAPTER SIXTEEN

NOW DAY 5: Monday 01/29 NIGHT

When the door closed behind the housekeeper, Sarah pressed her ear to the bedroom door and listened. *Maybe*, she thought, *the boy will come back.*

Sarah dropped her hand to the doorknob and hesitated.

What if Rodney's waiting in the hallway?

Her hand trembled.

She drew in a shaky breath and turned the knob gingerly, trying not to make a sound.

The door opened an inch.

Sarah took a deep breath, steeled herself, and opened the door enough to see down the hall toward the boy's room. His door was open an inch or two. She watched as it closed. He was still in there; he hadn't gone down for his snack.

Sarah forced herself to consider her options. *That kid is not Jeremy. What is he doing here and why? If I find out, maybe it'll help somehow. I need to know, but he's only a kid. I don't want Rodney to hurt him. I'll be careful.*

She stepped out of the bedroom, softly closed the door behind herself, and walked down the hallway. Pausing at the top of the stairs, she heard sounds from the kitchen and the droning of the television. She hurried the last few feet and stopped in front of the boy's bedroom door. Not daring to even tap, she opened it, stepped inside, and closed the door.

The boy sat on the edge of the bed, his dark eyes wide and intent.

"Don't be afraid, Jeremiah," Sarah murmured, and she saw fear in his eyes. "You are Jeremiah Johanson, aren't you?"

"I'm not allowed to tell you that."

"It's okay, I won't tell Rodney or Mrs. Hendricks. I just want you to know that I borrowed your phone today and I had to delete your messages."

The boy stared at her. When she didn't continue, he said, "I'm not supposed to bring my phone here after school, but I forgot yesterday."

"It's okay. Mrs. Hendricks has it and she'll keep it hidden until she gets a chance to give it back to you."

The boy nodded. He pressed his hand to his mouth; relief flooded his eyes.

"Why are you here, Jeremiah?" Sarah watched as the boy dropped his gaze, shoulders hunched forward. He trembled and jammed his hands between his knees.

He shook his head from side to side. He whispered, "I can't tell you."

"I know you are afraid, but…"

"I'm not afraid," the boy said firmly. He looked up at Sarah. "I'm not doing anything wrong. I'm doing my job."

"Job?" Sarah's hand rose to her chest, fingers splayed across her breastbone. Her eyes narrowed as she considered the boy. "I found a list of reminders in one of your books."

The boy's eyes flashed to the bookcase, but he didn't move or make a sound.

"Why do you have a list of the people in this house?" Sarah took a step closer. "I think someone gave you that list so you would remember our names." She reached out and touched the boy's shoulder. "Look at me."

He lifted his head but didn't meet her gaze.

"Who gave you the list?"

"It's none of your business." He stood abruptly and glared at her.

Sarah stepped back, surprised by his tone.

"I know you aren't my son. So, where are your parents? Why are you living here?"

He sighed. "I am Jeremy, not Jeremiah. I live here because Rodney is my father and you are my mother. I want you to get well and remember me. I'm trying to remind you of who you are." He tilted his head and looked up; a slight smile lifted his lips. "I won't tell Father you used my phone if you don't tell him about the list."

Sarah paled. That sounded like blackmail. *How old is this kid?*

"I'm going downstairs now and you should go back to your room before Father comes to check on you." He stepped around Sarah, opened the bedroom door, and stepped into the hall.

Sarah followed him out the door and down the hallway. At the top of the stairs, the boy paused and put his finger to his lips. Sarah grimaced, her eyes flashing with a surge of anger and frustration.

Back in her bedroom, she crossed to the window and looked out at the snowy yard and woods. Nothing moved. "Mrs. Hendricks is right. I need to calm down and make a plan." Using her finger, she wrote

JEREMY in the frost on the window before she turned away and began to pace.

Pacing didn't help. Sarah was unable to think past her fear and anger. At last, she dropped down on the bed and curled into a ball. The sun set and the room grew dim, but she didn't move until another knock sounded on her door. Sarah didn't answer. She turned her head and watched as the door opened.

Rodney entered and flipped the light switch. The lamp on the table by the window came on. Sarah covered her eyes with her arm and groaned. She rolled onto her back and watched as Rodney crossed the room and placed a tray on the table.

"After your craziness this afternoon, I thought you'd prefer to rest, so I had Mrs. Hendricks prepare a tray for you."

Sarah stayed silent.

"Jeremy is quite concerned about you, Sarah. I had to remind him you're not feeling well, but this can't go on."

Sarah pushed herself up. Her stomach clenched as dread filled her thoughts. "What did he say?" she asked.

"He said you called him Jeremiah today?" Rodney walked slowly toward the bed, watching intently. "Why would you do that, Sarah?"

Be careful, she warned herself. "I don't think I did. He must have misunderstood."

"Perhaps." Rodney's lips twisted in a smile that didn't reach his eyes. "Or perhaps not. It's time for you to get up and eat now."

"No." Sarah shook her head. "This has to stop. I've been here five days, and I don't know how long I was in that hospital place. I don't know what game you're playing, but there is something very wrong here." She paused, realizing she was repeating the words Mrs.

Hendricks had used earlier. "I want my clothes and shoes and I want my son. My *real* son, not that boy."

"Still delusional, I see." He shook his head slowly. "I don't like to see you suffer, Sarah. You know I love you and I only ever have wanted to take care of you."

"Liar! You're drugging me! I know you are."

"Oh, Sarah," he said, sounding upset and sad, "I would never hurt you on purpose. I know we've had arguments in the past, but we've worked through those problems and we are happy now."

Sarah shook her head. "That's not true. We're divorced. You hate me and I hate you."

"'Hate' is a very strong word, Sarah. I admit I hate to see you like this." He turned away from the bed and crossed to the dinner tray. "I'm not drugging you." He lifted the wineglass and took a sip, set it down, then lifted a forkful full of vegetables to his lips and ate it. "There is nothing wrong with this food."

He crossed the room again and opened the door. "I'll leave you alone. Eat and get some sleep. Tomorrow will be a better day."

Sarah sat frozen as the door closed. She held her breath and listened. The lock clicked. She was locked in again.

Sarah glared at the food tray. "I'll starve before I eat or drink another thing that he touches," she vowed and slumped down in the slipper chair next to the window.

It was fully dark now. A bright crescent moon hung just above the tree line. The woods looked dense and ominous. Sarah watched the moon rise higher, causing the snowy yard to glow. The shadow of the house grew darker until the garage door opened, spilling light across the driveway.

Rodney's car pulled out.

She caught a glimpse of that boy in the passenger window. Where would they be going on a school night?

The sound of a knock caused Sarah to jump. Her heart thumped and she pressed her hand to her chest before she managed to call, "Come in."

Mrs. Hendricks said, "I've come for your tray. Are you finished?"

Sarah stood and crossed the room to be closer to the door. "Yes, come in," she repeated.

The doorknob jiggled.

"The door is locked. Please open it."

"I can't. It locks from the outside."

Her words were met with a long moment of silence. Then the housekeeper spoke again, her words clipped and angry: "Stay there. I'll be right back."

Sarah pushed down a nervous giggle. *Where else would I go?*

Leaning her back against the door, she stared at her reflection in the window and waited. Her thoughts chased around in circles. *Where is Jeremy? Why is Rodney doing this? How do I get out of here? Where is Jeremy?*

A scratching sound brought her attention back to the door. Sarah held her breath and listened.

"I don't have a key, but I think I can pick the lock," Mrs. Hendricks said. "It should only take a minute."

Sarah waited. *Can I trust this woman? Who is she? Does she know where Jeremy is?*

The lock clicked and the door swung open. Mrs. Hendricks knelt on the carpet, a small leather case filled with shiny little tools beside her. In her hand was a funny-shaped metal stick.

"Thank you." Sarah reached out and touched the metal pick. "I need to learn how to do that," she added.

"You're welcome, but that's not important right now. We need to talk before your husband gets back."

Sarah gaped, her lips parted, struggling to believe that she might have honestly found an ally.

"I think," Mrs. Hendricks said as she stood up and smiled at Sarah, "that tonight you need to trust me." She touched Sarah's arm. "I don't know what is going on, but I know something is wrong and I think you need help."

Sarah nodded, mute.

"Okay. Just listen. I googled Jeremiah Johnson."

Sarah's eyes widened.

"It wasn't easy, but I found the kid. He's a child actor. He's definitely not your son."

Sarah's knees gave way and she leaned against the door jamb. Mrs. Hendricks placed a steadying hand on her shoulder. "The kid is thirteen and small for his age, but he has acting credits going back almost ten years."

"But—"

Mrs. Hendricks held up a hand to stop her. "I get it. You want to know why. So do I, but tonight we don't have time to find out."

"I have to find my son."

"Yes, of course. I get that. But unless you have an idea where he is, all we have is your husband and this actor kid, and they haven't given you a clue, have they?"

"He's not my husband. We're divorced," Sarah protested.

Mrs. Hendricks shrugged. "Irrelevant at the moment. They've gone out, and Mr. Blake told me to go home, so I have to leave before they get back. Just listen."

Sarah nodded.

The housekeeper bent and retrieved a paper lunch bag from the hallway. "You didn't eat anything, did you?"

Sarah shook her head; distrust darkened her eyes.

"I'm sure you're right about the drugs. This is a sandwich and cookies." She held up the bag. "He hasn't touched them."

She entered the room and dumped the contents of the lunch bag on the nightstand. "If you don't eat it all, you need to get rid of what's left." She crumpled the empty bag and placed it in her apron pocket. "I'm going to flush some of the food from your dinner tray now and then I'll leave and lock the door again. When he comes up here, pretend to be asleep. He'll think you ate."

"But…" she objected.

"We don't have time for an argument, Sarah." Mrs. Hendricks crossed to the table and picked up the fork and dinner plate. Walking toward the bathroom, she continued, "I'll help you tomorrow. I promise. Tonight you need to do as I say."

Sarah straightened her shoulders, took a deep breath, and bit her lip, before exhaling in a rush. She clenched and unclenched her fists, fighting for calm. *I'm tired of everyone telling me what to do.*

The toilet flushed and then flushed again.

Mrs. Hendricks emerged and returned the now mostly empty dinner plate to the tray. She moved back to the doorway and faced Sarah. "In the morning, don't come downstairs until you are sure I'm here. Okay?"

"Why?"

Mrs. Hendricks reached for Sarah's hand and gave it a gentle squeeze. "I think it would be a good idea that until we figure this out, you aren't alone with that man."

Sarah's voice trembled as she asked, "Do you think he hurt Jeremy?"

"I hope not. Remember, eat your sandwich, and pretend to be asleep when he checks on you. Can you do that?"

Sarah nodded.

Mrs. Hendricks gave her a quick hug. "I'll use the picks to relock the door and he'll never know I was up here. You'll be safe until morning as long as he thinks you're asleep. Stay quiet and be careful."

She stepped into the hall and looked back at Sarah. "I really have to go now. Try to rest. I know this is hard. But I will help you, I promise."

Sarah waited, frozen until she heard the lock click into place. Then she crossed to the window, where she looked down at the driveway and waited until she saw the housekeeper's car leave. "It will be alright," she told herself, pressing her elbows tight to her sides to stop her trembling. "I can do this."

She watched the driveway, looking for lights, afraid that Rodney would return before she was ready. Sarah moved to the tray on the nightstand, picked up the sandwich, and attempted a bite. Her throat closed. She was too afraid to eat. Instead, she took the sandwich and cookies into the bathroom, broke them into small pieces, and flushed the toilet over and over until every crumb was gone.

Then she returned to the window and turned out the light. She changed into her nightgown and sat in the dark until, at last, Rodney's car swept up the drive. His passenger was gone.

Sarah rushed to the bed, pulled back the covers, lay down, and pulled the blankets up to her chin. She took deep breaths to calm her thumping heart and lay still, waiting for the bedroom door to open.

Sarah didn't have to wait long until she heard the unmistakable sound of Rodney unlocking the door. She remained perfectly still, her breath steady and soft, battling the urge to open her eyes. His footsteps were silent on the carpet as she sensed him drawing closer to the bed.

"Sarah," he whispered.

She gave no response and felt his hand brush against her cheek. She flinched.

"Are you awake?" he asked.

Sarah mumbled a bit, then turned her back to the door and lay on her side.

His hand caressed her shoulder.

She didn't stir.

After a long minute, Sarah heard the dishes on the tray clink. Opening her eyes just a slit, she could see Rodney's silhouette against the moonlit window. She watched as he pushed the curtain aside and studied the yard.

She thought, *He's looking for the man in the woods. I shouldn't have told him.*

Rodney dropped the curtain, picked up the tray, and crossed the room. Sarah shut her eyes. The door opened and the light from the hallway spilled in. Sarah rolled to her back, keeping her breaths deep and even, and listened to hear what he'd do next.

Behind her closed eyes, the light dimmed and then brightened, and she knew he was back in the room. The closet door opened. She risked peeking again and saw him hang clothing in the closet and place something in the dresser drawer. He stepped into the bathroom. The medicine cabinet opened and closed.

Sarah clenched her teeth to keep from shouting at him. She remembered Mrs. Hendricks's promise to help and forced herself to feign sleep. Rodney stopped by the bed, pulled the blanket up, and tucked it around her shoulder.

Sarah managed not to cringe.

He left the bedside and exited the room, pulling the door shut. The lock clicked into place.

CHAPTER SEVENTEEN

BEFORE: 6 ½ Years Ago

Lydia Ross ran her perfectly manicured fingertips through her sleek bob and sighed.

Sarah cringed. The visit with her mother wasn't going well, but then they never did. She pasted a smile on her face, determined to make an effort. "Is that a new dress? The color looks great on you."

Lydia posed for a moment and smiled at her reflection in the large mirror over the fireplace. "It is. Your father has always liked me to wear blue." Her eyes swept back to her daughter. She raised her hand to her throat and tapped one finger against the blue sapphire pendant she wore. "He gave me this on the day you were born."

Sarah knew this story, but she waited for her mother to finish.

"He'd chosen a ruby, since you were a July baby, but I never liked red."

Or me, Sarah thought.

"Don't make that face, Sarah. Everything isn't always about you." She cocked her head and gave a small click with her tongue. "Have you been off that sofa at all today?"

"I opened the door and greeted you, didn't I?"

"Don't get snippy with me, young lady."

Sarah muttered, "Sorry," as she leaned back against the cushions and swung her feet up onto the coffee table.

"It's almost five. Have you started Rodney's dinner?" Lydia asked.

Sarah shook her head. Her back ached. Her feet were swollen and she was tired of being pregnant. The thought of getting up and fixing dinner for Rodney was impossible. "We'll order takeout, Mother."

"This is not the time to ignore your husband, Sarah." Lydia shook her head and tsked. "Rodney has an important job. One that pays enough for you to live in this house and stay home with your child. The least you can do is clean yourself up and cook a good dinner."

When Sarah didn't respond, Lydia said, "You look very puffy. How much weight have you gained?"

"I'm eight months pregnant! Not fat!" Sarah glared at her mother.

"I know that, Sarah. But it's very hard to get rid of baby weight. We talked about this." Lydia studied her daughter. "If you want to have a long and happy marriage, like your father and I, you need to take care of your appearance. I only gained twelve pounds when I was pregnant with you, and my waist was back to twenty-one inches in less than a month."

"And you still wear a size two." Sarah realized that she sounded like a grumpy teenager and struggled to keep her voice calm as she continued, "I was never a size two. My waist was never twenty-one inches. And, my doctor says gaining twenty-five or thirty pounds will be fine."

"You've always been so touchy, Sarah. I'm only trying to help."

Now it was Sarah's turn to sigh. "I know." She swung her feet down from the coffee table, one at a time, and stood up. The room spun and she shut her eyes for a moment.

"I hope your son takes after Rodney. It wouldn't do to have a boy that cries as easily as you do."

"I'd rather have a sensitive son than a bully." Sarah rubbed her wrist and wondered what her mother would think of the bruise that Rodney had caused last week when she'd opened the wrong bottle of wine.

"I'm going to ignore that. I know you don't mean it the way it sounded. Rodney has been very patient with you. Your father and I can see how much he loves you. He's going to be a wonderful father. Now," Lydia brushed her hands together, saying, "you go clean yourself up and put on something that doesn't look like you've been sleeping in it all day. I'll get dinner started."

Sarah didn't protest. She didn't have the energy to argue anymore. She admitted to herself that she was grateful her mother would cook. Rodney would be in a much better mood if dinner wasn't takeout again.

As Sarah left the room, Lydia added, "And put on a little makeup. A man likes his wife to be as pretty as possible."

Sarah clenched her teeth and kept walking.

A long, hot shower eased the tension from her shoulders. She rubbed lotion on her belly and noted that the stretch marks were darker. Opening the bedroom door, she heard laughter and realized that Rodney was home.

"If you can't beat 'em, you might as well give in," she told herself and stepped back into the bathroom. She added mascara and a swipe of lipstick before going downstairs.

Rodney stood with a highball glass in his hand, leaning against the kitchen counter. Lydia was perched on a tall bar stool with her legs crossed high. One spiky high-heeled shoe dangled off her swinging toe. She, too, held a highball glass of dark brown liquor.

Rodney tilted his glass toward Lydia and said, "Oh yes, I know how she is."

Lydia giggled.

Sarah asked, "Who are we talking about?"

Lydia spun on her stool. "No one you know, Sarah. Rodney was just telling me about his day."

Rodney turned his eyes toward Sarah and took a slow drink. "Wasn't it lucky your mother stopped by and offered to cook dinner tonight? I don't think I could have faced another takeout meal."

"It smells wonderful, Mother."

"Nothing fancy." Lydia slid off the stool. "Just my semi-famous macaroni and cheese, a salad, and a pork chop for the man of the family. There was only one chop in the house, but you can fill up on salad, Sarah."

Sarah winced.

Rodney laughed.

Lydia downed the end of her cocktail and set the glass on the counter next to Rodney. "I have to go make dinner for my own husband now." She stood on her tiptoes and kissed his cheek. "Call me anytime you need my help."

Lydia gathered her purse and jacket, turned to Sarah, and said, "The table is set. Salad is in the refrigerator. Be sure to shake the dressing before you toss it. The casserole and chop will be done in fifteen minutes. You need to go to the grocery tomorrow." She waved toward Sarah.

Rodney chuckled. "You're amazing, Lydia. I'll walk you to your car." He glanced at Sarah. "I'll be right back. Make me another drink."

***

The thirty-eighth week of her pregnancy brought with it a sudden surge of energy. Sarah wandered around the house looking for tasks to occupy herself. Nothing in the house was out of place, her hospital bag was packed and ready to go, and she didn't feel like reading or watching television.

Entering the nursery, she spun the mobile over the crib and ran her hand across the soft blue blanket folded on the rail. She took in the zoo motif and smiled. Everything looked perfect. The room was ready and waiting for the birth of their son.

When her phone vibrated against her baby bulge, Sarah glanced at the caller ID. She dropped into the Kub Haywood nursing chair, propped her feet on the matching footstool, and answered. "Hi. Rodney."

"You sound chipper. You must be feeling better."

"I am," Sarah agreed. "I think I'm in the nesting period the baby book talks about. I feel like I could move a mountain."

Rodney chuckled.

"In fact, I think I'll drive to the store and get a pot roast for dinner. How does that sound."

"Delicious, but I'm calling to say I won't be home for dinner. I'll be quite late." He paused and then hurried on, "I have to entertain a new client tonight."

"I thought that you'd turned all the entertainment over to John."

Irritation filled his voice. "You never listen, do you!"

Sarah flinched.

Then she smiled, hoping it would be reflected in her voice. "I'm sorry. I guess I have a touch of pregnancy brain."

"Yeah, maybe. You've been more flaky than usual. I have to go."

The phone clicked off. Sarah struggled to her feet, rubbed the small of her back, and stretched. She studied the phone in her hand and called Claire.

Claire's bright greeting brought a real smile to Sarah's face.

"Hi yourself," she said. "Rodney's working tonight. Want to meet for an early dinner?"

"Absolutely. I'll be done here by five. Do you want me to come to you?"

"No. Let's meet in the city. This might be my last night out for a while. I'm big as a house, but I'll use an Uber."

They arranged to meet at a new place in Claire's neighborhood. Sarah glanced around the perfect nursery, rubbed her lower back again, and went to change clothes. She selected her favorite playlist—one that Rodney hated—and turned the volume up high. She grinned at herself and sang along as Shania Twain sang "Man! I Feel Like a Woman!"

***

The Uber driver took one look at Sarah and jumped out to open her door and help her into the car. "We aren't headed for the hospital, are we?" she asked.

Sarah laughed. "Nope, just out to dinner. I've still got a couple of weeks to go."

"You sure? I've got three kids, and that baby looks like it dropped."

Sarah rubbed her hand across her taut belly and beamed.

They chatted and shared pregnancy stories all the way to the restaurant.

The valet opened Sarah's door and offered her a hand. Sarah accepted the help and told the driver, "Thanks for the fun conversation. None of my friends are pregnant and it was great to talk to you about all this."

The driver laughed and wished her luck.

Claire swung her MGB into the drive and pulled to a stop as the Uber drove away. "Hey, Mama!" she called.

Sarah giggled and waited for Claire to give the valet her keys.

The women linked arms and entered the bistro.

Looking around, Sarah took in the black-and-white-tiled floor, the dark-paneled walls, and the zinc-topped bar. "I feel like I'm in Paris," she said.

"*Oui, madame*," Claire laughed.

They followed the hostess to a small round table near the back wall and settled themselves in the curved rattan chairs. A handsome waiter took their drink order, a carafe of Burgundy for Claire and still water for Sarah. As he departed, Claire raised her eyebrows and whispered, "*Ooh là là.*"

Sarah giggled. "Stop that."

They laughed together and fell into easy conversation.

Claire sipped her wine and entertained Sarah with tales about her clients.

Sarah relaxed.

Claire flirted with the waiter and ordered her dinner in perfect French.

The waiter grinned and poured more wine from the carafe into her glass. He turned to Sarah and asked politely, "And for you, Madame?"

"The boeuf bourguignon, please." She closed her menu, handed it to the waiter, and said to Claire, "I guess I need red meat tonight. I offered to make a pot roast, but Rodney had to work."

Claire raised her glass. "His loss is my gain. I miss hanging out with you. But I'm glad you got what you wanted."

"I guess, but there is truth to that old saying, 'be careful what you wish for.' Last year getting pregnant was all I wanted. I thought my marriage was perfect." She thought a moment before continuing. "I mean, I'm happy to be having a child, but..."

Claire waited and then prompted, "But..."

Sarah pressed her hand to her side. "I think it's just that the timing seems off. I know it's what I wanted, but the way it happened..."

Claire frowned. "Do you mean because you had just made up your mind to go back to work? Or, something else? Is everything okay between you and Rodney?"

The waiter interrupted with their food and by the time they were settled again, Sarah had rethought telling Claire about her marriage. She smiled and said, "Everything is fine. I'm just being silly. This smells wonderful."

Claire didn't let it go. "You know you can tell me anything, don't you?"

Sarah nodded and asked Claire about her newest listings. The next hour passed quickly as they talked about everything but marriage and pregnancy. The waiter swept away their dinner plates and suggested dessert. They declined and asked for the check.

Sarah excused herself to use the restroom. She pushed back her chair and placed a hand on the table to help her rise.

Claire grabbed her hand. "Stop! Don't get up yet."

"What?"

"Don't look, but Rodney just came in with some woman."

Sarah laughed. "It's okay. She's a new client. He's entertaining her tonight." Sarah pulled her hand away from Claire's grasp. "I'll stop by his table and say hi."

Claire moved her hand to Sarah's wrist. "I don't think it's a client, honey. He just gave her a long kiss."

"He what!" Sarah jerked her head around and caught Rodney in the act of kissing the woman again. "Shit!" Anger flared in her eyes. Her face paled and her hands trembled. She took in a deep breath and pressed her hand against the pain in her side.

"Are you okay?" Claire asked.

"Just a cramp. What are they doing now?"

Claire turned her head and saw Rodney turn his head and drop his gaze from their table. "I think he saw us."

The color drained from Sarah's face.

"Look at me, Sarah," Claire demanded. "You need to breathe. Maybe there's an explanation."

Pressing her hands to her mouth, Sarah shook her head.

Claire kept talking and sneaked another look across the room. "I think they are leaving."

"Is he looking at us?"

"No. I don't think he knows we saw him. They're walking toward the door." She lifted her glass and drained it. "Are you okay? What do you want to do?"

"What I want is a stiff drink and a gun to shoot the bastard!" Sarah dropped her hands to the tabletop.

"Whoa, probably not a good idea," Claire said.

"Yeah, but you asked." Sarah puffed her cheeks and blew out a breath. "What I'm going to do is go to the bathroom and throw cold water on my face, and then I need to tell you some things about my marriage." As she pushed her chair back, the waiter hurried to her side and held out his hand to help her to her feet. Sarah pushed her hair behind her ears and grinned at Claire. "You'd better pour yourself another glass of wine, girl. You're going to need it."

Sarah closed herself in a stall and leaned against the wall. Her fists clenched and unclenched as she struggled to calm herself. Her belly cramped and she muttered, "Damn Braxton Hicks," as she rubbed the cramp away.

Moving to the toilet, she pulled down her underwear and noticed a trace of blood. *Whoever said pregnancy was fun got it all wrong*, she thought.

She washed her hands and headed back to the table.

The cramp moved from her lower belly to her back.

She hesitated.

Claire looked up and jumped to her feet when Sarah's face paled.

Sarah gasped and grabbed for the table she was passing as a gush of fluid rushed down her leg.

The couple at the table looked up, startled. The man jumped to his feet, placed his arm around Sarah, and eased her into his chair. "There you go," he said. "Looks like you're going to have your baby tonight."

"I can't!"

He chuckled. "I don't think you have much choice."

Claire arrived at the table and stooped to hug Sarah.

The waiter pulled out his phone. "Should I call 911?"

"Hold on a second." The man moved his hand to Sarah's wrist and counted her pulse.

His wife spoke up. "My husband's a doctor. Let's all step back and give him a chance to talk to this young lady."

"Thank goodness," Claire said, but she didn't let go of Sarah.

"How long have you been in labor? How close are the pains?" the doctor asked.

Sarah dug her fist into her lower back as she answered, "I'm not in labor. Just some Braxton Hicks and then one cramp and the water broke. Oh, and a little blood in the bathroom."

The doctor smiled and patted her arm. "Then I think you have plenty of time, but you should call your doctor and head for the hospital. I'm sure he'll want to check you." He looked around the restaurant. "Is your husband here?"

"No," Claire answered. "We were just having a girls-night-out dinner. I'll drive her to the hospital."

Claire gathered their belongings and handed her claim ticket to the waiter. "Can you get my car?"

"Sure thing." His French accent disappeared in his excitement to help.

"Ready to walk?" the doctor asked.

Sarah nodded, and he held out his hand to steady her as she stood. "Don't worry," he said. "Babies know when they are ready to be born." He glanced at his wife. "I'll be right back."

She nodded. "Good luck, dear."

"I'm so embarrassed," Sarah murmured.

"No need. Most natural thing in the world." The doctor tucked her arm in his and escorted her toward the exit.

Sarah kept her eyes down and didn't look at any of the diners.

Someone started clapping. Others joined in. She blushed as she looked up and waved. A smile lit her face.

"That's better." The doctor gave his approval.

Claire's car was waiting out front, and the waiter stood holding the door for Sarah.

"We forgot to pay," Claire said, turning back.

"Don't worry. You just drive carefully and get your friend to the hospital. I'll square it with the restaurant." He squeezed Sarah's hand one more time. "You'll have quite a story to tell your child."

"Thank you," Sarah said.

"My pleasure." He closed the door and tapped on the roof.

Claire put the car in drive and pulled into the traffic. "You should call Rodney," she said.

Sarah pulled her phone from her bag. "I'm not calling that bastard. I'm calling my doctor."

***

Sarah stirred when she felt the nurse lift her arm and slip on the blood pressure cuff. She opened her eyes and looked at the infant crib pulled up close to her bed. She smiled and reached out to touch the newborn's chest.

"You have a beautiful baby boy, Mrs. Blake."

Sarah looked around the room and shifted her gaze to the nurse. "Where's Claire?" she asked.

"She went home for a bit while you were sleeping. She said to tell you she'd be back soon."

The cuff tightened around her bicep and Sarah frowned.

"Are you okay? Are you in pain?" the nurse asked, swiping a temporal thermometer across Sarah's forehead. The monitor at the head of the bed beeped as it recorded the stats. The cuff deflated.

"I'm fine. Just a bit sore."

The baby gave a little squeak.

"Your young man is awake."

"His name is Jeremy."

"Right. I believe Jeremy would like to try nursing." She reached for the bed controls and pushed the button to raise Sarah's head, and then scooped up the swaddled baby.

Sarah held up her hand. "Wait. I need to use the bathroom first."

The nurse nodded and asked, "Do you need help?"

Moving slowly, Sarah swung her legs around and stood. She shook her head and crossed to the bathroom, pulled the door shut, and stared at herself in the mirror.

"I'm a mother," she said. A smile played across her face. Then she frowned. "With an abusive, cheating husband."

The sound of the baby crying jerked her from her thoughts.

The nurse knocked on the door and asked, "Everything okay?"

Nothing is okay, Sarah thought, but answered, "Everything's fine. I'll be right out."

With the nurse's help, Sarah settled herself on the bed and opened her arms for the baby. She cuddled him close and felt the pull when he latched on and began to suck.

The door opened, and Claire grinned at Sarah from behind a large bouquet of flowers and balloons. "Wow!" she said. "You had a baby!"

Sarah and the nurse laughed.

"Sorry. That sounded really stupid. Of course, you had a baby. I knew that." Claire set the vase on the windowsill and watched as Sarah lifted the baby to her shoulder and rubbed his back until he burped. "Wow!" she said again.

Sarah smiled. "Jeremy," she asked, "would you like to meet your godmother, Auntie Claire?"

The baby burped again.

"I'll take that as a yes," Sarah said, and she looked at Claire. "Would you like to hold him?"

"Absolutely."

The nurse glanced at Claire. "Wash your hands first." She moved to lift Jeremy from Sarah's arms and waited for Claire to comply before placing him in Claire's.

Claire smiled down at the baby.

"You're a natural at this," the nurse said. "Do you have children?"

"Nope. Just nieces and nephews, and now Jeremy." Without lifting her eyes from the baby, she said, "He's beautiful, Sarah. He looks just like your dad."

The nurse slipped out of the room as Claire stroked a finger across Jeremy's cheek and said, "It's almost five a.m. Have you called Rodney?"

"I don't want to talk to him." Sarah pulled the blankets higher and scowled.

Claire studied Sarah's face. "I get that, but even though he's a jerk, he must be wondering where you are."

"He's probably not even home yet."

Claire's eyes darkened. She shook her head and clicked her tongue. "Does he stay out all night?"

"Sometimes," Sarah admitted. "We sleep in separate bedrooms now. I don't think he'd know if I'm home or not until he wants breakfast at seven."

"Still," Claire chose her words carefully, "you need to tell him."

"Can't you do it?"

"I could, but…"

"Yah, I guess that wouldn't be a good idea. I'll call him now." Sarah pulled the wheeled table closer and picked up her phone, opened it, and pressed Rodney's number.

Claire walked with the baby to the window and turned her back. She tried not to listen as Sarah left a message. "Rodney. I had the baby at one thirty-three this morning," she said and hung up. Claire turned back to face Sarah. She raised an eyebrow and waited.

"Short and sweet," Sarah declared. "He can figure out the rest. I'm going to sleep now. You can stay if you want."

Claire laid Jeremy in his bassinet, covered him carefully with the tiny blue blanket, and then sat on the side of Sarah's bed. She brushed

Sarah's hair back with a gentle hand. "I'll stay until Rodney gets here."

Sarah's eyes drifted shut. Claire moved to the reclining chair and kept watch until she, too, fell asleep.

The two were awakened abruptly when the door slammed against the wall. Startled, Claire pushed the recliner upright with a resounding clunk. Sarah sat up and gave a small gasp. Jeremy burst into loud wails. Rodney strode toward the bed. Sarah cringed backward against the pillows.

"What in the world is going on in here?" an angry nurse asked as she entered the room.

Rodney stopped in mid-stride and smiled down at the woman. "I'm sorry," he said. "I was just excited to see my son. I didn't mean to upset anyone."

The nurse reached into the basinet and picked up the screaming child. She held him close and bounced a bit. "Hush now," she said, "no need to be afraid. It's just Daddy, who is a little late to the party but anxious to meet you, young man."

Sarah saw Rodney clench his fist and shove his hand into his pocket. The smile he managed didn't reach his eyes. "I was working and my wife didn't call."

"It happens." The nurse shrugged. "Mommy, I think you should nurse this one and then your husband can get acquainted with him." She handed Sarah a wet wipe for her hands and waited for Sarah to open her gown.

Rodney turned away as he spoke to Claire. "Come outside with me and tell me what happened."

Claire exchanged a look with Sarah and gave her a thumbs-up as she followed Rodney into the hall. Rodney didn't look at his wife or son but headed to the door. Claire stopped to hug Sarah, but when he turned and glared at her, she followed him into a deserted waiting room.

"I want you out of here, but first—" Rodney kept his voice low.

Claire interrupted. "Wait a minute. I'm here for your wife, not for you. I'll leave when she asks me to leave and not before."

"What the hell happened? Why didn't she call me when labor started?"

Claire let sarcasm color her voice as she answered, "Because you were busy."

"I was working."

"Is that what you call it?" Claire tilted her head and glared. "It didn't look like work, but you did look busy."

"I was entertaining a client last night. Sarah knows that."

Claire arched her eyebrows. "I never kiss my clients."

Rodney sank down on a convenient sofa. "Did Sarah see?"

For a second Claire almost felt sorry for this man, but then she remembered the look on Sarah's face when she'd turned and seen him kissing the other woman. "Yes," she answered.

Rodney cradled his head in his hands and stayed quiet for a long minute.

Claire waited for an explanation.

Instead, Rodney pushed himself to his feet and hissed, "I want you out of here. If you weren't always insisting that Sarah go out with you, she would have been home where she belongs and none of this would have happened."

"That's ridiculous! You were out with another women when your wife was about to give birth. I'm not the bad guy here."

"That," Rodney stabbed a finger at her, "is exactly what I'm talking about. You have no idea what it takes to be married and you never will. No man could stand to be around a bitch like you."

Claire recoiled. "My life is none of your business. Sarah needs my friendship. I'm going to be Jeremy's godmother."

"You will over my dead body. I want you out of our lives and I want it now."

Claire turned her back and headed for the door. "We'll see about that," she taunted.

Rodney grabbed her arm and squeezed.

Claire jerked away. "You ever touch me again and I'll sue your ass off."

"Sorry." Rodney dropped his hand. "I'm trying to protect my family. I love Sarah and I know I should have been there last night."

"And not out with another woman?"

"She is just a client," he protested.

"Right." Claire hurried back to the room with Rodney close behind.

CHAPTER EIGHTEEN

NOW DAY 6: Tuesday 01/30 MORNING

Sarah lay restless, tossing and turning, her gaze fixed on the ceiling as the interminable night dragged on. Her stomach rumbled. She wished she'd eaten the sandwich the housekeeper had provided. Sarah contemplated getting dressed, but that seemed to be when Rodney unlocked the door each day. Mrs. Hendricks's admonition about never being alone with Rodney made sense. Turning on the shower felt too risky; she didn't want to reveal to him that she was awake.

At last, the patch of sky she could see from the bed brightened. She heard car tires crunching over the snow in the driveway. A dog barked. *Ajax,* she thought, *do you know where Jeremy is? Is he safe?*

A soft click drew Sarah's attention to the door. Had he unlocked it? She wondered if it was safe to go downstairs. She drew in careful deep breaths and stayed put. The door didn't open. She pushed the duvet out of her way, slid off the bed, tiptoed to the door, and pressed her ear against it to listen. She heard nothing and tried the knob—it turned easily.

Sarah dropped her hand without opening the door and walked across the room, pulled back the window drape, and looked down. Mrs. Hendricks's car was parked in clear view. Her shoulders relaxed and she blew out the breath she hadn't known she was holding.

"Good morning, darling."

Sarah jumped and dropped the drape. She spun around. Rodney, dressed for work, leaned casually against the frame of the now open door.

"Did you sleep well?"

"I won't sleep well until—" Sarah caught herself and stopped. "Until I get my memory back," she finished.

His lips twisted in a sneer as he strode across the room and flung the drape open. "What were you looking at?"

Sarah struggled to keep her tone light. "Nothing."

She took a step away, but Rodney reached out and grabbed her arm. She froze. "Look at me!" he demanded.

Sarah took in a trembling breath and forced herself to meet his eyes.

"Is your phantom man in the woods out there again?"

Afraid to speak, Sarah shook her head.

His hand tightened, trapping her in place, as he turned his gaze back to the window and scanned the tree line.

Sarah's stomach growled.

He regarded her with a mix of disdain and frustration, shaking his head. "You're a complete mess. I'm leaving for work now, but I've already spoken to Mrs. Hendricks. If there is a repeat of yesterday's behavior she'll be out of a job. And, let me be clear," he warned, narrowing his eyes and frowning, "you will not enjoy the consequences. Is that understood?"

She nodded, afraid to speak.

Rodney let go of Sarah's arm and stormed out of the bedroom.

Sarah rubbed her arm and forced back tears. She waited by the window until his car pulled out of the garage and drove away. Then, without getting dressed, she hurried downstairs and joined Mrs. Hendricks in the kitchen.

***

Sarah poured herself a cup of coffee and sat down in front of the plate of scrambled eggs and toast on the kitchen table. "Thank you, Mrs. Hendricks," she said. Her stomach rumbled again. "I'm starving." She lifted her fork, then hesitated and laid it down. "What if Jeremy is hungry? He must be so scared."

"Your husband is Jeremy's father. No matter what game he's playing, I doubt he would hurt his own child." She filled a mug with coffee and sat down across from Sarah. "Was he ever abusive in the past?"

"To me, but not to Jeremy, at least not physically." She pulled up the sleeve of her robe and revealed the red bruise that encircled her arm. "But he's changed. He seems, um, different, more angry."

Mrs. Hendricks reached for Sarah's arm and gently touched the dark red handprint that encircled her bicep. "That looks painful."

Sarah nodded and pulled the sleeve back down. "It doesn't matter what he does to me as long as I find Jeremy."

"I want to help you with that, but I need to understand. Why do you believe Rodney has anything to do with Jeremy's disappearance?"

"All of this," Sarah waved her hand to indicate the house and yard, "is a lie. I've never been here before. And you know it, too. You told me you found that boy's acting credits."

"Yes." Mrs. Hendricks nodded. "That kid is definitely not Jeremy Blake, but I'm not sure he's Jeremiah Johanson, either."

"But last night you said…"

"I know what I said." She sighed and pushed her hair back behind her ears. "You might as well call me Judy; I'm tired of hearing you call me Mrs. Hendricks."

"Okay, Judy, tell me what you know, please."

"I wish I could, but I'm not sure I know anything that's true. We need to figure this out together. Let's start at the beginning. Tell me everything you remember about the last night you spent at home with Jeremy."

Swallowing the last forkful of eggs, Sarah nodded her agreement. "It was just a regular Friday night."

"Do you remember the date?"

"It was payday, so January fifteenth."

"Fifteenth?"

"Yes, I'm sure it was. I get paid on the first and the fifteenth."

"Do you realize what today's date is?"

Sarah shook her head. "You know Rodney has been keeping me away from anything that shows the date."

Judy kept her eyes fixed on Sarah's face. "Wasn't the date on the kid's phone?"

"Maybe, but I didn't notice it."

Judy tapped her calendar. "It is January thirtieth, Sarah." She watched Sarah consider her revelation. "This is the sixth day you've been here. If it's true that you had an accident and ended up in the hospital only a week or a few days before Rodney brought you home, and that the boy living here is not your son, where has Jeremy been for those missing days?"

"I remember being with Jeremy and then I woke up in a hospital, and the nurse brought me clothes, and then we came here. Right away."

"I don't think that could be right." Judy shook her head. "It doesn't make sense. Start on January fifteenth. What did you do at work that day?" She opened the calendar app on her phone and opened the month display for January.

"I don't know, probably the same thing I do every day." Sarah propped her elbows on the table and massaged her temples. "What difference does that make? Jeremy wasn't at work with me."

"Then where was he?" Judy turned the calendar so Sarah could see the screen. "The fifteenth was a Monday, Martin Luther King Day. The schools would have been closed."

"But I know it was payday because I picked Jeremy up from Extended Day at the school and we went to the grocery. I let him choose his own dinner. I only do that on the first and the fifteenth, when I get paid."

"Didn't you tell me you work for the Parks Department?" Sarah nodded. "Is your paycheck auto-deposited to the bank?" She nodded again. "I think you may have been right when you said it was Friday, but that would mean the last night you saw Jeremy was January twelfth. If I'm right, we are looking at twelve, or maybe thirteen, missing days." Judy picked her words with care as she said, "Let's assume for a minute that it was Friday, a Friday before a long holiday weekend. Did anything special happen at work that day?"

Impatience colored Sarah's voice. "How is that going to help us figure out where Jeremy is now?"

Judy cocked her head, her lips curled in a smile. "Maybe it won't, but if you can remember the events of the day before, it might lead to your remembering exactly what happened the day he disappeared."

"I know exactly what happened. I woke up. And Jeremy was gone. There isn't anything else to tell."

"I think there is. Memory is a strange thing and even though you don't believe it, I'll bet you remember more than you think you do. Humor me. Try to think about your last day with Jeremy."

Sarah closed her eyes for a moment and sighed. Then, opening her eyes slowly, she focused on the kitchen wall, staring into the past. "It was cold in the house and Jeremy was mad because he wanted hot chocolate and I said we didn't have time. He wanted to wear his cowboy boots. I didn't want him to because I knew it was going to snow and they have slippery soles. He was stomping around, telling me I'd be sorry if I didn't let him. He sounded so much like Rodney that I yelled at him to stop." A tear escaped and she brushed it away. "He said I was a bad mommy."

Judy stayed quiet, waiting for Sarah to continue.

"When I dropped him at school, he was still mad." Sarah rose and crossed to the counter to fill her coffee mug. She lifted the pot toward Judy, who shook her head no. Sarah sat back down. "I took a late lunch and went to the pub with Becca. She's a single mom, too, and when I told her about my morning, she laughed and said 'kids can be assholes.' It made me feel better."

Sarah stopped talking and twisted her mug in circles. "We had a couple of beers," she admitted, "and then we went back to work. On Friday, I'm off at four, so I picked up Jeremy and we went to the grocery and home, just like I said."

"What did you talk about? Was Jeremy still mad at you?"

"No, he was fine. I let him choose a frozen dinner and a dessert. On the way home, he chattered about a cowboy he saw at school."

"A cowboy?" Judy asked.

"I think he said the cowboy was by the fence without his horse—I didn't really pay attention; I'd poured myself a vodka tonic and I was putting away the groceries. I let him eat dinner in front of the TV and we watched some dumb kids' movie about a dog. It was just a regular Friday night."

"What about bedtime?"

"What about it?" Sarah leaned back and crossed her arms over her chest.

Judy studied her and waited.

Sarah squirmed and blew out a breath that lifted her bangs. "It was Friday night; I was tired."

Judy lifted an eyebrow and waited.

"I had a couple of drinks, okay?" Color rose in her cheeks. "I kind of drifted off. The movie was boring. I woke up about ten, and Jeremy was watching *South Park* and eating a bag of chips."

"Were you upset?"

"Yeah, I guess so. He's not allowed to watch that."

Judy scrutinized Sarah as she asked, "What happened next?"

"I made him brush his teeth and go to bed. He was really mad and said he was going to run away." Tears rolled down Sarah's cheeks. "I told him I didn't care, but he'd have to wait until morning."

Sarah clenched her fists and tapped them on the table as she fought to control herself. "What if that's the last thing I ever get to say to my son?"

Judy didn't try to comfort her. Instead, she asked, "Did he go to sleep?"

Sarah nodded.

"Did you check on him during the night?"

"After he stomped off, I made another drink and took it into my room so I could read in bed. I fell asleep about midnight."

"Did you hear anything in the night? A car? Or maybe the dog? The dog was at your house with you, right?"

"Of course, Ajax was at the house. He always slept in Jeremy's room." She thought a moment and continued. "I don't remember hearing anything. Do you think Rodney kidnapped him in the night?"

Judy ignored her question. "Tell me about the cowboy," she said.

"What cowboy?"

"You said that Jeremy told you there had been a cowboy at his school."

Sarah sat up straighter. "I don't think that means anything. He's always talking about seeing cowboys." She shook her head. "That's why he wanted to wear his boots, in case he saw the cowboy. He's cowboy obsessed right now."

Judy leaned forward. "Think carefully, Sarah. Have you seen anyone that Jeremy would call a cowboy? At the school or in your neighborhood?"

Sarah lifted her mug. The coffee sloshed and spilled across the table. She whimpered and slapped her free hand over her trembling lips.

CHAPTER NINETEEN

BEFORE: 6 ½ Years Ago

Holding Jeremy close to her heart, Sarah sat staring at the dark TV until her eyes drifted shut. Around them, the chaos of a new baby was evident. Her half-empty teacup rested on the arm of the sofa, an open bag of diapers sat at her feet, and the laundry basket full of unfolded baby clothes was on the coffee table along with a half-eaten sandwich and her phone.

Jeremy squeaked. Sarah's eyes popped open. "Please sleep," she whispered to the bundle in her arms. She rocked him, swaying side to side, too tired to stand.

The phone chimed and lit up with Claire's smiling face. Sarah stretched to reach it, careful not to disturb the baby. "Hey."

"Hey, yourself, Mama. How are you and your bundle of joy?"

Sarah looked down at the baby and shifted him to her shoulder. "Alive," she managed to answer.

"That's good." Claire chuckled. "I have a present for my godson, but I thought I should call before I come to visit. Is this afternoon a good time?"

When Sarah didn't answer, Claire continued, "I'm showing a house near you in a few minutes, and then I thought I'd stop by and admire Jeremy. So, around two? I can be gone before Rodney gets home."

"The house is a mess," Sarah protested.

Claire sighed. "You know I don't care about that. Your mess is everyone else's super-clean house."

"Not anymore. If Rodney could see this..." Sarah's eyes drifted around the room. She drew in a deep breath, closed her eyes, and leaned back against the sofa cushion. Jeremy stirred but didn't wake. "Come, please." She ended the call and allowed herself to sleep.

What seemed like only moments later, Sarah jerked awake as Jeremy's furious demand for attention penetrated her dreams. She straightened from her slumped position on the sofa, lifted her sweatshirt, and unhooked her bra. Holding Jeremy in the cross-cradle position, she brought him to her breast.

Jeremy arched his back and refused to latch.

Sarah tried again and when he latched on, his quick sucking caused her to gasp in pain.

The doorbell rang.

Jeremy pulled away and screamed.

Sarah burst into tears. She laid the baby on the sofa and hurried to open the door.

"Whoa," Claire said, stepping through the open doorway and opening her arms.

Sarah burrowed into Claire's hug and continued to sob.

Jeremy screamed louder.

Claire kept one arm around Sarah and moved her toward the living room. Her eyes took in the chaos. "Sit," she commanded and guided Sarah to a chair. She turned, picked up the baby, and bounced him up and down. He stopped crying and stared at this new person.

Sarah watched, dumbfounded. "How did you do that?"

"I'm the oldest of five, remember? It won't last long. He's just surprised. Is it time for a bottle?"

Sarah shook her head. "No bottle. I'm supposed to be nursing, but it hurts so much and he never sleeps."

"Have you been for his first checkup?"

Sarah nodded.

"What does the doctor say?"

"To give it time. That he'd settle in if I relax." Sarah wiped the tears from her face and blew her nose on a tissue. "He wanted me to see a lactation specialist, but Rodney said we don't need one."

Claire frowned. "What is wrong with that man?"

"My mom agrees with him. She said I should just drink a beer and relax, but everything I read says that's not a good idea." Sarah sat on the sofa and lifted her arms. "Give him to me and I'll try again before he starts screaming."

"I'm no expert, but I think a lot of first-time mothers talk to a lactation consultant."

"There was one at the hospital. She showed me some stuff, but it doesn't always work." Sarah gazed down at the baby and brought him to her breast. She winced as he latched on. Tears rolled down her cheeks.

"Oh, honey," Claire said, reaching for a tissue and wiping Sarah's cheek. "I think you need some help. Where is Rodney anyway? Didn't he take time off?"

"Yes, two days, but he has some big contracts in the works and he needs to be at work."

Claire clicked her tongue and scowled. "Right. Does he at least get home early and help at night?"

"I'm sure he would, but he had to go to Cincinnati for a meeting. He'll be home on Saturday."

"This child isn't even three weeks old. What kind of father leaves for a business trip and doesn't arrange for someone to help his wife?"

"He said I could call my mother if I need anything, but…well, you know how she is."

"Got it." Claire smiled her agreement. "But if Jeremy doesn't eat, he won't sleep, and if he doesn't sleep, neither do you."

Sarah smiled down at her son. "He's sleeping now."

Claire nodded. "Okay." She reached for Jeremy. "Give him to me and you go take a shower, and then we are going to call your pediatrician and get some help."

When Claire heard the water turn on she lowered Jeremy into his bassinet, carried the laundry and diapers to the nursery, and folded the clean clothing and blankets, placing them into the drawers. The shower turned off and Claire returned to the living room. She glanced at Jeremy and assured herself he was still asleep. Then she picked up Sarah's phone and the dirty dishes and took them to the kitchen.

The room was a mess. A partially disassembled breast pump lay on the table. Shards from a broken baby bottle were scattered across the floor. Dirty cups, glasses, and plates of half-eaten food filled the sink and covered the countertop.

"Yikes," Claire muttered. She swept up the glass, took out the garbage, then filled the dishwasher and turned it on.

"You didn't have to do that," Sarah said from the doorway.

"Friends help friends." Claire smiled at her. "You look better. Is Jeremy still asleep?"

Sarah nodded.

"Sit down. You need to eat. I'm making you your favorite—tomato soup and grilled cheese—and while I finish that, you need to call the doctor and ask for an emergency consult."

"But—" Sarah protested.

"But nothing. Sit." Claire pointed to the table. She handed Sarah her phone. "Call now."

Claire folded her arms and waited until Sarah had dialed and was speaking to someone in the doctor's office. She turned away and busied herself, listening all the while.

"Hi, this is Sarah Blake."

After a pause, she said, "I think he's fine, but—but I don't think he's getting enough to eat."

…"About every half hour."

…"He falls asleep, but he wakes up screaming."

…"Yes, please. When can she see us?"

…"Today? My husband is out of town and—"

Claire turned and said, "I can drive you."

Sarah shook her head and listened. "Oh, okay. I'll be here. Thank you." She laid the phone on the table and rubbed her temples. "She's coming here. Tonight."

Claire placed the bowl of soup in front of Sarah.

Jeremy whimpered.

Claire flipped the grilled cheese sandwich and slid it onto a plate.

"You eat. I'll get him and change his diaper. Then I'll stay until the nurse is here."

When the doorbell announced the nurse's arrival, Sarah and Jeremy were both asleep. Neither stirred as Claire answered the door and invited the woman in, explaining that she wasn't the mother.

"I'm Eliza Gomez and I work with Dr. Barlow, Jeremy's pediatrician," the woman announced. She let go of the handle of the roller bag she was pulling, fished a business card from her pocket, and handed it to Claire.

Claire noted the picture of Eliza holding a young child and read the inscription. "I see you're a registered nurse, but what does 'certified by IBCLC' mean?"

"In the United States, lactation consultants are not licensed and come from a variety of backgrounds. I'm a licensed RN and have taken the additional training and supervised hours to qualify for certification from the International Board of Lactation Consultant Examiners."

Claire nodded.

Eliza glanced into the living room and smiled at Sarah and Jeremy. "Let's go into another room and you can tell me what's going on while we allow Mother to sleep. It won't be long before the baby is ready for a feed."

Claire led the way to the kitchen, waved Eliza to a bar stool, and offered her something to drink.

Eliza unzipped the outer pocket of her roller bag and removed a pad of paper and a chart file. She opened the file and read the first page before turning back to Claire. "Are you related to the family?"

Claire shook her head and perched on a stool. "Just a friend. I stopped to see Sarah and Jeremy, and…" Her voice trailed off. "Sarah and I are close friends. She asked me to be Jeremy's godmother."

"I see." Eliza's dark eyes studied Claire for a long moment. "Then you must be very good friends. When Sarah called, she indicated that she is worried about Jeremy."

"She says breastfeeding is very painful, too."

Eliza made a note on the pad. "Most new mothers experience a bit of discomfort in the first week or two, but nursing should not be painful. I see the breast pump on the counter. Do you know how often she pumps?"

Claire shook her head.

Liza stood and crossed the kitchen to pick up the pump and examine it. "Can you help me find the baby bottles? And, please, put on a big pot of water for me, Claire? There appears to be some residue in the tubing, so I'll replace that, and I'd like to wash and sterilize all the other parts."

"Sure thing." Claire searched the cupboards and drawers and found a large soup kettle. After asking if it was big enough, she filled it halfway with water and placed it on the stovetop to heat.

Eliza busied herself with scrubbing the pump parts and then placed them in the now boiling water. Claire opened cupboards and continued her search for bottles.

"Hello," Sarah said, entering the kitchen with Jeremy fussing in her arms.

Eliza introduced herself and Claire reached for the baby when Sarah said, "I need to go to the bathroom before I feed him."

"You go ahead. I'll set up the scale. I want to weigh him before he nurses."

Eliza opened her roller bag and extracted the scale. Sarah returned, and Eliza asked her to undress the baby. Sarah complied and then placed Jeremy on the scale. He startled, arms and legs flying.

Eliza placed her hand on his tummy and said, "I'm sorry, Jeremy. This will only take a minute and then Mommy will feed you."

Jeremy screamed.

Once Jeremy was dressed again and calmer, Eliza asked, "Where are you most comfortable nursing, Sarah?"

"Umm, I guess the sofa is good."

"Okay. Let's go into the living room and then I'll observe Jeremy while he nurses and we can figure out what you need to make this a good experience for both of you. Claire, please turn off the stove wait about five minutes, and then use the tongs to remove the pump parts and place them on a clean towel. Sarah, we were unable to locate any baby bottles. Do you have a supply?"

Sarah shook her head. "I had one in the baby kit the hospital gave me, but I dropped it this morning and it broke."

"I have a few sterile bottles with me. We can use those for milk storage. Have you been pumping your milk?"

"I tried, but I can't." Tears filled her eyes. "It hurts too much."

"Jeremy is not back to his birth weight yet, but that's understandable if you are having trouble nursing. Don't worry; a lot of first-time mothers experience discomfort when the baby latches on incorrectly. I'm here to help."

Eliza spent the next hour working with Sarah, showing her ways to encourage Jeremy to latch on and nurse without falling asleep.

When Jeremy was no longer willing to nurse, she had Sarah place him in his bassinet and then showed her how to use the breast pump correctly. "If you express all the milk after every feeding, your milk production will increase, Jeremy will eat more and begin to gain weight, and then you will be able to go longer between feedings. The milk you pump can be frozen and your husband will be able to do some of the feeding so that you can rest. In just a few months, the baby will be sleeping through the night."

"Months?" Sarah blurted.

Eliza chuckled. "Trust me, once Jeremy is sleeping three or four hours at a time it will get easier. I know that right now he needs you every hour, but it will get better, and your discomfort will decrease."

Sarah laid her head against the back of her chair, closed her eyes, and sighed.

Eliza patted her hand. "I'm going now, but I can come back whenever you need me. Just remember everything I showed you. Your next appointment with Dr. Barlow is in three days, and we'll need to see Jeremy to be sure he is gaining weight."

She checked her bag, clicked it closed, and studied Sarah, who was asleep. She turned to Claire and asked, "Can you stay until Daddy gets home?"

"He won't be home until Saturday."

"Oh dear, that's not ideal. New mommies need support. Is there someone else, Sarah's mother perhaps?"

Claire shook her head. "Don't worry, I'll figure out something. Thank you for coming."

"You have my card. Call me if you need me." Eliza waved goodbye and let herself out.

The door clicked shut and Jeremy woke with a howl. Sarah jerked awake. She glared at the baby. "I can't do this, Claire. He never sleeps more than a few minutes. I'm tired and I hate nursing."

"Okay." Claire didn't question Sarah's decision. "What do you want me to do?"

"I think if I switch to formula, he'll get enough to eat and then he'll sleep."

Claire waited.

"Will you go to Safeway and buy formula and bottles?"

"Of course I will. If that's what you want. What kind should I buy?"

"It's all the same—just get something for newborns, and hurry."

Claire gave Sarah a quick hug, grabbed her purse and coat, and headed for the door. "Hang in there. I'll be right back."

CHAPTER TWENTY

NOW DAY 6: Tuesday 01/30 AFTERNOON

"Look at me, Sarah," Judy commanded.

Sarah dropped her hand from her lips and took a deep breath, struggling for control as she forced herself to make eye contact with Judy.

Judy nodded. "That's better. You need to tell me everything you can remember. You said Jeremy is obsessed with cowboys. Tell me about that?"

"*Toy Story* was streaming a while ago."

"The movie?"

Sarah nodded and continued, "Yeah. He watched it like a million times. He loved Woody."

Judy tilted her head. A look of puzzlement crossed her face.

Sarah smiled and explained, "You know, Woody. The lonesome cowboy."

Judy clicked her tongue. "I guess I know what you mean. I haven't seen the movies, but I've seen the ads. Kind of skinny guy with a sheriff's badge, right?"

"Yes. Jeremy started talking about cowboys all the time. He told his dad that all he wanted for Christmas was a Woody action figure." Sarah paused and frowned. "Rodney wasn't crazy about the idea; he told Jeremy he was too old to play with dolls."

"Did you give Jeremy Woody for Christmas?"

Nodding again, Sarah admitted, "I did, but I didn't tell Rodney and neither did Jeremy. We decided it would be our secret." Sarah watched doubt pass over Judy's face. She sat up straighter and said, "I can tell you think it was wrong to tell Jeremy to lie to his father, but sometimes a white lie is safer than the truth."

"Did Rodney ever find out you'd lied about the doll?"

"Action figure," Sarah corrected. "No. It never came up. He's not around, and he just assumes that if he tells us to do something, we do it."

Judy's phone vibrated on the table. She flipped it over and glanced at the screen. "Nothing important," she said, and swiped the message away. "Did you give him the cowboy boots for Christmas, too?"

Sarah's eyes lit up. "Yes. I found them at Costco. They looked just like Woody's, but without the spurs. Jeremy loved them. He wanted to wear them all the time."

"One more question about Woody and the boots: how does a six-year-old keep a secret about something he loves so much from his father?"

"You have to talk to someone to tell them secrets."

"Rodney didn't see Jeremy on Christmas?"

"No. He went skiing with friends."

Judy raised her eyebrows but didn't comment. Instead, she asked, "Before Christmas was Jeremy talking about seeing the cowboy?"

"I don't think so. But it started right after. During the winter break, while I was at work, he went to the Holiday Day Camp that the Parks Department runs in Pateros. They have horses, so naturally he met a real cowboy." Sarah smiled at the thought.

"Did this cowboy have a name?"

Sarah searched her memory. "I think it might have been Rusty," she paused, "or maybe that was the horse."

Judy sighed and rapped her fist against the table. "Okay, this is going nowhere. Maybe the cowboy has nothing to do with anything. Let's go back to the night you believe Jeremy disappeared. You're sure your husband is lying, so let's assume Jeremy didn't run away."

"Ex-husband," Sarah murmured.

"Tell me about the divorce. How long were you married?"

"A little more than five years. We split right before Jeremy's fourth birthday." Sarah looked away. "I didn't cope very well with having a baby and I admit I drank too much. We saw a marriage counselor and I tried to be a better wife, but…" She sighed and shrugged. "Things had gotten very bad. One night I decided I had to leave and the next time Rodney went out of town, I took Jeremy and fled. When he found us he was extremely angry."

"Where did you go?"

"To an Airbnb in Ocean Shores. My grandparents used to take me there when I was a kid, and I knew Rodney didn't like the beach. I just needed time to think." Sarah spun her coffee cup in a circle. "It was only a few days before he figured out where we went. After I got out of the hospital, I found an attorney and she filed for a restraining order."

Judy held up her hand in a stop gesture. "Hold it. Go back. I think you missed a few things. Why were you in the hospital?"

Sarah bit her lip and fiddled with her cup again. "He didn't mean to hurt me," she said softly. "I overreacted when he knocked on the door and demanded to come in. I tried to close the door, but he pushed against it and I fell. I broke a couple of ribs and my nose."

Judy reached across the table and stopped Sarah's hands. "He abused you?"

Sarah's face flushed. She pulled her hands away from Judy and took a deep breath, steeling herself to continue. She gave a small nod. "When we were married, I was twenty-seven, Rodney was forty-one. He said he loved me and I believed him. He wanted to marry right away, and it seemed so romantic. He was jealous and possessive, but that seemed romantic, too. I thought I was in love and by the time I realized I wasn't, it was too late. I was a mess, and I was afraid of him."

Sarah stood, hugging herself and rubbing her hands up and down her arms. She crossed the kitchen to look out at the snowy yard. "Claire knew that he was hurting me. She was going to help me, but I couldn't leave when I found out I was pregnant. Rodney really wanted us to have a baby and I thought that the baby would fix everything."

She turned the tap at the sink and watched the water gush down the drain.

Keeping her gaze focused on the water, she said, "It wasn't better."

Judy asked, "Did you and Jeremy go back home?"

Sarah kept her eyes averted and struggled for composure.

Judy waited.

Mutely, Sarah shook her head from side to side. Her fingers clenched and unclenched under the stream of water, as she struggled with what she needed to say. Finally, after gathering her courage, she twisted the tap off and turned to face Judy.

Tears filled her eyes and she brushed them away, shaking her head. "No. I refused. My mother thought it was my fault and that I was ruining my life and Jeremy's. She kept saying a boy needs a father and that I'd never be able to cope as a single mom." Lifting her eyes, she looked directly at Judy. "But she was wrong. I moved into the cabin on Alta Lake, enrolled Jeremy in the local school, got a job, and filed for divorce. Rodney wanted custody of Jeremy. He tried to prove that my drinking was our only problem, but my attorney presented my hospital records. Rodney's attorney maintained it was an accident, not abuse. We were granted a divorce with joint custody."

"How often does he see Jeremy?"

"Our agreement is that Jeremy will spend every other weekend with him. For about six months, he picked up Jeremy on Fridays for his weekend and brought him home Sunday afternoon. Then it changed to about once a month, usually just for a pizza. He still lives in Seattle and that's a long drive. Sometimes he calls and asks to speak to Jeremy so they can FaceTime."

"If your divorce and custody arrangement isn't causing issues between you and your ex, why would he be angry enough to set up this whole ruse?" Judy waved her hand in a circle, seeming to take in the house, Sarah, and herself. "If what Rodney is telling me and what he told the police yesterday is a pack of lies, there has to be a reason."

Sarah hesitated, running her fingers through her hair and rubbing at the back of her neck. She returned to the table, seated herself across from Judy, and cleared her throat. "I need to know why you want to know all of this. You work for Rodney. How do I know I can trust you?"

Judy eyed Sarah and shrugged. "I guess you'll just have to take my word for it. I haven't done anything to hurt you and I found out that the kid is an actor, didn't I?"

Sarah nodded.

"I was hired by Mr. Blake just a couple of days before he brought you home from the hospital." Judy maintained eye contact and spoke slowly. "I only met the kid the morning you arrived."

"Didn't you think it was strange that Rodney needed someone to babysit his wife?"

"Actually, no. You'd be surprised what rich people expect from their hired help."

"It's almost like you know too much."

Judy frowned. "Too much about what?"

"Me, Rodney, the drugs in my food, how to find that kid on the internet. You're too calm." Sarah kept her gaze focused on Judy. "You ask too many questions."

"My mother always said, 'Curiosity killed the cat, but satisfaction brought him back.' I think you need help and I'm willing to help. You don't have to trust me, but this will be easier if you do."

Sarah's eyes narrowed. "Exactly what is this?"

"That's the question." Judy grinned. "And, the only one here who knows the answer is you. So, are you going to keep answering my questions or are you going to sit around and wait to see what happens?"

Speechless and angry, Sarah slapped her palm on the table.

Judy waited and watched as Sarah pushed back her shoulders, sat up straighter, and raised her head. Then she said, "Kids don't usually wander off in the night, especially in a storm. I assume your son would leave the house with his father, but is there anyone else he'd trust? Friends? Grandparents? Other relatives?"

"My mother, I suppose. Maybe his teacher, or Claire."

"Who's Claire?"

"She used to be my best friend. I haven't seen her for a year or more."

CHAPTER TWENTY-ONE

BEFORE: 6 ½ Years Ago

Sarah sprawled on the sofa, her phone balanced on her stomach and a glass of wine at hand on the coffee table. The baby monitor emitted a soft squeal from nine-month-old Jeremy. Sarah shifted and sat up. "He's waking up, Claire. I gotta go, but first, tell me what's happening in the real world."

Claire laughed. "The real world is highly overrated. Why don't you and your son come have lunch with me tomorrow?"

"It's so much work to bring everything he needs. Can't you come here for happy hour and dinner?" When Sarah heard Claire's hesitation, she added, "Rodney is in Phoenix this week. He won't be home until Friday night. We haven't had a girls' night since Jeremy was born. Please, come. It'll be fun."

"Umm…"

"Come on, say yes. I miss you."

Claire laughed. "Okay, if you're sure Rodney won't mind. You know he told me to stay out of your life and Jeremy's. I don't want to get you in trouble."

"Don't be silly. You're my best friend and Jeremy's godmother. You are always welcome here." Sarah took a breath and continued,

"Rodney didn't mean those things he said at the christening. He was just embarrassed because I couldn't make Jeremy quit crying and because of the stupid toast my dad made."

"Got it," Claire said. "I'll drive over right after work tomorrow, and be at your house about six. I'll bring all our favorite deli food."

Sarah laughed. "That's a generous offer. I have eggs and baby food in the house, but I really could go to the grocery and serve you a decent meal."

"No need for any trouble. It'll just be fun to see you and catch up."

They said goodbye and hung up.

Sarah drained the wine from her glass and swayed slightly as she walked to the nursery to tend to Jeremy.

***

The next morning, for the first time in weeks, Sarah was awake before the baby. She stretched and smiled, pulled a sweatshirt over her pajamas, peeked into the nursery, and hurried downstairs to enjoy a cup of coffee.

Sarah stopped in the kitchen doorway, surprised at the mess illuminated by the bright sunlight. Dirty dishes were stacked in the sink, the garbage can overflowed, and the countertop looked sticky.

Maybe Rodney has a point, she thought. *I do need to get a grip.*

After starting the coffeemaker, Sarah rinsed the pile of dirty dishes, put them in the dishwasher, wiped down the counters, and washed out the sink. She poured herself a mug of coffee and leaned back against the counter, gazing out at the backyard.

Motherhood hadn't turned out to be at all what she had expected. She'd believed having a child would be fun and that she and Rodney would finally be happy. But, Rodney paid no attention to Jeremy. Whenever she was busy with the baby, he demanded something and became angry if she protested.

If Jeremy was awake when Rodney came home, he closed himself in his office, emerging only to fire a volley of accusations at her. He complained about everything, most often focusing on her inability to be a "good mother," and that she hadn't regained her pre-baby figure. And no matter how often she apologized and promised to do better, it was never enough.

Her thoughts turned to the christening. Her mother had wanted the ceremony and a party. She'd convinced them it was important for Jeremy's future. So, even though Sarah and Rodney didn't attend church, when Jeremy was six months old, they'd agreed. Rodney had suggested his attorney, James Cullen, and his wife be named as the godparents. Sarah agreed that James could be the godfather but wanted Claire to be named godmother. The disagreement had turned ugly, with Rodney declaring he'd never allow Claire to have anything to do with his child. He'd accused Claire of "sticking her nose in where it didn't belong," claiming she was nothing but a troublemaker.

For once, Sarah hadn't backed down. When they met with her mother to finalize the invitations, Sarah reminded him that when they'd married without Claire as her maid of honor, he'd promised she could be the godmother to their first child. Rodney had sputtered a bit, but Lydia assured him it really didn't matter, saying, "It's not as if the godparents do anything. It's just a lovely tradition, a way to present our grandson to the world." And so, he had agreed.

On the first Saturday in June, Sarah dressed Jeremy in the tiny white suit her mother provided and squeezed herself into her only dress that still fit. As she applied full makeup for the first time since the baby's birth, her mood lifted. The first six months had passed in a blur, but now Jeremy slept from 10 p.m. until 6 or 7 a.m., and Sarah was getting enough sleep and feeling much better. Most days were just plain repetitious and boring: feed the baby, change the baby, play with the baby, feed the baby, change the baby, and squeeze in a little housework or laundry when he was sleeping.

Driving with Rodney to her parents' home, Jeremy had slept like an angel. For once, her mother had refrained from commenting on Sarah's choice of outfits. Her parents, Steve and Lydia, had cooed over the baby, and Sarah relaxed on the drive to the church.

The christening service was brief, and everything had gone perfectly. Jeremy had looked adorable and Sarah had been excited to show him off. They'd driven from the church to her parents' home and formed a receiving line. Lydia had created her usual amazing party look and the house was festive with flowers and baby-blue ribbons. Rodney held Jeremy and accepted congratulations from the guests. Minutes later, Jeremy whimpered. Rodney scowled. Sarah tensed. Jeremy's whimper grew to a cry. She took the baby from Rodney and bounced him gently. Jeremy hiccupped and stopped crying.

Someone said, "Looks like you're raising a mama's boy."

Rodney frowned; his jaw clenched. He glared at Sarah and reached for the baby. She surrendered him.

Jeremy wailed. The guests chuckled.

Claire raised her arms toward the baby and said, "I'll give him a bottle, Sarah. You stay and greet your guests."

"My son needs his mother, not you." Rodney thrust Jeremy toward Sarah; his eyes glinted with anger.

Sarah flinched but managed to smile as she took the baby and said, "Come with us, Claire. You can hold him while I get the bottle ready."

By the time Jeremy was fed and changed, the reception line had broken apart and guests were filling their plates from the brunch buffet and drifting into small groups. When Sarah and Claire reappeared with Jeremy, Steve proposed a toast to his grandson. The caterer made sure everyone had a glass of champagne.

Steve threw his arm around Rodney's shoulder and raised his glass. "I'd like to make a toast to the newest member of the family. Congratulations on the birth of your son, Jeremy Scott Blake. With the guidance of his godfather and, of course, his grandfather, I know he will become a fine man. To Jeremy." Steve clinked his glass against Rodney's and drank. "I'm not sure why the child has been christened without a family name, but you can name the next one after me," he paused, "or yourself."

The crowd chuckled and Rodney grinned, but the smile didn't reach his eyes and Sarah felt her anxiety rise. She gulped down her champagne, accepted another glass, and stayed as far from Rodney as she could.

By 5 p.m. the guests were gone, leaving only the new godparents and the family. The Cullens made their farewells. Claire kissed Jeremy's head and gave Sarah a last hug. "We need to talk," she whispered, and then said in a normal tone, "See you soon. Now I'm officially in the family and I want to get to know my godson."

Rodney put down the plate he'd been holding and turned to the women. "I'll walk you out, Claire." He pulled the front door open and waited for her to exit.

Sarah handed Jeremy to her mother. "I'll go too. I could use some fresh air."

"As you wish," Rodney said.

He pulled the door shut behind them and spoke through clenched teeth. "You," he pointed at Claire, "need to butt out. I won't have you interfering in my son's life anymore. My wife doesn't need your advice on anything. Wasn't it enough that you waited to call me until after he was born, or that you gave him that fancy-pants sissy name?"

Claire's mouth opened.

Sarah jumped in. "Those were my decisions, Rodney. Having just seen you kissing some other woman, I didn't want you at his birth. He is my son as much as he is yours. You can't tell my best friend she isn't welcome in my house."

"We'll see about that." Rodney glared down at Sarah. He grabbed her arm and spun her toward the house.

Sarah flinched but tried to hide her fear. She looked back over her shoulder and said, "I'll call you, Claire. Drive safe."

Later, when she called Claire and apologized for Rodney's behavior, Claire assured her it was okay. Since then, they'd talked a few minutes every week, but this was the first time Sarah had dared make plans with Claire.

The baby monitor lit up and caught her attention. Jeremy was stirring. She dumped her now cold coffee into the sink and vowed it would be a good day. Tonight she'd tell Claire about her plan to leave Rodney, to get a divorce and start a new life.

"Today," she promised herself, "I won't have a drink until Claire is here and Jeremy is down for the night."

***

Jeremy smiled and cooed, pulled himself to standing using the edge of the coffee table, and entertained them with his baby babble. All conversation centered on him until his bedtime. While Sarah took Jeremy to his room and tucked him in, Claire arranged the deli feast she'd purchased on a tray, carried it into the living room, and made them each a cocktail.

Sarah returned to the living room and sank down on the sofa, grabbed a piece of cheese, and tucked one leg under herself. She leaned forward and picked up her glass. "Here's to friendship," she said, raising her glass and taking a long drink.

"I'm your friend, Sarah, but I never see you anymore."

"I know. I'm sorry. That will change now that the kid is older." She took another deep drink. "I'm going to go back to work. I don't want any more children, and I need to make plans for our future." She sipped again. "Mine and Jeremy's."

Sarah leaned forward to place her drink on the coffee table. She fidgeted with the glass until it was centered on a coaster. Without looking a Claire, she said, "I want to get a divorce."

Claire narrowed her eyes and waited. She reached for a cracker and spread it with pâté.

Sarah scooped a few nuts from the tray. She juggled them from one hand to the other and then placed them on her napkin. "Aren't you going to say anything?" she asked.

"I'm not sure what to say. Almost two years ago we had this same conversation. And then you stayed with Rodney and had his baby. I know you're unhappy, and I'll help you in any way I can. But...you have to make your own decisions."

"I'm not just unhappy, Claire. I'm miserable!" She drained her glass, untwisted her legs, and stood up. Holding out her hand, she said, "I'm getting a refill. Want one?"

"Not yet."

"Suit yourself. I'll be right back."

In the kitchen, Sarah downed a shot of vodka and mixed a tall vodka and tonic. She stirred the drink, tasted it, and added a splash more alcohol, then carried it to the living room.

Sarah resumed her seat and the conversation. "It was a mistake to have a baby. I know that now, but at the time I believed it would fix everything that had gone wrong with my marriage."

Claire opened her mouth as if to speak, but stopped herself.

Sarah flushed. "You told me not to marry him so fast, but he told me he needed me, that he'd never been so much in love before and that he liked everything about me, that he wanted to take care of me for the rest of my life." She paused and wiped away a tear. Bringing her glass up in a mock toast, she said, "Here's to my stupidity." She took deep swallows of the alcohol and set the glass down.

The glass teetered, half off the coaster. Claire moved quickly and righted the drink. "You aren't stupid, Sarah."

"All the years I watched how my mother manipulated my dad, how he would never stand up for what he believed, I knew I didn't want a marriage like theirs. And, I think that's why I chose a man who manipulates me."

"You may have a shaky marriage right now but you have a beautiful baby boy. Life is never perfect all the time. You just need to figure out what is making you unhappy and then fix it."

Anger filled Sarah's words. "Rodney is making me unhappy. I'm afraid of…" Her voice dwindled to nothing.

"Afraid of Rodney? Is he hurting you?" Claire leaned closer and touched Sarah's arm.

Sarah dropped her eyes and reached for her drink.

Claire covered the glass with her hand. "Tell me, Sarah. What are you afraid of?"

Sarah hugged a throw pillow to her chest and looked away.

Claire moved closer and wrapped an arm around Sarah's shoulders. She gave her a squeeze. "I took a psych class once where the teacher kept quoting Helen Keller and saying, 'Alone we can do so little; together we can do so much.' If you don't tell me what's wrong, I can't help you figure it out."

Sarah nodded. "Remember that I'd planned to leave Rodney right before I found out I was pregnant? The pregnancy didn't happen at a good time. I mean, I'm glad I have Jeremy now, but…" She struggled to think of how to explain. "Once I was pregnant, Rodney stayed away."

Claire squeezed her hand.

Sarah continued to avoid eye contact. "He swears that woman we saw him with the night Jeremy was born didn't mean anything. We hadn't been sleeping together for months. My restless sleep habits made it impossible for Rodney to get enough sleep and he moved his stuff to the guest room." Sarah reached for her drink. "He's still sleeping in the guest room."

"And, now?" Claire asked.

"Now, if we talk, we fight. About everything." Sarah finished her drink. "My mom and dad agree with Rodney that I'm a terrible wife and mother. She says I'm lucky to have any man at all in my life. I wanted to go to a marriage counselor. But, Rodney and Lydia made fun of people who can't solve their own problems. They convinced me that I was having 'baby blues.' Rodney said he was sorry he'd been so hard to live with, that when the doctor told him he had a low sperm count, he'd gotten very depressed. He said he was sorry he hadn't told me how sad he was. He didn't mean to hurt me and he promised he never would again. I believed him. So we didn't go."

"What the—? I never did like your mother!"

Sarah laughed. "The feeling is mutual. She and Rodney both think you are a terrible influence."

"This isn't high school. Next birthday we'll both be thirty. So what is it you're afraid of?"

"I'm afraid to stay and I'm afraid to tell Rodney I want to leave."

Claire removed Sarah's empty glass from her hand. "I'm going to make us each a fresh drink. And then we'll figure this out."

CHAPTER TWENTY-TWO

NOW DAY 6: Tuesday 01/30 AFTERNOON

Judy said, "Instead of focusing on the night Jeremy disappeared, let's talk about the divorce. Tell me how Claire helped and why you haven't seen her for a year." Judy drummed her fingernails on the tabletop and waited for Sarah to answer. Then she prompted, "So what happened a year ago?"

Inhaling deeply, her nostrils flaring, Sarah said, "If you must know, I fucked up!"

Judy waited and watched as Sarah struggled to get herself under control.

"The divorce was a long time coming. I knew I needed to leave before Jeremy was born and I just couldn't do it. I had a million excuses, and Rodney was right. I was drinking too much. When Jeremy was a little over a year old, I spent six weeks in a residential rehab program."

Judy nodded her encouragement.

"Rodney was sure he could get full custody of Jeremy after that, and my mother thought so, too. So, I believed them and agreed to try to work things out. At the rehab center, we had to go to counseling a couple of times, but Rodney's schedule kept him too busy to attend. The counselor seemed to think I just needed to change."

Judy raised an eyebrow but didn't interrupt.

"Claire was super supportive and offered me help when I kept saying I would leave. But every time I tried to get free, I got scared and went back to Rodney. Until three years ago."

"Was that when you took Jeremy and fled to Ocean Shores and ended up in the hospital, because of Rodny's abuse?"

"Yes. When I was released from the hospital, I knew I had to change my life. I filed for divorce. Rodney threatened and raged, but I didn't give in. Jeremy and I moved to the cabin at Alta Lake. We were happy. Claire came out to visit a few times, and Jeremy and I went into Seattle for the weekend a couple of times. I started working for the Parks Department and life seemed good. Jeremy was doing well. I hadn't made any friends, so it was usually just Jeremy and me. Claire started dating someone and she was too busy to come out as often. I guess it was lonely, but it was better because I wasn't afraid all the time."

Sarah took a deep breath and finished in a rush. "The day I received the final divorce papers, I bought a bottle of vodka. I knew I shouldn't, but I did. At first, I only had a drink on Friday night, but…pretty soon I was having a drink every night.

"One night, when Claire called, she realized something was wrong and asked me if I was drinking. I denied it, of course, but she showed up at the cabin a couple of hours later. I was drunk and she was tired of my nonsense. We had a big fight. She told me she didn't want to have anything to do with me until I got sober and stayed that way. I called her a hypocrite and a few other names, but the upshot is that we haven't spoken in over a year."

Sarah sighed and looked off in the distance, her eyes unfocused. "I miss her. If I'm honest, I knew the marriage was bad from the start. Somebody once said, 'Marry in haste, repent at leisure.' That's exactly what I did." Sarah kept her eyes down and fiddled with her fingers as she continued, "None of the past seems to justify Rodney taking Jeremy now. I mean, I was drinking the night Jeremy disappeared, but Rodney didn't know. He hadn't seen us since before Christmas."

"Do you think he could have been watching you and Jeremy, that he was just waiting for a chance?"

"Sure, but why do all this? If he still wanted custody, why pretend we are married, and why is that fake Jeremy here?"

Judy's phone vibrated on the table. She flipped it face up. Glancing at the message, she pursed her lips and asked, "Where is Claire now?"

"When I tried to reach her two days ago using that kid's phone, her office just said she was out of the country."

"One more thing: do you think there is a chance Claire and Rodney could be working together?"

"Not in a million years! That's crazy! They can't stand each other. Rodney always called her a troublemaker. He didn't even want her in our house. Claire's my friend."

"Maybe then, but what about now?"

"No way!"

Judy tapped on her phone and turned the screen to face Sarah. "Is this Claire?"

Sarah nodded. "But…"

Judy flicked the screen to the next picture and held it out again. "Is this Rodney with Claire?"

Sarah gasped. "When was that? Why do you have their pictures?"

Leaping to her feet, her chair crashed to the floor. She grabbed the phone from Judy. "Who the hell are you? What's going on?"

Judy rose from the table and lifted her hand toward Sarah as she said, "You need to calm down."

"Or what?" Sarah sputtered. "You'll drug me? What's your part in all this?"

"I'm on your side. I only want to help you."

"You can start by telling me who sent you that picture."

"I suppose it's not enough to say a friend."

Jabbing her forefinger against the phone, Sarah demanded, "Where did this come from?"

"I don't know. You can see it came from a blocked number."

"Why should I believe anything you say?" Sarah starred down at the image. "This looks like it was taken inside my cabin." Bewildered, she turned the phone so Judy could see the image.

"What makes you think it was taken at the cabin?"

Sarah studied the photo again. "I know my own house. That's my fireplace."

Taking her phone from Sarah, Judy flicked back and forth between the two images, "I think these were taken at the same time. Claire definitely has on the same outfit. But…" She stopped and frowned.

"But, what?"

"Your husband says that the cabin burned down six years ago, when your grandparents died."

"How many times do I have to tell you? Rodney is NOT my husband. We are divorced. My son is missing. Jeremy and I lived in that cabin when he went missing. And, my grandfather died six years ago. But my grandmother only died less than a year ago. There is nothing wrong with my memory!"

"Sorry." Judy spread her fingers in surrender. "When do you think these pictures were taken? Could they have been taken while you and Jeremy were living there?"

"Not a chance. They were never there at the same time. Besides, Claire and Rodney hate each other."

Judy turned the image back toward Sarah. Rodney stood, holding Claire's wrist and pulling her close to his side. Claire gazed up at him. Rodney's eyes, intense and unwavering, were focused directly at the viewer. "Does this look like hate to you?" Judy asked.

"You know it doesn't." Sarah pushed her hair up and off her neck, squared her shoulders, and picked up her toppled chair. "Sit down," she commanded. "It's time you tell me who you are and what you know. You work for Rodney, don't you?"

"Not exactly." This time it was Judy who rose and paced the kitchen. "I mean, it's true that I'm working for Rodney as a housekeeper, but I'm also working with an organization that is investigating him."

Perplexed, Sarah focused on Judy, waiting for more.

Judy paused at the sink, pushed the curtain aside, and scanned the yard.

"What organization?" Sarah scowled. "Are you with whoever that is in the woods?"

"Maybe. It seems likely, but…" She turned, shook her head, and said slowly, "I'm a detective with the financial crimes division of the Seattle Police."

"What are you doing here? Are you investigating Rodney? Why?"

Judy nodded. "I can't give you details."

"Got it. You think Rodney is up to something." Sarah pursed her lips and narrowed her eyes. "What would a financial crime have to do with this charade?"

"Not sure, but as I told you last night, it's obvious to me that something is going on in this house. Nothing adds up. I intend to get to the bottom of it."

"And find Jeremy?"

"Exactly." Judy glanced at the clock. "Rodney will be here in about an hour. I'm going to start dinner."

Sarah flashed a mischievous grin at Judy, her eyes sparkling with delight. "From police detective to chief cook and bottle washer? I'm truly impressed!"

Judy laughed. "Okay, tell me everything you can remember about waking up in the hospital and finding Jeremy gone, while I work."

Sarah sobered. "I've been thinking about that. I'm not sure I was ever in a real hospital. I didn't see anything but the one room and a bathroom. It looked like a regular hospital room and the bed was a hospital bed—you know, with the rails and things. There was some kind of beeping monitor, I think, and I had an IV in my hand. Rodney and a nurse were there."

Hesitating, Sarah considered a moment before speaking again: "I think I asked right away if they'd found Jeremy, and Rodney pooh-poohed the idea that he was lost. It was very confusing, and I was sort of dizzy. My head ached. The nurse took out the IV and helped me into the bathroom. A doctor came in and he and Rodney seemed very chummy, laughing and talking. The nurse gave me my clothes and told me not to ask questions. Rodney came back with a wheelchair." Confusion filled her eyes. "I woke up in Rodney's car in front of this house." She cocked her head, waiting for Judy's reaction.

"Okay, I get that that's all you remember for now." Judy gestured with the potato peeler. "But there must be more. It seems unlikely that you were unconscious for ten or more days. If Jeremy disappeared on January twelfth or the morning of the thirteenth, where were you?"

"I think I woke up in the cabin a couple of times. Rodney was there and someone else."

"Claire?"

"I think it was a man. I thought I heard the sheriff." Sarah frowned, "I don't know. Everything is so fuzzy. Once it might have been my mother."

Judy held out the potato peeler. "Finish peeling. I need to make a couple of phone calls."

Sarah accepted the peeler and moved to the sink.

"Be right back," Judy said. Then she picked up her phone and left the kitchen.

Sarah finished peeling the potatoes and dropped them into a pot of water. Movement at the edge of the woods caught her attention. "Ajax," she whispered. The dog sat, partially concealed, watching the house. The wind picked up, sending a flurry of snow cascading from the branches of the trees. The setting sun caused the snow to glitter. Tears flooded Sarah's eyes. "Please, find Jeremy," she said aloud. Ajax rose, barked once, and trotted into the woods.

Returning to the kitchen, her brows furrowed, Judy said, "There's a problem. We're not sure you're safe here, but my boss needs time to arrange a few things before we can move you. He thinks it would be wise for me to delay my departure tonight, at least until you are safely in your room. In the morning, I can bring you a coat and some shoes or boots to wear and we can leave as soon as Rodney goes to work."

"Ajax is in the woods again," Sarah said.

Judy frowned. "Nice, but a dog can't protect you. Do you think you can stay in this house one more night? I'll hide my personal phone in your room, so you'll be able to call if anything upsets you. We don't think, in this current situation, that Rodney is violent. It seems more likely he's using you and Jeremy to get what he wants, that he needs you for some reason."

"Now that I have someone who believes me, I'm not afraid of him anymore." Sarah hesitated and asked, "If he needs me, how can you be sure that getting me out of here will help us find Jeremy?"

"I can't promise anything, but we believe that removing you will force his hand."

"Listen, I trust you, sort of, but I don't think Jeremy is your priority." Placing her hands on her hips, Sarah fixed her gaze on Judy. "I need to be here. I won't leave until you get him to talk. But I'll accept your phone for the night and the coat and shoes."

"My boss isn't going to like that, but we can't force you to do anything."

"I'm staying put. Rodney knows I can't run without shoes, so he's confident he has me trapped. Maybe I can get him to talk if you tell me what you need to know."

"That is definitely not a good idea. If he has committed a crime, we need uncorrupted evidence in order to charge and prosecute. A wife," Judy stopped and held up her hand as Sarah opened her mouth to protest, "even an ex-wife, is not an appropriate part of that process."

"Okay, don't tell me." Sarah's eyes flashed with anger. "I just want my son back."

"The safety of a child is always the highest priority. I can assure you that, now that we have determined that Jeremy is missing, we'll have a team devoted to finding out what happened and where your child is now." Judy crossed to the closet, opened the door, and pulled a phone from her coat pocket. "Take this upstairs and hide it. If you are afraid for any reason, call the contact labeled AAA and tell whoever answers that Detective Hendricks is needed. They'll take care of the rest. And whatever you do, don't let Rodney know about the phone."

Sarah accepted the phone and turned to leave. Then she spun around and asked Judy, "How much trouble is Rodney in?"

The sun's red glow filtered through the kitchen window, and for a moment the light danced across the countertops and sparked off the blade of a large chopping knife. For a long moment the women locked eyes and considered each other. Judy looked away first and said, "A lot. You need to believe me when I say you can't trust him."

CHAPTER TWENTY-THREE

NOW DAY 6 Tuesday 01/30 EVENING

The last light of the sunset faded, and the sky darkened. In her bedroom, Sarah nestled the phone into the hidden crevice between the cushion and the back of the slipper chair by the window. No one had found that boy's phone, she reasoned, so perhaps this hiding place would work again. Leaving the table lamp unlit, Sarah pulled aside the drape. The silhouettes of the trees dissolved into a solid dark, dense shadow. As she watched, Ajax left the woods and crossed the yard, heading somewhere behind the house.

Sarah dropped the curtain and hurried to the stairwell window, hoping to see where Ajax went. But he had disappeared. The sound of Judy setting the table in the dining room drifted up the stairs.

The front door opened and closed.

Rodney was home.

Sarah's pulse quickened. She stayed motionless, listening as Rodney's footsteps moved toward the kitchen. Judy greeted him and offered a cocktail. Sarah summoned her courage. She took two deep breaths, letting each out slowly, and headed down the stairs and into the kitchen.

"Hey, Sarah," Rodney greeted her, his voice laced with a friendly, casual tone that didn't reach his eyes.

"Hi," she replied, forcing herself to meet his gaze. "Where's the … Jeremy?"

"Your son is having dinner with a friend. They played in a basketball game at the school this afternoon. I'll pick him up later."

Sarah nodded. Since when did Jeremy play basketball? She had to keep her wits about her; she couldn't let Rodney know she was suspicious. The feeling that Rodney was watching her too closely as if he knew more than he let on, persisted. She eyed his cocktail.

"Would you like a drink, darling?" He raised his glass and sipped, his smile tight, savoring her discomfort.

"No, thank you."

Rodney ignored her and turned to Judy. "Bring my wife a gin and tonic. We'll be in my office," he ordered. "Come along, Sarah." Stepping to her side, he placed his free hand on the small of her back.

Sarah felt his slight push and tried not to cringe. They moved down the hallway to the locked French doors of his office. As he sorted through his keys, she asked, "How was your day?" her voice steady despite the turmoil in her stomach.

Rodney swung the door open and gestured for her to enter. "Funny you should ask." He placed his drink on the desk and waited for Sarah to sit. "I talked to your mother today." He sat behind the desk, picked up his glass, and watched her reaction.

"I haven't seen her in months. Not since Thanksgiving," she said, her casual tone belying the storm brewing inside her. What game was he playing?

Judy interrupted and, keeping her back turned to Rodney, handed Sarah a tall, crystal glass. Her lips formed the words "be careful."

Sarah sipped from the glass, recognizing that it was only tonic water, no gin. "Thank you, Mrs. Hendricks," she said. "It's delicious."

Judy nodded, turned to leave, and hesitated at the doorway. "Dinner is ready any time, sir."

"Got it. We'll be in when we finish our cocktails."

Sarah kept her eyes averted and asked, "What did Mother have to say?"

"Your memory really is faulty. You see your mother every week. You two are always shopping or having lunch. But since the accident, and in light of your current condition, your parents are worried about you." His cold gaze stayed focused on her face as he studied her reaction. "They leave on their cruise soon and she wanted to be sure that you are capable of caring for yourself and our son."

Sarah bit her lip to keep from protesting. Her relationship with her mother had been iffy at best; she knew there'd been no weekly visits. *She certainly wasn't concerned when I called.*

Rodney's sneer widened. "Don't worry, I assured her you are in good hands." He lifted his glass. "Drink up. We don't want to keep Mrs. Hendricks waiting."

"I'll take it with me to dinner." Rising from her chair, Sarah moved to the doorway.

Rodney plucked her glass from her hand. "Go ahead. I'll freshen your drink and be with you in a moment."

Afraid to protest, Sarah left the office and walked the few feet to the dining room. Judy waited by the table. Sarah whispered, "He's doing something to my drink."

Judy glanced at the hallway. It was still empty. She whispered, "Don't drink it. I'll think of something." Then she raised her voice to a normal tone and added, "Should I wait for Mr. Blake before I serve?"

"No need to wait." Rodney entered the dining room and crossed to Sarah. He placed her drink on the table and pulled out her chair. "I'm here, right where I belong."

Sarah took her seat. The sensation of Rodney's fingers on the back of her neck made her shiver. Jerking away, she reached for her cocktail, then remembered in time and picked up her napkin instead. Forcing herself to look at Rodney, she kept her voice steady and said, "I didn't know my parents were planning a cruise. Where are they going?"

Rodney gave an impatient sigh. "Your mother is going to Greece. She leaves in the morning."

"Isn't Dad going along? I thought you said 'they'?"

"I think that was the original plan, but Lydia said he's preparing for a big trial and has chosen not to go." Rodney stopped talking and frowned at Mrs. Hendricks. "We're ready for dinner whenever you are," he said, his words dripping with sarcasm.

Judy startled. "Sorry, sir." She hurried out of the room.

Rodney drained his cocktail glass and pushed it aside. "Drink up, darling."

Sarah cringed and reluctantly lifted her glass.

Rodney's phone buzzed. He pulled it from his pocket and looked down, a brief flicker of annoyance crossing his face before he regained his composure. "Excuse me for a moment," he said, stepping away, and leaving the dining room to take the call.

As soon as the office door closed behind Rodney, Judy appeared with their salads and a decanter of wine on a serving tray. Placing the tray on the table, she scooped up Sarah's cocktail and dumped its contents into the floral arrangement on the sideboard.

Sarah suppressed a nervous giggle. "Those flowers are silk."

Judy winked. "Then the drink won't kill them." She moved back to the table, poured the wine, and placed the salads.

The office door opened.

Judy composed herself and asked, "Will there be anything else?"

"No thank you." Sarah lifted her glass and sipped the wine.

"Keep your guard up," Judy whispered. "I'll be right here."

Sarah steeled herself, preparing for whatever lay ahead, as Rodney returned, a satisfied smile on his face.

He paused, taking in the wine and the salads. "Is this the St. Julien Bordeaux?" He glared at Judy. "I asked for it to be served with the roast, not the salad."

"I'm sorry, Rodney," Sarah interrupted. "I finished my cocktail and I asked Mrs. Hendricks to pour it now."

Rodney shook his head and said, "The trouble with marrying a younger woman is they have no class. Honestly, who knew pairing wine with food required an advanced degree?" Sighing, he resumed his place at the table.

Sarah forced herself not to react. Instead, she sipped the wine and said, "It's very good." Replacing her glass, she lifted her fork and began to eat the salad. "Was your call important?" she asked, discreetly glancing at Judy, who gave her a tiny, reassuring nod and left the dining room.

"Just work. I have to tie up a few loose ends before the weekend." Rodney concentrated on his salad and gazed out the dining room window into the dark backyard.

Sarah thought about the pictures Judy had shown her. She fiddled with her napkin and tried to think of a way to ask Rodney when he'd last seen Claire.

"Mrs. Hendricks?" Rodney's stern call interrupted Sarah's thoughts.

Judy scurried into the room.

Rodney rose from the table and crossed to the window. "That dog is out there again." He whirled around, and his eyes jerked between the two women. "Have you been feeding that mutt?"

Sarah stood and hurried to the window.

"Of course not," Judy said, and crossed to look out the window. "I don't see anything."

"I don't either," Sarah said.

Rodney grabbed Sarah's arm. "Are you calling me a liar?"

Sarah squirmed to be free.

Judy stepped closer.

Rodney dropped Sarah's arm and demanded, "Why would he hang around if no one is feeding him?"

"Usually, a dog stays near his owner," Judy said. "They are pretty territorial. Maybe he lives around here or he's looking for someone."

"There's not another house within miles. He must be lost," Rodney said. "I'll call the pound tomorrow and have him picked up."

He looked out the window again and then pulled the drapes closed. "Sit down. Finish your dinner, Sarah. I have to pick up Jeremy soon."

Sarah kept her eyes on her food as she chanted silently, *Ajax, find Jeremy. Please, please, please find Jeremy.* Feeling Rodney's stare, she compelled herself to look at him. Aloud she said, "How long will Mother be cruising?"

"I assured her that I'd take care of you, one way or another, and she didn't need to worry about Jeremy. She'll be gone for another month or more."

"Another? Has she already gone somewhere?"

He pointed his fork at her. "Stop asking so many questions."

Sarah paled.

Judy entered with their plated dinners. She deftly removed the salad plates and forks and slid the dinners into place. "I have a lovely mousse for dessert. You didn't mention what you'd like with the roast, but my husband always likes a touch of chocolate."

Rodney made a great show of looking at his watch. "There won't be time for anything else. I need to pick up Jeremy."

"Of course, sir."

Sarah smiled at Judy. "Perhaps Jeremy would like a snack when he and his father return."

"Nonsense," Rodney said. "It'll be after ten. He'll need to get to bed." He studied Sarah. "In fact, you look a bit drawn yourself. Haven't you been sleeping well?"

"I guess not," Sarah admitted, thinking, *how can I sleep when my son is missing and nothing makes sense?*

"I think you need to go to bed early."

Sarah faked a yawn. "Perhaps that would be a good idea." She ate a few bites and pushed her plate away. Watching Rodney wolf down his dinner, she sipped her wine and waited for him to finish.

When he folded his napkin and pushed back his chair, she said, "There don't seem to be any of my books in your house."

Fury crossed Rodney's face. His fist clenched around the napkin and then dropped it on the table. "The doctor suggested that we remove the books from your room. He felt reading would make your headaches more severe."

"But I don't have a headache, and you know I like to read in bed before sleeping."

"I have the new Jodi Picoult in my car," Judy said. "If your husband thinks it okay, I wouldn't mind lending it to you."

Rodney grimaced and shrugged. "Fine, but if your head hurts tomorrow, don't blame me."

Rodney stood and Sarah rose with him. "I'll go up now and get ready for bed. If I'm still awake when you and Jeremy get home, I'd like to say good night to him."

Rodney frowned.

"I'll just finish in here and then I'll get that book from my car and bring it up. Would you care for a nice cup of tea?" Judy asked.

"That would be lovely, Mrs. Hendricks." Sarah smiled at the housekeeper and shifted her gaze to her husband. "Drive safe, Rodney." She stepped around him and headed for the doorway.

"I'll be up in a minute to say good night." Rodney watched closely, but Sarah refused to react.

She smiled slightly and murmured, "Great."

***

Back in her bedroom, Sarah longed for her favorite flannel pajamas, the ones printed with cowboys and horses. Jeremy had picked them out, and she'd purchased matching pj's for him. Her heart clenched at the memory of his delight. Tonight, there was nothing in the closet but another one of the flimsy white silk gowns. Sarah removed her makeup and brushed her teeth, stalling in the hope that Rodney would come before she needed to wear the revealing nightwear.

Finally giving up, she changed out of her clothes and into the gown. She pulled the cashmere sweater she'd been wearing all day over it and slipped under the covers just as the door opened.

Rodney's eyes raked over her and then examined the room. Finding nothing amiss, he came to the bedside, carrying the Picoult book and a steaming teacup.

He placed the book on the nightstand and waited for her to accept the cup.

Sarah inhaled the steam. "It smells heavenly."

"It's Egyptian chamomile with a splash of milk and honey." Rodney kept his gaze locked on hers. "Mrs. Hendricks added a splash of brandy. She said it would help you sleep."

Sarah inhaled another breath of the spicy brew.

"Taste it!" Rodney commanded.

Sarah took a cautious sip. She smiled, relieved that the taste was as sweet as the smell. "Thank you."

Rodney leaned down and kissed her forehead. "That will warm you up and you can take off that ridiculous sweater. I'll check on you when I get home."

"Good night, Rodney." She watched him leave the room and waited, listening. The lock clicked and his footsteps retreated. Sarah pushed the covers back and crossed the bedroom, still holding the tea.

The light from the garage door flooded the yard and she saw Rodney drive away. His high beams flashed off something in the woods. Sarah squinted, but nothing moved.

Judy had been right: the tea was a nice treat. It tasted of apple and spice. She took another drink and set it on the nightstand. Feeling warmer now, and with Rodney not likely to return, she slipped off the sweater, piled her pillows against the headboard, and snuggled under the fluffy duvet.

She reached for the cup of tea. A knock sounded on the door and the knob jiggled. Judy's voice reached her: "Don't drink the tea."

Sarah scrambled out of the bed and stumbled to the door. "I already had some. He said you made it."

"How much did you drink? Are you alright?"

"Just a few sips." Sarah looked at the cup. "Maybe a quarter of the tea. Unlock the door and help me."

"I can't. My lock set is gone from the drawer I hid it in and I don't have a key for this door. Do you feel funny, or dizzy? Is your vision blurry?"

Sarah blinked back tears. "Maybe a little. What should I do?"

"Quickly, go in the bathroom and make yourself throw up. Do it now."

Sarah whispered, "Okay," and hurried to the bathroom. She knelt on the floor and stuck her finger down her throat, coughing and gagging until a gush of golden tea and bile rushed out and splashed in the toilet. She wiped her mouth with the back of her hand and forced herself to do it again and then a third time, until her stomach ached and her throat burned. Using the rim of the sink, Sarah pulled herself up. She rinsed her mouth with glass after glass of water. Tears ran down her cheeks and she scrubbed them away. "God damn him to hell," she said to her reflection. "I want my son back. I'll make the bastard pay for this."

Returning to the door, she said, "Are you still there?"

"I am. Are you okay? Did you get it all up?"

"I think so. I can't throw up any more."

"I'll break open the door and we can leave right now. We'll figure out another way to prove his guilt."

"No. I told you, I don't care if you prove he's a criminal. He has my son. I'm not leaving until we find Jeremy—the *real* Jeremy. That's all I care about. I won't let him win. I have your phone, and he thinks I'm drugged. He won't do anything else tonight."

Silence greeted Sarah's outburst.

After a long pause, Judy said, "Okay. Call the AAA number if anything happens. We'll be outside the house all night, watching and listening. And whatever you do, don't eat or drink anything else he gives you. Promise?"

"I promise." Sarah nodded even though she knew Judy couldn't see her. "I'll see you in the morning."

"Good night, Sarah. Take care of yourself. I'll be back by 6:30."

***

Sarah sat in the chair by the window. She was afraid to turn on a light and read. Instead, she strained to see any movement in the yard or the woods. If Judy had told the truth, whoever was watching was very good at hiding.

Time passed slowly. Sarah pulled the phone from its hiding place and kept track. Shortly after midnight, headlights swept into the yard. Stuffing the phone back into place, she hurried to the bed and buried herself in the duvet.

Minutes later, the bedroom door opened. Sarah closed her eyes to a narrow slit and kept her breathing deep and slow. Rodney picked up the teacup. Sarah's heart stopped—had she forgotten to dump the contents? Rodney set the cup down and laid his hand against her cheek. She moaned softly and turned her head away.

Rodney leaned closer, his eyes glinting in the light from the hall. "I know you're not asleep. I thought you'd enjoy your special treat, but I guess not," he said, his tone dripping with implication.

She opened her eyes, meeting his gaze with a steely resolve. "What do you want, Rodney?"

His face twisted with surprise. "I want you to realize how foolish you are," he snapped, stepping back as if her defiance had thrown him off balance. "If you don't cooperate, you might never see Jeremy again. You need to stop resisting."

"You can't keep my son from me."

"We'll see about that. Since you're not sleeping tonight, you'll have plenty of time to reconsider and think about the consequences of your behavior.

He stepped away from the bed, strode across the room, and slammed the door shut.

The weight of the moment crashing down on her, an overwhelming tide of fear and revulsion rose within her.

Sarah heard the click of the lock engage.

CHAPTER TWENTY-FOUR

NOW DAY 7: Wednesday 01/31 MORNING

Unable to sleep, her mind churning with fear, Sarah spent the rest of the night alternating between staring out the window and pacing. She coached herself to stay calm. She thought about calling the emergency number, but what if she was trusting the wrong people? Judy said she was a police detective, but there was no proof. Sarah hadn't seen an ID, or another policeman, and who'd sent her that picture of Claire and Rodney? At last, when the phone showed 4 a.m., she forced herself to lie down and drifted into a fitful sleep.

The sound of the bedroom door opening jarred her awake. The room was dim with early morning light. The faint scent of Rodney's cologne alerted her to his presence. She kept her breathing steady, feigning sleep while mentally preparing for the confrontation she sensed was about to unfold.

"Wake up," he whispered, his voice low and dangerous.

She shifted slightly, responding with a soft murmur, "Mmm…," in an attempt to maintain her ruse.

"This is your last chance. If you want your son back, you need to stop fighting me, Sarah." Rodney leaned closer.

She could feel his breath against her hair as he continued, "You need to understand your position in all of this. It's not too late to make this easier for yourself."

His words made her stomach turn. She wanted to scream, to lash out; instead, she focused on keeping her mind sharp. She'd need to remember everything.

"You really should have just played the good little wife. You could have avoided all this. I would have taken care of you. But you insist on causing trouble."

She opened her eyes. "Do you think I'm afraid of you?" she challenged, her voice steady despite the tremors in her hands. "You're not invincible, Rodney. You can't just take my son and expect me to sit back quietly."

"Do you really think you can fight me? Everyone knows you're an unstable alcoholic, a bad mother."

She sat up and glared at him. "I'm not weak or helpless. I know what you are, Rodney. You'll never break me, and you'll never win. I will find my son and you'll get what's coming to you."

His expression shifted for a moment from mockery to a begrudging respect. "This is far from over, Sarah." He strode back to the open door. "There are far worse fates than death. Remember that."

As the door closed behind him, panic surged through her, but she refused to give in.

Sarah grabbed the phone from its hiding place, hid in the bathroom, and called the contact Judy had given her for emergencies.

"Stay strong, stay focused," she whispered to herself. "You'll get through this."

"Yes?" a deep male voice answered.

"I need Detective Hendricks, please."

"Yes, ma'am. Are you safe?"

Sarah's voice quivered as she said, "I think so."

"It is 6:15 a.m. She'll be there in five. Would you like me to stay on the line with you?"

"No. I have to hide the phone. If Rodney finds it he'll kill me."

"Be care—"

The voice cut off as Sarah disconnected.

Pressing her ear to the door, she strained to hear any sounds outside the bathroom. What if Rodney had come back? What if he'd heard her call?

She counted to one hundred and eased the bathroom door open a crack. The dimly lit bedroom seemed empty, but she couldn't shake the feeling that Rodney was lurking nearby, waiting for her.

Gathering her courage, she stepped out and scanned her bedroom. The early morning sunlight spilled into the room, brightening the corners where shadows lingered, but there was no sign of him.

She hurried to the chair and with trembling fingers, tucked the phone back into the crevice between the cushion and the back. If Rodney did return, she needed to act natural—she couldn't give him any reason to suspect that she had contacted Judy. She needed to get dressed and go down for coffee.

A tap sounded on the door.

Sarah froze.

The door swung open.

This time, it was Judy.

"Good morning," the detective said softly, stepping inside. "You okay?" Judy gestured for her to be quiet, closing the door behind her. "I'm here, and I'm going to help you," she whispered. "We need to talk quickly. What happened?"

"He threatened me. He told me to cooperate or I'd never see Jeremy again, that there are fates worse than death."

"Did he say he has Jeremy? Did he say where?"

Sarah could feel the urgency in the detective's tone. "Not exactly, but he said if I quit fighting and did as he said, I'd see Jeremy again."

Judy's eyes scanned the room. "Listen carefully. Rodney is suspected of embezzling client funds. The force is starting to piece it together, but we need to move quickly."

Sarah's mind raced, trying to process the implications of Judy's words. "Embezzlement. How much? Why?"

"I can't disclose details," Judy said, her voice low. "But it's serious. He's been under investigation for a while now, and the noose is tightening. If he suspects you're working with us, he'll escalate things quickly."

"What should I do?" Sarah asked, her heart sinking at the thought of what Rodney might do if he found out she was working with the police.

"Until he's out of the house this morning, you need to act natural. Put on a robe and come down for coffee." Judy picked up the cup from the nightstand. "I'll take this down with me. If he sees me, he'll think I'm just doing my job, tidying the house. We need to test it to find out what he's giving you."

Judy opened the door and stepped into the hall. Raising her voice, she asked, "Do you need anything else, Mrs. Blake?" Leaning closer, her voice a whisper, she said, "I won't let him hurt you. And we *will* find Jeremy." She winked and said in a normal tone, "The coffee will be ready in a minute." Judy pulled the bedroom door shut with a solid click.

Sarah's knees wobbled and she sank to the side of the bed. Tremors shook her thin frame. Tears threatened. She brushed them away. "Get a grip," she told herself, realizing these were the exact words Claire had used a million times in the past. Sarah muttered, "What the hell is going on? If Rodney did something terrible, is Claire involved?"

She pulled on her robe, slid her feet into the slippers, and squared her shoulders. Still unsure of who, if anyone, she could trust in what felt like a maze of deceit, she vowed to be brave and do whatever was necessary to reclaim Jeremy from Rodney's grasp. Two could play the deceit game.

***

As Sarah approached the kitchen, she could hear Rodney asking Judy, "When you left after dinner last night, did you notice anyone outside?"

"Outside? You mean in the yard?"

Sarah paused, waiting and listening.

"Or in the woods?"

Judy's voice sounded ordinary, as if there was nothing worrisome about the questions Rodney was asking. "No, no one. It was getting dark. I looked for that dog, but I didn't see him either. Not even the usual wildlife. Why? Did you see someone when you left?"

"I thought I saw something, but...I must have been mistaken." Rodney's response was sharp and irritated. "You know how the mind can play tricks in the dark. It was probably just my imagination."

Sarah wasn't convinced. Judy had admitted the house was being watched. What had Rodney seen?

She entered the kitchen, accepted a mug of coffee, and sat down at the table. Her gaze flicked to the window behind Rodney. She shivered at the thought of who or what might be in the woods.

She had to find a way to uncover the truth before she lost Jeremy to Rodney's manipulations.

Sarah kept her voice casual as she asked, "Where's the boy this morning?" She watched anger flick across Rodney's face as she taunted him.

Judy's jaw tensed. Her eyebrows drew together in a frown. She gave a tiny shake of her head.

Sarah ignored her. "I don't care what you're up to, Rodney, but I do care that you've dragged Jeremy into your mess. If my son is injured in any way I'll see that you pay for it. You may think you can play these games without consequences, but I'll make sure everyone knows the truth about who you are."

Rodney's eyes widened, his jaw slack in disbelief. He regained his composure, a smirk creeping across his face. "My, my, aren't you the brave one this morning. You seem to have forgotten—I always come out on top."

He set his coffee mug on the counter and brushed past Sarah, almost knocking her off her feet. "I'll be home early tonight. Don't stir up any trouble."

The women watched from the kitchen window until Rodney had driven away. Then Judy sat down and studied Sarah for a long moment. Taking a deep breath, she asked, "What the hell do you think you're doing?"

Sarah leaned back and folded her arms across her chest. "I'm taking charge of my life."

Judy rolled her eyes and pointed a finger at her. "You have no idea, what you're getting into."

"Then tell me. Tell me everything you know."

Judy's expression hardened. "I can't do that. This is an active investigation and you're part of it."

"That seems like all the more reason for you to tell me. I'll help you if you help me."

"Sarah, this isn't a made-for-TV movie—you can't strike a bargain with law enforcement."

A rap sounded against the glass in the back door.

Sarah jumped.

Judy waved the man at the door inside. "My partner, Jason Stevens."

He wiped his feet on the mat and smiled at Sarah. "Good morning." Turning to Judy, he asked, "Where's the evidence you want tested?"

"In the cupboard over the refrigerator. There's still tea in it."

Jason slipped on plastic gloves, retrieved the teacup, and placed it in an evidence bag. "I'll just run this out to the team and be right back. I've got surveillance following Blake. We'll have plenty of warning if he heads this way." Jason opened the back door and continued, "We're talking to that creep watching from the woods. He's claiming to be a local cop but he doesn't have an ID. I put Jeffers on that."

Sarah waited until the door closed behind him. Then she asked Judy, "If you're a detective and that guy in the woods is some kind of investigator, aren't you on the same side? Why don't you know who he is?"

"That would be the question in a nutshell. I know who I am and I think that guy is lying." She pulled her phone from her pocket and tapped in a call.

Sarah stayed silent listening for clues, trying to determine who to trust.

"Yeah." Jason's voice boomed from the speaker of Judy's phone.

"You still got the woods guy out there?"

"Yep, ready to transport in a few. Jeffers is pulling into the drive now."

"Stand him somewhere we can see him from the kitchen. I want Sarah to get a good look at him." She stood up and turned to Sarah. "Come over to the window."

Sarah complied.

"Take a good look. Do you recognize that man?"

Sarah started to shake her head no, but then said, "Wait. I think maybe I do. Have him take off that ski hat."

"You hear her, Jason?"

"Yep."

Judy and Sarah watched as Jason said something to the man, who reached up and removed his knit hat. A thick thatch of red hair spilled out and tumbled to his shoulders.

Color drained from Sarah's face. She steadied herself on the counter. "I think that might be Jeremy's cowboy. He said Rusty's hair looked like Grandma Lydia's."

"Well, he's certainly not police with that mop. Read him his rights and take him in, Jason. We may be looking at a kidnapping charge."

Judy guided Sarah away from the window. "My boss is getting a warrant to search this property. You should go upstairs and get dressed."

Mutely, Sarah pressed her lips together and struggled to make sense of what was happening around her. "But," she stammered, "we know Jeremy isn't in this house."

"We won't be looking for your son. We'll be looking for evidence of Rodney's crimes. We need to get you out of here and to someplace safe, somewhere Rodney can't find you."

Sarah hesitated, panic threatening to spill over. "But what about Jeremy? I can't just leave—"

"Trust me, I won't abandon him," Judy assured her. "If we find the evidence we believe is here, Rodney will be arrested. Then we will get a warrant for his office and any other property he owns. Do you understand?"

"No. You need to understand—my son is missing!" Sarah was shouting now. "He's been missing for nineteen days! You said so yourself. Why isn't anyone looking for Jeremy?"

"We've alerted the FBI and the local police. They are looking into your allegations. But remember, Rodney claims that the boy living in this house is your son Jeremy."

"You know he isn't Jeremy! You told me he is an actor. Make someone believe you."

"That's exactly what I plan to do. But first, we have to find the evidence of Rodney's crimes, including kidnapping and false imprisonment."

CHAPTER TWENTY-FIVE

NOW DAY 7: Wednesday 01/31 AFTERNOON

By the time Sarah had showered, dressed, and left her bedroom, the house was teeming with police. The locked doors along the upstairs hallway were all flung open. Sarah thought about the map she'd drawn and wanted to see what the locked rooms contained. To the right, the open French doors allowed her a view of the room the boy had told her was the master bedroom. It contained nothing but a bed with a bare mattress and a stack of boxes. A young man, wearing a jacket with the Seattle Police logo on the left shoulder and plastic gloves, looked up and gave her a quick nod before returning his attention to the boxes.

Retracing her steps past her bedroom, Sarah stopped and glanced into the room across the hall. It was empty. The next two rooms were guest rooms, immaculate but as impersonal as those in any hotel, each with a spa-like bathroom, towels neatly hung, and a crystal accessory set arranged on a silver tray.

From the boy's room she could hear the murmur of voices. Pausing, she tried and failed to make out the words. Stepping inside,

Sarah watched as a man searched through dresser drawers. He said, "I wish my kid kept his room this neat."

The woman he addressed laughed. "Yeah, it's way too tidy in here." She busily removed books from the bookcase, flipping each one open, shaking it a bit to see if anything dropped out, and then added it to the growing stack on the floor.

"The first day, I found a list inside one of the boy's books," Sarah said.

The searchers turned to look at her. The man's eyes swept up and down her body and came to focus on her face.

The woman looked at the book in her hand and then at Sarah. "Oh yeah, what'd it say?"

"I think it was a list of things the boy was supposed to remember." Sarah crossed the room and pointed at one of the books. "That one. *A Wrinkle in Time.*"

The agent pulled the book from the shelf.

"The note's not in there anymore," Sarah said. "I hid it."

"Why would you do that?"

Sarah shrugged. "I knew he wasn't my son and the note seemed to mean I was right. I thought I could use it to prove Rodney was lying to me."

"Does Hendricks know about this?"

"No."

"Okay, let's see it."

Sarah led the way back to her bedroom. She lifted the lamp and removed the folded paper. She handed it to the woman, who opened the square quickly and read the list. She pulled an evidence bag from her pocket, labeled it, and slipped the paper inside. "I'm going to get

Hendricks up here, and then I need you to tell us exactly when and where you found this."

***

Judy and the others listened carefully to Sarah's explanation. After only a few questions, Judy asked Sarah to accompany her downstairs so the police could complete their search.

As they walked together down the stairs, Sarah asked, "Have you found anything yet?"

"Some things. We'll be taking the documents and Rodney's computer with us. Forensics will analyze them and log everything in as evidence, and the CFEs will take a look at all the financial records."

"CFEs?"

"Certified fraud examiners. We've gathered enough to ask for a warrant to be issued for Rodney's arrest and to search his office."

Hope flared across Sarah's face. "Do you know where Jeremy is?"

Judy shook her head. "I'm afraid not. So far we have no proof of his disappearance."

Sarah covered her mouth with her hands and drew in a quick gasp.

"We have another problem, too." Judy kept her gaze focused on Sarah as she said, "This cabin you claim is yours, we haven't found any record of property registered in your name. Not anywhere in Washington."

"It's not actually mine. It's in a trust my grandparents set up for Jeremy. They knew about my marriage and about my drinking problem. I don't think they trusted either Rodney or me. My grandmother was the trustee and now that she's gone, I think it is their attorney. I know I have the right to live in the cabin as long as I like. But I can't sell it."

"If you've been living there, I assume you know the location and how to get there. I need the address and your permission to search the premises."

"But…"

"No buts. Rodney is being arrested as we speak. Jeremy isn't here and he may well be at this cabin of yours. The FBI has been informed that Jeremy is missing. They work with the locals if there is a kidnapping case. You go upstairs and gather anything personal that you want, and I'll coordinate with the FBI."

Sarah stepped back and tilted her chin up, her jaw tight. "The cabin is on Short Drive. Just off Alta Lake Road. There's a sign that says Eagle's Rest, and our cabin is number seventeen." Her shoulders dropped. "I don't have anything personal up there." She pointed at the ceiling.

"Oh, right. Of course, you don't." Judy raised her voice and called, "Jason."

"Right here," Jason answered as he stepped from Rodney's office into the entry. Judy waved him back into the office and followed him.

She dropped her voice, speaking quietly. "Where are we with the guy in the woods?"

"We ran his prints. He's Kent Williams, a local lowlife with a list of petty stuff. Minor jail time. No outstanding warrant. But we've got him on impersonating a cop and we can make a case for stalking. He's been in those woods a few days with a bunch of high-tech surveillance equipment. I sent someone to the school to see if a teacher would remember him hanging around."

"Any idea who he's working for?"

"Not yet. Jeffers will keep pressing him, but we'll have to transport Williams to Seattle soon." Jason pulled off his plastic gloves, turning them inside out and stuffing them in his pocket. "Blake's under arrest and screaming for his lawyer. His office is stripped and locked down and we're done in here. Everything is bagged and tagged. The vans will be here in a few and we'll transport everything to Seattle."

"Both this house and his local office are crime scenes that need to be watched tonight. The kid is still missing, and somehow that links to this." Judy waved her hand at the bags and boxes accumulating in the hallway. She caught sight of Sarah listening at the door and flushed. "Sorry, Sarah. I should have said Jeremy."

Brushing tears away, Sarah nodded. "Is there anything in any of those bags that pertains to my son—clothes, toys, anything?"

"No, ma'am. We did find women's clothing in Blake's bedroom." He glanced at Sarah's slippered feet. "No shoes or coat."

"He was putting just one outfit at a time in my closet. At night, he came in and took away what I'd worn and laid out something else. None of that stuff is mine."

Jason's brows knit together in a frown. "Control freak?"

Sarah nodded.

Judy turned to Jason. "The FBI will take charge of the investigation into Jeremy's disappearance. The cabin will be their crime scene. I'd like to get up there first."

Jason nodded his understanding.

"I have a coat and shoes for Sarah," Judy continued. "We are leaving now. I'll call them from the road and give them directions to the cabin."

"Got it," Jason said. "I'll be right behind you."

***

Highway 97 from Rodney's house on the outskirts of Wenatchee to Lake Alta followed the Columbia River through the valley and then past towering pines and rugged snow-capped peaks. As they traveled north, Judy spoke on the phone, first to her boss and then to an FBI agent. Sarah listened carefully, hoping to glean more information.

When Judy hung up, Sarah asked, "Exactly what is Rodney charged with?"

"Suspicion of embezzlement."

"What about kidnapping? What about locking me up and drugging me?" Sarah's voice escalated, laced with urgency as she pressed for answers.

"Right this minute, we have proof that he embezzled customer funds and diverted them into his own accounts. The FBI will determine if Jeremy's disappearance is a kidnapping. As for drugging you and holding you hostage, we need to have proof that his intentions were unlawful."

"He locked me in my room and drugged me. What else could they be?"

"Rodney will claim he was acting under the advice of your doctor. We need to subpoena your medical records, and we need proof of your divorce and the custody arrangement."

"The divorce was filed in King County. It's a public record. Can't you just ask for it?" Irritation colored Sarah's voice. "Why does everything take so long?"

"We requested the full divorce record this morning. You need to understand that until two days ago we were only gathering evidence on the embezzlement charges." Judy kept her eyes on the road and kept her voice even. "He bought that house about six months ago. Everyone we've spoken with believes he lives there with you and Jeremy."

"What the hell? Didn't you ask my friends, my mother?"

"Nope. We had no reason to be suspicious. His business and work colleagues all believe you guys are married and that you are ill or unstable."

Sarah sat silent and digested this information. Taking a breath, she asked, "What about my job or Jeremy's school?"

"Didn't check. Our focus was entirely on the missing money. Rodney's boss pressed charges and we began our investigation. There was no reason to doubt the personal information he provided. When I took the undercover position, it was to determine who Blake was working with. Never once did it come up that you were anything other than his wife. He told me that you'd tried to kill yourself, had mental health and memory issues, that you needed to be watched carefully until you'd fully recovered. We weren't suspicious about anything until you found that kid's phone."

Sarah turned in her seat and studied Judy's profile. "Do you believe me now?"

Silence stretched between them. When Judy spoke, she seemed to consider each word: "I believe you believe everything you've told me. But the timeline doesn't make sense."

Sarah chewed on her lower lip and kept her eyes on the passing trees. At last, she asked, "Do you think I had some kind of psychotic break? That maybe I was in a hospital for a month but don't remember it?"

"Do you think that's true?" Judy asked.

Sarah shook her head. "No, not really."

"It always comes back to why Rodney tried to convince you that that kid was Jeremy. If we figure that out…" Judy's voice trailed off.

"We're getting close," Sarah said. "The turn is right beyond the corner."

Judy slowed and made the turn.

Sarah pointed. "It's that one."

Judy swung into the drive and stopped. The car ticked in the silence. The woods looked close and desolate. "I don't see any car tracks or footprints. The place looks deserted." She swung open her door. "Does anyone else live out here?"

"Not full time," Sarah said, opening her door and stepping out. "Most of the other cabins are summer only. I think that green one down there," she pointed farther down the road, "is winterized. We see people over there sometimes."

"Pretty lonely out here," Judy said. "You got a key for this place?"

Sarah moaned. "I don't have shoes or a coat—where would I keep a key?"

Judy moved to the trunk and popped it open. "I can probably break it open, but without a search warrant, that would be iffy."

"The trust may own it, but I live here legally," Sarah said. "You have my permission to break in."

"And, lucky for us, I put a new lock pick set in here last night." Judy grinned at Sarah, retrieved the lock picks, and moved to the door. "Let's see what we can find. If your son has been living here, it should be obvious."

Judy inserted the curved tool, turned it, and the cabin door swung open. They hesitated on the threshold, allowing their eyes to adjust to the dim light. "I need you to go first," Judy instructed. "Look around and tell me if you see anything unusual."

It was chilly inside; the heat must have been off for days. Sarah shivered and pulled her borrowed coat closer. She flipped a switch by the door and an overhead light came on. Not a single item was out of place, from the neatly arranged furniture to the gleaming kitchen counter. "It's too clean," she murmured, frowning. "Where's all our stuff?"

They moved through the living room, where a cozy fireplace stood empty, logs piled beside it. There were no traces of personal belongings, no toys that might belong to a child, and no signs of life.

"This is Jeremy's room," Sarah said, twisting the doorknob to reveal a small bed covered in a plaid blanket. A toy box stood open and empty at the foot of the bed. The shelves under the window were bare. Sarah crossed to the closet and flung it open. Empty hangers rattled together. She whirled around, her face a mask of confusion. "Where is everything? What does this mean?"

"It looks like whoever lived here moved out."

"Damn it! *I* live here. I live here with Jeremy and we sure as hell didn't move out!"

Sarah dashed out of the bedroom and charged across the living room toward the closed door on the other side. She grasped the knob and twisted. "It's locked." Her eyes wide, she slammed her hand against the door. "Why would it be locked?"

"Only one way to find out," Judy said. "I'll use the picks and you turn up the heat in here." Judy watched as Sarah returned to the wall outside Jeremy's room and adjusted the thermostat. Somewhere a heat pump rumbled to life. "You okay?" Judy asked.

Sarah didn't answer. She stared straight ahead, her pupils dilated, her breathing shallow and too fast.

Judy hurried to her side. Wrapping an arm around Sarah, she forced her to sit and pushed her head between her knees. "Slow and easy, Sarah. Just breathe slow and easy. In through your nose, out through your mouth. There you go. Again, slow and easy. Okay now?" Judy removed her hand from the back of Sarah's neck and asked again, "Okay?"

Sarah blew out, puffing her cheeks. "Yeah. Thanks."

Judy patted her back. "I'm going to open that door. You just keep breathing."

A loud banging on the front door exploded into the room.

"FBI! Open the door." The male voice was deep and commanding.

"Damn it, they're here already," Judy muttered, and then called out, "It's open. Come on in."

The door flew open and banged against the wall.

Judy laughed. "Andy Jones, welcome."

"Shit," the tall, dark man filling the door said with a grin. "When they said Seattle PD was involved, I should have known it was you, Hendricks. Are we going to have any trouble?"

"Not if you play nice. Where's the rest of the team, Andy?"

"I was already in Wenatchee. The closest field office is Tri-Cities. It'll take the others another hour to get here." Andy approached Sarah and introduced himself. "I understand that your six-year-old son,

Jeremy, is missing. When was the last time you saw your son, Mrs. Blake?"

"I think it was January twelfth, when I put him to bed."

Andy's face hardened; his dark eyes narrowed. "January twelfth—that's over two weeks ago."

"Exactly nineteen days," Judy supplied.

Andy pulled out his phone. "Okay if I record our conversation, ma'am?"

Sarah nodded and moved to the sofa.

Andy sat facing her. He tapped his phone a few times and placed it on the coffee table. He stated the date, time, and his name. Then he added, "In the room are Seattle PD Detective Judith Hendricks and Mrs. Sarah Blake."

"Please, call me Sarah. I'm divorced."

Andy glanced at Judy. "Okay, Sarah. You stated the last time you saw your son was the night of January twelfth, this year. Is that correct?" Sarah nodded. "Please answer aloud for the record."

Sarah cleared her throat and said, "Yes, about nine-thirty, when I put him to bed."

"Why haven't you reported his disappearance until now?"

"I tried, but no one believed me." She brushed away her tears. "Somehow I lost almost two weeks. Rodney says I'm crazy. And everyone believes him."

Judy interrupted. "The Seattle PD are working a concurrent case that involves Rodney Blake, the ex-husband, father of the boy. Sarah's apparent confusion over her identity and that of her son did not appear to be related to the crime under investigation. Two days ago we became aware that something in addition to our case might be happening. Until yesterday morning, we were unsure if the child living in the home was Sarah's son or an impostor as she claimed."

"Okay, what happened yesterday?"

"We discovered that the child Blake was claiming as his son is actually a child actor, hired to play the part of Jeremy Blake."

"That's twenty-four hours ago."

"We still have no proof that Jeremy is missing. His father or someone else may have secreted him from the mother."

Sarah gasped and started a protest.

Judy waved her to silence. "Until half an hour ago, when we arrived here, we believed this cabin didn't exist, that it had burned to the ground six years ago. What I do know for sure is that Blake has been drugging his wife—ex-wife, that the actor kid was hired to impersonate Jeremy, and that none of that makes any sense when it comes to the embezzlement case. But all of it means something is very wrong."

Sarah sprang to her feet. "I'm sick of this! You act like I'm an idiot. Ajax is hanging out at Rodney's house and I think he knows where Jeremy is. And what about the man in the woods? You arrested him—he must know something? Then there's Claire and that damn picture?"

The officers sat dumbfounded by her outburst.

"Figure out why Rodney was embezzling." She pointed at Judy. "You said yourself that he must need me under his control for some reason. Well, what's the reason? You arrested him. Make him talk."

Andy cocked his head. "She has a point, Hendricks. How many times have we all heard 'follow the money'? It may be a cliché, but embezzlement is certainly about the money." He turned to Sarah. "Who's Ajax?"

"Jeremy's dog. He was with me when I searched for Jeremy in the woods. When I woke up, Rodney denied we had a dog, but he's hanging out at Rodney's house."

"Rodney says he never saw that dog before," Judy chimed in.

Sarah scowled at Judy. "Rodney lies! Admit it, you know he lies. How about if you guys start believing me instead of him."

All three turned as the front door opened and Jason Stevens arrived. "Yo, feels tense in here." He looked from one to the other and shrugged. "Judy, I need to talk to you."

Andy turned off the recorder, stood, and stretched his hand toward Jason. "Andy Jones, FBI. A missing person trumps financial crime; it's time for you guys to share what you know. If this kid has been missing nineteen days, time may be running out."

Jason shook Andy's hand and waited for Judy to say something.

The silence stretched for a long moment. Judy nodded to Andy. "You're right." Her look transferred to Jason. "What have you got?"

"Blake has lawyered up. We have evidence of the embezzlement and transfer of the money to his own accounts on both his home computer and his work computer. In addition, we've found a couple more things that forensics is attempting to confirm now." Jason paused, opened a notepad, and considered Sarah.

She bit her lip and said, "Go ahead. I can take it."

"The tea contained a strong doze of estazolam. Not enough to kill, but enough to insure a deep sleep. We found a prescription bottle with your name on it, Sarah. There's only one set of fingerprints on the bottle. They match Blake." He consulted his pad again. "Looks like

Williams, the guy in the woods, is working for a local loan shark. He claims Blake owes some big money for gambling debts and that he was watching Blake's movements and reporting to his boss. He's denying any knowledge of the kid, but one of the teachers from the Pateros school recognized him. Says he's been hanging around since before Christmas. Jeffers will keep the pressure on until we find out everything he knows."

Judy said, "The embezzlement may have been to cover his gambling debts."

"Seems likely. We'll try to tie them together. The gambling may have gone on a long time and we know the embezzlement started over a year ago." Jason paused again. "But there is something else. Sarah, we found correspondence with a law firm that was sent to you. It was a letter confirming that they had filed your grandmother's death certificate and her will with the probate court. Do you remember reading that letter?"

Sarah looked puzzled. "She died last August. I received a payment of a few thousand dollars from an insurance company. They said I was the named beneficiary. I used it to pay off my car and put the rest in the bank. I was never notified of a will."

"The letter went to Mrs. Sarah Blake, care of Rodney Blake, at his office address in Seattle. It mentions that your grandmother left a sizable estate. All of it to you."

Sarah shook her head, frustration bubbling up. "What does that have to do with Jeremy's disappearance?"

"Rodney's concealment of your inheritance raises concerns that his recent claims of being legally married to you may be an attempt to access that money."

Andy interrupted. "If Williams was hanging around Jeremy's school, the FBI needs to interrogate him." He pulled his phone from his pocket. "I'll divert one of my team. We'll also need access to the father. What has Blake told you?"

"He's not talking without his attorney and we haven't questioned him at all on the disappearance of his child," Jason said.

"First things first," Judy said. "We need to determine if there *is* a missing child. Did you get to the kid actor?"

"I was getting to that," Jason said.

Sarah's face flushed with anger. "What is wrong with you people? What do I need to do to get you to look for Jeremy?"

Jason ignored her outburst and continued, "Yes, we talked to the actor in the presence of his mother. There is something fishy there. They agree that he was hired to pretend to be Jeremy Blake for a few days. The mother admitted that the job came from an agent." Jason looked at his notepad. "A guy called Clyde Garson. Not the kid's usual agent. She says she thought it was a really weird request, but he assured her that Blake was only trying to help his wife get her memory back and the money was really good."

"Did you contact the agent?" Andy asked.

"We haven't found him yet. No sign of him on the internet, which is problematic."

"Okay then." Andy looked between the policemen. "Anything else?"

Neither answered.

"Sarah has a good point. We need to give her the benefit of the doubt. This cabin, yard, and the surrounding area is an FBI crime scene. From here on out we treat it as one. Nobody touches anything until I give the word."

Judy and Jason nodded.

Sarah kept her eyes glued to Andy and brushing her tears away, she said, "Thank you."

Andy turned to Judy. "When you arrived at the cabin, describe the scene."

"Sarah found the cabin with no hesitation. The driveway and yard were covered in unbroken snow. No tire tracks or footprints. I asked for and was given permission by the presumed legal resident to search the property. Because she had no key and did not volunteer that a key was hidden, I opened the door with a pick set."

She gestured toward the living area. "Sarah appeared to be familiar with the cabin. She knew where to find the light switches and the thermostat. She also commented on how clean and uninhabited the room is. We proceeded to the bedroom on the right. The door was unlocked, but the room was completely empty of personal items except for a plaid blanket covering a child's bed."

"Did you touch anything?

Sarah volunteered, "I lifted the lid on Jeremy's toy box and opened the closet door. They are both empty."

Andy nodded.

Judy continued, "We moved to the second bedroom. It's locked, and you arrived before I got a chance to unlock that door."

The sound of cars arriving drew their attention to the window.

"Reinforcements," Andy said. He turned to Sarah. "We are going to search every square inch of this cabin and fingerprint everything. While the other agents do that, I am going to ask you questions—a lot of questions. Our priority is to locate your son and in doing so, find out why and how he disappeared."

"And, who took him?" Sarah asked.

"Yes. I'd like to resume recording our conversation. Are you in agreement?"

"Of course."

Andy gave instructions for the FBI agents to process the declared crime scene and led the way to the kitchen table. He pulled out a chair for Sarah. Glancing over his shoulder at Judy and Jason, he asked, "Do you want to sit in on this, Hendricks?"

"Andy," an agent called.

They turned. The second bedroom had been unlocked and the door stood open. The room was full. A jumble of bags and boxes were stacked on every available surface, including on an unmade hospital bed. A vital signs monitor, still plugged into the wall, sat on a wheeled cart. Pushed into a corner was an IV pole, hung with partially empty bags and an infusion pump. A folded wheelchair leaned against the bed.

"Shit," Jason breathed out. "What went down in there?"

Judy said, "Sarah, I think you may have been right when you told me about the hospital not being a real hospital."

"Hospital?" Andy asked. He looked from Judy to Sarah and said, "It's time to tell me everything you can. Start with when you first noticed Jeremy was missing."

CHAPTER TWENTY-SIX

NOW DAY 7: Wednesday 01/31 EVENING

Two hours later, Sarah was exhausted. She'd answered all of Andy's questions, had told him everything she could remember about her life with Jeremy in the weeks and days before waking in the cabin and finding him gone. They'd talked about her terrible fear as she stumbled after Ajax, searching in the woods. And then how she woke to find that everything she knew and believed had disappeared and that days were missing from her life.

"Okay, Sarah." Andy stretched his arms above his head and leaned back in his chair. "For now, we are going to proceed under the belief that your story is factual. Your son was abducted, between the hours of ten p.m. January twelfth and seven a.m. January thirteenth by an unknown person or persons."

Plopping his chair back onto all four legs, he continued. "Sarah, this cabin will remain a crime scene for another day or two. Is there someplace you'd like to stay? Perhaps with friends or family?"

"Rodney is in jail, so I guess I can still use his house."

"Good idea. We're setting up our command center there anyway." Andy smiled warmly. "Any problem, Hendricks?"

"We've got him on a seventy-two-hour hold that started about eleven a.m. today, so we're clear for a couple of days," Judy said. "Right now, we have the embezzlement charges and with the drugs in the tea, we can get unlawful detainment. The prosecutor's office will need to decide on the crime or crimes to pursue for prosecution. I'll be Seattle PD's liaison to the FBI and stick with you guys. Jason, you can head back to Wenatchee and keep us informed as things move there."

Andy nodded. "The FBI will take all of the cabin evidence to our lab in Seattle and coordinate with Seattle PD there. We'll need to move fast. This kid has been missing a long time and so far we haven't found a trail."

Andy passed his hand over his jaw and continued, "The fact that there hasn't been a ransom demand points to a parental abduction of the kid. The FBI needs to be in on processing the evidence from Blake's house and office."

Sarah listened, her eyes going back and forth, as the officers talked about their plans. "Jeremy," she said. "The kid is Jeremy."

"Sorry, ma'am." Andy had the grace to look abashed. "We need a recent picture of Jeremy."

Sarah's eyes swept the bare room. "His school picture was on the mantel. Whoever removed our belongings must have done something with it."

Andy rose and crossed to the bedroom. Stopping at the door, he asked, "You guys find any pictures in those boxes?"

"Yeah, that one." The agent pointed. "Nothing's been fingerprinted yet."

"Got it. Give me some gloves." Andy looked over his shoulder at Sarah and beckoned.

She stood and walked to him slowly, her face pale with fear.

"You stand right here in the doorway. I'm going to go through that box and you tell me what things mean. Can you do that?"

Sarah nodded.

Andy pulled on the gloves, entered the bedroom, and crossed to the indicated box. He pulled open the flaps, reached in, and lifted out a framed picture. Glancing down at it, his lips lifted in a smile. "Cute kid," he said, turning the picture toward Sarah. "Is this Jeremy's school picture?"

Sarah nodded. Tears flowed. She hugged herself to control the trembling and then reached for the picture.

"Sorry," Andy said, holding it out of reach. "I'm sure your prints are already on this, but we need to preserve the chain of evidence."

Sarah's hand dropped.

Holding the frame by its outer edges, Andy handed it to the agent. "Photograph this, dust it, and then get that picture out of the frame. We'll send it out with a BOLO and a nationwide Amber Alert.

"Sarah, we can head back to Rodney's house. By the time we get there, the team will have established it as our primary command center."

Sarah winced. She bit her lip and gave a tiny nod.

"We know how to find a child, Sarah. I promise we are moving rapidly and we will do our best to find your Jeremy. Are you ready to go?"

"Wait. What about that picture of Claire?" Sarah asked. "Isn't that a clue?"

"Maybe," Judy acknowledged.

Andy glared at her. "Care to share?"

Judy opened her phone gallery and found the images of Claire and Rodney. She handed the phone to Andy. "Claire was Sarah's best friend until about a year ago. Sarah thinks both photos may have been taken here."

Andy scrolled back and forth. He studied the images and then said, "Looks like it to me, too. This one," he tapped the picture of Claire by herself and pointed, "is right over there by the sink. And, this one is definitely in front of the fireplace." He handed the phone to Sarah. "Do you agree?"

"Yes, but Claire and Rodney were never in this cabin at the same time."

"Never?"

"Never. They hated each other." Sarah studied the photos again. "In this one by the fireplace, you can see the corner of Jeremy's school picture. I put it here the night Jeremy brought the pictures home from school."

"When was that?"

Sarah brushed away a tear. "Right after Christmas break." Her voice broke as she said, "Rodney and Claire must have been here since Jeremy disappeared."

"Or," Jason spoke up, "*when* Jeremy disappeared."

"Where did these photos come from?" Andy asked Judy.

"They came on a text message from a blocked caller, about 5:30 yesterday afternoon. We're tracing the call, but so far no luck. It wasn't a priority before, but I'll tell them to push now."

"Wait!" Sarah broke in. "Did you see this?" Sarah had enlarged the photo of Claire by the sink. "I think that is Jeremy reflected in the window."

Judy grabbed the phone. She and Andy stared at the picture.

"I can see two reflections," Andy said.

Sarah bent close. "It looks like Rodney is taking the picture and Jeremy is behind him."

"You might be right," Andy agreed. "Forensics can make this much clearer."

"I have another question," Sarah said. "If my clothes are in those bags or boxes, can I take some of them with me to the house, and what about my car?"

The agent working in the bedroom, who'd been listening as they talked, said, "Lots of women's stuff in these bags, but we have to process everything before we can release anything. It'll be a while."

"Sorry, Sarah, but he's right," Judy said. "We can stop at a store on the way to the house if you can purchase what you need quickly."

"I don't want to slow anything down. If you let me keep this coat and shoes, at least I'll be able to go outside."

"No problem. If you make a list, I can have someone else do the shopping."

"That's a plan," Andy said. "What kind of car do you drive and where do you usually park it?"

"It's a 2023 Subaru Forester. It should be in the garage. Through that door." She pointed across the kitchen.

Jason hurried to the door and swung it open. The garage was empty. He whipped out his notebook. "Do you know the license number? We'll add it to the BOLO and the Amber Alert."

Sarah provided the information.

***

Andy directed Sarah to ride with him and told Judy they'd follow her car. Sarah rode staring out the window without seeing anything. Andy left her in peace, asking only if she was okay.

Arriving at the house, Sarah was surprised by the number of vehicles in the drive. "Who are all these people?"

As he parked, Andy answered, "FBI, state and local police. It doesn't look like the media are here yet, but I'm sure it won't be long." He reached to open his door and paused. "There will be an FBI agent assigned from Victim's Services that will assist and support you as we move through this investigation."

Sarah blew out a deep breath and swallowed hard. "Okay."

"Just ask if you have any questions. Tell us if you see, hear, or remember anything. Anything at all may be important." He smiled at her. "Okay. Let's go."

Sarah opened her car door and stepped out.

A joyful bark echoed from the woods, filling the air with excitement. Sarah spun around, her heart racing. "Ajax!" she called out, her voice bright with anticipation. A whirlwind of brown and black fur burst from the tree line, streaking across the yard with unbridled joy. Ajax raced toward her, his excited barks filling the air.

Sarah knelt in the wet snow, her heart swelling as Ajax launched himself into her arms. His tail wagged furiously, a blur of happiness, while he showered her face with affectionate licks, wiping away the tears that had escaped.

Andy laughed as he watched. "So, this is the dog Blake says doesn't belong to you or Jeremy." He grinned as he helped Sarah to her feet. "I'd say that dog is sure he knows you. We need to figure out how he found his way here."

Accompanied by Ajax, they entered the house. Jason, Judy, and Jeffers were already there, along with at least a dozen other agents and local police. Sarah was introduced to the group of law enforcement as they bustled about the large living room, pushing furniture out of the way and setting up equipment. Ajax stayed close to Sarah, watching everyone.

A policewoman arrived with Target bags full of sweatpants and shirts, socks, and warm pajamas. Sarah accepted them gratefully and went up to her room to change. The room was sealed with crime scene tape. A young officer stopped her from opening the door. "Sorry, we're not done in there. You can change in the boy's room."

Ajax following at her heels, Sarah moved down the hall and entered the bedroom. Ajax whined. "It's okay," Sarah soothed him. "They'll find Jeremy soon." Ajax stayed in the doorway, standing tall, his ears perked up as he sniffed the air. He gave three short barks.

The young officer they'd encountered in the hallway approached. "What's up, boy?" he asked.

Ajax looked between them and whined again.

"He knows something," Sarah said, reaching out and petting the dog. "Ajax, find Jeremy."

Ajax paced to the bed and then back to Sarah, keeping his eyes on her with every step.

The officer touched his shoulder radio and spoke into it. "Upstairs. The dog's on to something."

Voices lifted from below and they heard the sound of footsteps running up the stairs.

"Find Jeremy," Sarah said again.

Ajax hurried to the bed, lay down, and pushed his head and shoulders into the space underneath. His tail thumped the floor as he tried to wiggle into the small space. He whined.

The policeman clicked on his flashlight and lay down next to the dog.

Andy burst through the door. "What have you got?" he asked.

"There is something under here, way back in the far corner. I can't reach it." He stood up. "We need to pull the bunks away from the wall."

More agents and officers were now crowding the room and peering through the door. Andy glanced at the group. "A couple of you move this bed, carefully."

Sarah pressed her hand over her mouth.

The bed moved. Ajax leapt onto the lower berth and then down into the wall space. Andy moved to stop him, but it was too late. The dog had captured his prize. He pulled something from the crevice and shook it triumphantly.

"Gaffy!" Sarah shouted.

Ajax dropped the toy at Andy's feet and returned to Sarah's side. She dropped to her knees, hugging the dog and sobbing.

Andy laid his hand on Sarah's shoulder. "Does the toy belong to Jeremy?" he asked.

Unable to talk, Sarah could only nod. Andy helped her to her feet and guided her out of the room. "Come with me. We need to let them do their job. We'll talk downstairs."

Sarah stumbled after the agent, following him to the living room. The furniture had been pushed back against the walls. Tables covered in computers and telephones crowded the room. Andy indicated a chair and waited for Sarah to bring her tears under control. Ajax sat pressed against her legs. Her hand strayed to his head and stayed there.

Judy joined Andy as he began his questioning. "Can you tell me about the toy, Sarah?"

She nodded. "It's Gaffy. Jeremy's giraffe. He's had it since he was a baby. It used to go everywhere with him, and even now he can't go to sleep without it." Desperation filled her voice. "Why would it be at this house?"

"It may mean Jeremy was here at some time. Did he ever visit his father in this house?"

"Of course not. I didn't even know this house existed."

"Did Blake ever mention buying a new home when he picked up Jeremy?"

"I told you, no. I thought he still lived in Seattle. Jeremy hasn't spent a night with Rodney in months."

"Was the giraffe in the cabin when you found Jeremy missing?"

Sarah squirmed in her chair. "I don't know," she admitted. "I don't think I looked for it. I remember the bed was unmade." She closed her eyes, trying to picture the morning. "I grabbed my coat and rushed outside. The wind was howling and driving the snow. I didn't have my boots. I was afraid Jeremy didn't have his coat and mittens."

"Did you see his coat in the cabin?"

"I'm not sure. I just remember thinking he might be outside without them."

Ajax gave a sharp bark and laid his head on her knee.

"I followed Ajax. He was barking and running into the woods and back to me. He seemed to want me to follow him."

"What made you think that?"

"Because," Sarah lifted her eyes and looked directly at Andy, "it was Ajax's barking that woke me up. He was in Jeremy's room and the door was shut so he couldn't get out. As soon as I opened the door, he dashed to the front door and barked until I opened it. He was frantic and headed straight across the road and into the trees. I ran after him."

"Are you sure? You didn't mention this before."

"Positive. I just remembered."

"Okay. How do you think the giraffe got to this house?"

Sarah hesitated. "Whoever took Jeremy must have brought him here?"

Judy interrupted, suggesting, "Is it possible that the dog followed the kidnapper here and has been hanging around waiting for the kid to show up?"

"Unlikely. That's about sixty miles, but dogs can do some pretty amazing things. Are there any outbuildings on this property?" Andy asked, looking toward the other agents in the room.

"None," Jason responded.

Andy clicked his tongue. "We need to get Blake to talk and find this Claire Hamilton. Any word on her whereabouts?"

"Andy," one of the agents manning the phones called. "We've got some lab results."

As he read from the screen, everyone in the room turned to hear his report. "The contents of the IV bags still on the pole have been identified. One bag contains an intravenous nutrition supplement and the other is a saline solution heavily laced with clonazolam. It's a high-potency, long-lasting drug. Strong enough to keep anyone sedated and to produce memory problems. Residue on the needle matches Sarah's blood type. We've got unidentified fingerprints on both bags. Forensics is tracing the supplier. The hospital equipment, bed, pole, monitors—all of it came from a medical equipment rental place in Wenatchee. Dispatch has sent people to find out who rented it and when."

"Anything else?" Before the agent could reply, Andy's phone rang. He answered, "Agent Jones," then listened a minute. "Send it to me and then get a team over there and open it up." Taking the phone from his ear, he watched the screen and then opened a text. "Got it. Get moving."

Andy held up his phone for the others to see. "It's a receipt. Dated two weeks ago. They found it in the cabin. Looks like it's for some kind of storage unit."

Judy's brow furrowed as she reached for Andy's phone and studied the receipt. "It's located just outside of Wenatchee. Rented on January tenth—that's two days before the abduction."

"Could Rodney be hiding Jeremy there?" Sarah asked, her mind racing with implications.

The agents exchanged looks.

Judy spoke first. "Let's not speculate. They'll open the unit and let us know. It shouldn't take long."

CHAPTER TWENTY-SEVEN

NOW DAY 7: Wednesday 01/31 NIGHT

Sarah curled up on a chair in the corner of the living room and focused on the gathering dusk. Ajax stayed by her side. She picked up a book and put it down without reading a word.

Around 5 p.m., Andy approached and introduced Sarah to her Victim Services liaison, Michele Breckenridge. Sarah nodded, unable to force a smile, her eyes reflecting her exhaustion and despair. Excusing himself, Andy left the women alone.

Michele seated herself and spoke quietly. "Sarah, we're going to do everything we can to find Jeremy. I'm here to help you in any way with anything you need. We will want you to speak to the press soon."

"Tonight?" Sarah's voice wavered.

"Probably not until tomorrow morning, but I want you to be prepared. I'll help you craft a plea for information. We have few facts about who abducted Jeremy or exactly when. The public may be our best chance right now. Someone may have seen or heard something; even the smallest detail can help."

Sarah studied Michele, taking in the dark, curly hair that framed her face and the way her brilliant blue eyes sparkled with determination. There was something reassuring about her presence, a quiet strength that made Sarah feel slightly more at ease in the chaos surrounding her. "If it will help you find Jeremy, I'll do and say anything you want."

She leaned her head against the back of the chair and closed her eyes for a moment, then opened them wide and fixed Michele in her stare. "I know it was Rodney. He thinks he can control me, but I'm not afraid of him anymore."

Andy's voice rang out, calling for attention. The voices in the command center stilled. He waited for a moment, his eyes roaming the room and focusing on each agent in turn. "We're going to need to broaden our search grid, get more eyes on the ground. Williams, that creep in the woods, told us the dog has been staying close to the house for the past six days, maybe longer. We believe Jeremy was brought to this house, so we need to find the proof. We've contacted the local search-and-rescue teams. They'll be here at first light tomorrow. The more people looking, the better."

The tension in the room shifted as a pair of agents burst in.

"We've got news," one reported, a mixture of urgency and control in his voice. "The locals have the storage unit and the surrounding property secure. We don't have word on what's inside"

Andy said, "We've traced the medical equipment rental. It was rented on January tenth, in the name of Sarah Blake. Delivered to the cabin on January thirteenth."

Sarah clenched her hands into fists and stifled an outburst. Her heart sank.

Sarah watched Andy's jaw tighten as his eyes narrowed and he studied her.

A phone on the desk rang. The agent who answered listened a second, looked at Andy, and said, "The storage room is open. Do you want it on the speaker?"

"Yep." He motioned to Michele, who moved closer to Sarah. "This is FBI Special Agent Andy Jones. Who am I speaking with?"

"Deputy Sheriff Colin Boyle, Sir. Chelan County."

"What've you got?"

"Place is clean, except for a red 2023 Subaru Forester, license…"

Sarah stood and made a terrible moaning sound. Michele wrapped an arm around her and held her up as her knees sagged.

Andy kept his eyes on Sarah as he asked, "Anything in the car?"

"Yes, sir. A pile of blankets, what looks like some food wrappers, and some kid's stuff, a woman's jacket. We didn't touch anything or open the doors yet."

Andy stepped closer to the phone and pushed the button to take it off speaker. He turned his back to Sarah and said just above a whisper, "Open it carefully and check for a body. Button up the scene and don't touch anything else. We'll be there in twenty minutes."

Andy turned from the phone and surveyed the room. "Judy, Jason, Smith, and Anderson, let's go. Everyone else, you know what to do." The named agents grabbed their outerwear and hurried out of the house.

Sarah looked bleakly after them. *Rodney's trying to frame me for something. He wants people to think I'm crazy.* Fear filled her eyes. Turning to Michele she said, "I didn't rent any medical equipment.

Why would I do that? Please, just find Jeremy. He's only six years old. Wherever he is, I'm not there. He's got to be frightened."

Michelle nodded. "We have no evidence that he's been injured. Let's concentrate on that."

***

Time dragged by. Someone brought in pizzas and the smell made Sarah gag. Michele tried to get her to eat, but Sarah refused. Instead, she paced the floor, waiting for word from the storage unit. At last, Andy called to say he'd sent pictures and asked Sarah to identify what they'd found.

A file was opened on one of the computers. The agents watched and took notes as Sarah identified Jeremy's winter coat, hat, and mittens, his pajamas, a blanket from the cabin, and finally his cowboy boots. She broke down and sobbed in relief as Andy reported that they had found no sign of foul play.

Someone asked about fingerprints and Andy just shook his head. "Working on that. We'll know more in the morning. But the storage unit was rented by a Sarah Blake on January eighteenth—that's six days after the abduction date."

Sarah sputtered.

Andy continued, "We talked to the desk clerk who rented the unit. He's not on duty until midnight. But he's sure it was a woman, he's not sure how old. Said she was short, slim, with long curly blond hair, wearing a Patagonia ski jacket."

"I don't own a jacket like that," Sarah protested.

Andy ignored her outburst. "There is a woman's size small Patagonia jacket in the car. The guy said she claimed that she was leaving the country for a long skiing vacation in Switzerland and wanted the car protected in storage while she was gone. Get a picture of Sarah and we'll show it to him when he gets to work."

"You got it, boss. Anything else?"

"Not now." Andy hung up without speaking again.

Sarah grabbed Michele's arm. "He thinks I did something, doesn't he? I love my son. I'd never hurt him."

"No one is accusing you of anything, Sarah. Let me take a couple of pictures of you for Andy to use and then we'll have to wait. If you didn't rent the storage unit you have nothing to worry about."

Sarah felt everyone's eyes on her as Michele took the pictures and sent them off. Her stomach clenched with fear. What if Rodney had done something terrible and was blaming it on her? Everyone always believed him.

Michele made tea, but Sarah pushed it aside.

Her bedroom had been put back in order after its thorough search, and about 11 p.m. Michele persuaded Sarah to go upstairs and rest. Ajax, still staying close to Sarah, walked up with them.

"Would you like me to stay with you for a bit?" Michele asked.

"You don't need to." Sarah plucked at her clothing. "I hate these clothes,"

Surprise crossed Michele's face.

"These aren't my clothes. Rodney kept me locked up and made me wear this stuff. I never wear clothes like this; well, I guess I did when we were married." She looked around the room. "A policewoman gave me a bag of sweats and stuff, but then Ajax found Gaffy and I never got to change. Do you think you can find out what happened to the clothes?"

"Sure thing. Why don't you take a shower and I'll find the bags and bring you a cup of tea. It'll help you relax."

Sarah's spine stiffened. "No tea," she said, then entered the bathroom and closed the door behind herself. Ajax lay blocking the bathroom door and kept his eyes on Michele until she left the room.

Sarah showered and wrapped herself in a towel. She pulled her wet hair into a ponytail and opened the bathroom door. Ajax thumped his tail on the floor and stood up. Sarah rubbed between his ears. The Target bags lay on the bed. She checked the bedroom door and was relieved to find it unlocked. Opening it a crack, she looked out. The upstairs hallway was empty and dark. Voices drifted up from downstairs.

Dressed in sweats and a tee shirt, Sarah lay down on the bed. She signaled for Ajax to join her. He jumped up, turned around in a circle, and then curled tight to her side. Sarah scratched behind his ears and whispered, "I didn't do anything bad. Tomorrow we will find Jeremy." Ajax licked her fingers and placed his head on her arm. Sarah sighed and adjusted her breathing to match the dog's. They drifted to sleep.

Michele tapped lightly and opened the door. Ajax lifted his head. Sarah slept on, too exhausted to pull a blanket over herself.

***

By 2 a.m., the task force had reconvened in the command center. The smell of brewing coffee filled the air and boxes of pastry and doughnuts littered the tables. Whiteboards had been brought in and set up. Notes covered them but seemed to make little sense.

Andy, the lack of sleep showing on his face, lifted his coffee mug, took a swallow of the strong brew, made a face of disgust, and said,

"Okay, let's recap what we've got and then get a couple of hours of sleep. Judy, where's Seattle PD on the embezzlement and can you tie it to the abduction?"

"Blake's employer filed the original complaint a year ago. He was suspicious of Blake and we found plenty of evidence to support his complaint. We've traced $765,000 over twenty-one months. Our case is solid. Blake kept excellent records of his crime."

"Idiot," someone said. The others chuckled.

Judy continued, "He's been placing bets on sporting events for years. About two years ago he started losing big money. He kept track of his betting, too. Like I said, excellent record-keeping skills. Our guess is that the people he owed got serious when the debt reached twenty-five grand. He paid the debt with company funds. His streak of bad luck continued, and soon he was using embezzled money to place his bets. His employer started asking questions and in July of last year, his bets increased in size; he was most likely thinking a big win would allow him to pay back the money he was stealing and no one would ever know."

"That never works," Jason commented.

Judy finished, "It didn't work for Blake, either. According to his own records, his current gambling debt is over a hundred thousand dollars. He purchased this house, using stolen money, in December. I'm guessing it's part of some scheme he's dreamed up to get his hands on Sarah's inheritance."

Someone whistled.

Andy took over the briefing. "We are building a case for the false imprisonment of his ex, but the abduction is still a blank. Blake, of course, isn't talking. However, we know from Sarah that he diverted the notification that she was named in the will. We spoke with the grandmother's attorney and learned that Blake misrepresented himself as her legal husband."

He looked at Judy. "We agree that it seems likely that when he discovered the size of the inheritance Sarah's grandmother had left, he immediately began figuring a way to get his hands on the cash. The will was filed for probate in October. Of course, the attorney can't talk about the terms, but we were able to get a copy of the will. Sarah inherits everything."

Andy yawned and rubbed his jaw. "Blake's boss told us that around the Seattle office, which is Blake's official workplace, he's been saying that he reconciled with his wife and they purchased a home together."

He glanced at his notes. "He took some time off in January and when he returned, told everyone that his wife had been in an auto accident and was in the hospital over here in Wenatchee. That coincides with the disappearance of Jeremy and the time Sarah may have been kept captive in the cabin."

Andy drew lines and arrows on the whiteboard connecting ideas and thoughts as he spoke. "Blake was encouraged to work from here in order to be with his family. His secretary said she got the impression that the accident had been Sarah's fault or—in her words—'maybe a suicide attempt.' He's been off work the past ten days, unavailable to the office, purportedly taking care of family business. Giving him the opportunity to set up this house, the fake kid, the housekeeper, all of it. I'd like to know what this guy was thinking, what he was planning."

One of the FBI agents asked, "How did Seattle PD find out about this house?"

"Simple," Judy answered. "We followed him here and discovered that he's the owner of record. He doesn't own anything in Seattle. The house he lived in with Sarah sold almost two years ago. He lives in an apartment in Pioneer Square."

Judy looked at Jason, who nodded his confirmation.

She continued, "We heard him place a call to an employment agency for a temporary housekeeper to assist while his wife was recovering and took advantage of the request to place me undercover."

Michele asked, "Do you have a wiretap on his phone?"

Jason shook his head. "No evidence until now that we might have needed one." He grinned. "We were just eavesdropping in a coffee shop and got lucky."

"What about the guy in the woods? What's his story?" an agent asked.

Jeffers spoke up. "Williams is still not talking. He's got an attorney. But his police record shows that he's connected to the gambling syndicate that Blake owes money to. Best guess is he's watching the house for his boss. We'll interview him again in the morning and let him know he may be implicated in a kidnapping. If he's innocent, he'll talk."

"Anybody got anything else?" Andy asked. No one moved. "Okay, if you're not on duty, go home, sack out for a couple of hours, and we'll hit it again in the morning. I'm sleeping here, so wake me if anything happens."

CHAPTER TWENTY-EIGHT

NOW DAY 8: Thursday 02/01

By first light, the yard was again teeming with vehicles and people. A few of the searchers focused on Sarah as she watched from the front steps. Officers kept them from approaching.

Special Agent Casey, wearing an FBI jacket and beanie, explained that the search would encompass the yard and woods surrounding the house. Grids were assigned. "You know the drill. We believe it's been at least seven days since the boy was in this house and there has been snowfall during that time. Keep your eyes peeled for anything hidden in the snow. Evidence of the boy or of anyone passing through the area is of interest. The tracking dogs will go first." Casey held up Gaffy and waved the dog handlers forward. The dogs sniffed the toy and sat, indicating they were ready. "Good luck, everybody."

Ajax gave a single bark but stayed at Sarah's side.

Michele touched Sarah's arm, causing her to jump. "Sorry," Michele said, "I didn't mean to startle you. Come inside now and let the teams do their work. The press conference is scheduled for 10 a.m. I've prepared your statement."

***

Sarah practiced the statement three times, each time choking on the words. Then Michele suggested she take a break and put on some makeup.

"Makeup!" Sarah said, shocked.

"I just thought it might make you feel better, more confident, and less worried about speaking to the press."

"I'm asking for help. Someone somewhere must know something. I don't care what I look like."

Michele kept her voice low and calm. "Okay. They are setting up the press conference now; we'll begin as soon as Andy and Judy arrive. We have a few minutes if you'd like a cup of coffee or something to eat."

"I'm fine." Sarah pulled the scrunchie from her ponytail, ran her fingers through her hair to smooth it, and replaced the scrunchie. "I'll just wait." She held out her hand to Michele. "Let me read that a couple more times."

Michele handed her the typed page. Then she went to the kitchen and prepared herself a cup of coffee, leaving Sarah alone.

Sarah watched the searchers in the yard and waited. News vans for all the major networks arrived and disgorged their passengers and equipment. Andy and Judy pulled up and were immediately accosted by the press. They hurried past the reporters, refusing all questions.

When the press had been ushered in and they'd settled down, Sarah followed Judy and Andy to the table. Sarah sat and listened as Andy addressed the attendees: "I am FBI Special Agent Andrew Jones, head of the Child Abduction Rapid Deployment Team that has been assigned to the abduction of Jeremy Blake, age six. You have been supplied with his photo and relevant details. In a moment Jeremy's mother, Sarah Blake, will make a public plea for information. Please hold your questions until the end of her statement. At that time we will do our best to answer your questions. Thank you." He turned to Sarah and nodded. "Sarah, please, read your statement."

Sarah picked up Gaffy from the table and cradled him in her arms. She blinked rapidly as the cameras flashed. Squeezing Gaffy tight, she read: "Good morning. Thank you for helping. I'm Sarah Blake. My son, Jeremy Scott Blake, is missing. I put him to bed on January twelfth of this year. In the morning, he was gone from our home on Alta Lake. I searched for him and was unable to locate him.

"Jeremy is six years old, with brown eyes and light brown hair. There is a tiny heart-shaped birthmark on the inside of his left wrist. He loves school and attends first grade at Pateros Elementary. Jeremy was wearing blue flannel pajamas printed with cowboys and horses when I put him to bed. He may be wearing his red puffer jacket and a Seattle Seahawks navy-blue and lime knit hat with a lime pom-pom. He is a smart, funny boy, obsessed with cowboys and LEGOs. He is afraid of robots and can't sleep without Gaffy."

She held up the stuffed giraffe and then cuddled it again, giving herself the courage to continue.

"The screen is showing Jeremy's first-grade picture, taken only a few weeks ago, and the toll-free number for the Missing Child Hotline. We are asking for anyone with information—no matter how small or insignificant it may be—to come forward. Your help could make all the difference in bringing Jeremy home safely."

Sarah dashed tears from her eyes. Her voice quivered as she said, "We are desperate for your help. Keep an eye out for Jeremy and share our story far and wide. Please, help us find Jeremy. If you suspect something or have information, no matter how minor, contact the local authorities or call the toll-free number on your screen to reach the Missing Child Hotline. Remember, any help is crucial in this desperate time."

Looking directly at the camera, no longer reading from the script, tears streaming unattended, Sarah finished, "Jeremy, I love you forever. Stay brave and strong. The police are helping me look for you. If you can find a phone, you know my phone number. Please call me. I love you and I miss you."

Sarah dropped her gaze and sobbed, shoulders shaking, hands trembling. Michele stepped behind her at the table and placed her hands on Sarah's shoulders.

The cameras refocused on Andy as he stepped forward. "I'll take questions now."

People shouted from all directions. Andy pointed at people and answered questions, one after another.

"Why are you calling it an abduction, not a kidnapping?"

"There has been no ransom demand."

"Is the suspect a family member?"

"No comment."

"Why is Seattle PD working this missing person case? It's not their jurisdiction."

"Seattle is working on a separate case that may be related."

"Related, how?"

"I will not discuss open cases. Please keep your questions related to finding Jeremy Blake."

"What took so long to start looking? January twelfth is a long time ago."

"Twenty days. We were unaware that a child was missing until yesterday."

"Sarah, what took so long? Where have you been?"

Sarah sat up straight, anxious to tell her story.

Michele squeezed her shoulder and hissed, "Don't answer that."

"Do you have a suspect? Is it the mother?"

"We do not have anyone in custody at this time."

"But the father has been detained, right?"

Andy held up his hand to stop the barrage. "That is all the time we have. Please spread the picture of Jeremy, his description, and his last known whereabouts. If you hear or see anything that may point to Jeremy's location or his abductor, call your local authorities at once. Thank you."

Michele pulled Sarah to her feet and keeping an arm around her, moved her from the command center to the kitchen.

Sarah slumped down in the breakfast nook and propped her head up with her hands. "Did you hear that guy ask if I'm a suspect in Jeremy's disappearance?"

"I did," Michele answered, opening the refrigerator to look for creamer. "I'm pouring myself a coffee. Want some?"

Ignoring the question, Sarah asked, "Why would he think that?"

Judy tried to lighten the mood. "Too many movies and cop shows, maybe."

Sarah rubbed her temples, easing the tension headache that was threatening. She twisted her neck to the left, then to the right, and rolled her head in a slow, full circle, seeking relief from the discomfort.

"Do you have a headache?" Michele asked.

"Sort of," Sarah admitted. "I probably just need caffeine."

Michele pulled a mug from the cupboard, filled it, and placed it on the table in front of Sarah. "How about something to eat, too?"

"Are you trying to distract me? Do the police think I did something to Jeremy?"

"It's their job to consider every possible angle."

"I had kind of a hard time adjusting to motherhood the first year of his life and I probably drink more than I should. But I would never hurt Jeremy. You can ask Claire; she knows."

"We would love to talk to Claire, but no one seems to know where she is." Michele sipped her coffee and kept her eyes focused on Sarah. "I do have one concern, though. You asked Jeremy to call your phone."

"It's the only phone number he knows."

"Okay, but you don't have a phone."

Sarah's mouth fell open, and her cheeks flushed as her eyes grew wide. "Oh shit! I forgot that. Where is my phone? Did they find it in Rodney's stuff?" She slammed her fist on the table. "I'm so stupid. What if he's trying to call right now and I don't answer?"

One of the agents from the command center appeared in the kitchen. "Everything okay in here?" he asked.

Michele explained the situation.

The agent smiled at Sarah. "I got this, ma'am. I'm Agent Joe Weller and I'm an IT guy. You tell me your phone number and we'll have your calls routed to us. It'll only take a minute."

Relief flooded Sarah and she stuttered her thanks, along with her number.

"How long has the phone been missing?"

"Um, I'm not sure. I only noticed it when Rodney brought me here. But, maybe since January twelfth. I must have had it before Jeremy went missing." She stopped and considered her answer. "At least I'm pretty sure I would have had it."

"Okay, we'll put a trace on your phone and get a copy of all the calls in and out from January twelfth to date. If Jeremy has tried to reach you, we'll know soon."

Weller hurried back to his computer to begin the trace.

Sarah shifted her gaze to the window. Andy was talking to Agent Casey, who was waving his hands, gesturing and pointing toward the woods behind the house. "I think they've found something." She pushed her coffee aside and hurried to the back door. Michele grabbed a jacket and followed. Ajax was close behind.

Seeing the women approach, Andy turned from Casey and said, "I'm sorry there's no sign of the boy yet. We've found a shelter that Williams has been using. I'm going back into town to question him now. We should know something soon." He strode away.

"Wait a second," Michele called.

Andy turned and listened as Michele updated him on the phone issue. He frowned and shot a look of disbelief at Sarah, then said, "Okay." He walked to his car, got in, slammed the door closed, and drove away.

Sarah hugged herself, rubbing her hands up and down her sweatshirt-clad arms.

"It's cold out here," Michele said. Come back in the house."

"But..." Sarah protested.

"I know it's hard to wait, but sometimes that's all you can do."

***

It was after 1 p.m. when Andy arrived back at the command center. "How's the mother holding up?" he asked Michele.

"About was well as she can, I guess. She doesn't complain, but she's got a headache. I talked her into lying down a few minutes ago."

"She need a doctor?"

"I don't think so. It's probably just stress. She's been waiting next to Weller. He was able to transfer any incoming calls on Sarah's phone to our line, but there's been no action. Her phone is turned off now and we are still waiting on the warrant so we can get its last location and the call record."

"I can't believe Seattle PD didn't start a phone trace as soon as they realized that kid was an actor and that Sarah's own phone was missing." Andy shook his head in disgust. "Check with Weller about the caller that sent the pictures to Hendricks. Maybe he can do something to speed that up."

Casey entered the house, carrying a cup of coffee and a sandwich. He set them down, shrugged off his jacket, and asked, "What did you get out of Williams?"

"He admitted he'd been hired to watch Blake. At first he denied any connection to the loan sharks, said it was just a random job. He claimed a PI, whose name he couldn't recall, approached him in a bar one night and hired him. I hit him with the kidnapping, and he changed his tune and admitted to working for the money lenders."

Andy drank deeply from his coffee mug and continued: "The loan sharks want their money. Blake has been stringing them along, claiming that his wife inherited big money and was going to give him what he needed. Then he told them she'd had an accident and was in a coma. They hired Williams to watch the house. He's been out here off and on for twelve days, reporting back on Blake's movements and his guests."

"Makes sense," Casey said. "He's got a nice shelter set up back in the woods. There's a bunch of surveillance equipment, but no pictures."

Michele laughed. "That's the trouble with the internet—all the photos are digital these days."

"We're working on the pictures, but we do have confirmation on a few things," Andy said. "When Williams arrived, Blake was living here with a kid. The second day, a woman in a Bentley showed up and the kid left with her. I showed him the picture of Claire. He denies ever seeing her at the house. Then a day later, another bigger, older, kid showed up with a suitcase and a different woman. At first, Williams thought it was Blake's wife and kid, but they only stayed an hour and left without the suitcase. His boss figured something funny was going on, and that's when Williams started living full-time in the woods."

"I'm getting confused," Casey said.

Andy moved to a clean whiteboard. "Assuming that Jeremy was the first boy Williams saw, this is how I understand the timeline." He began listing the calendar dates and filling in the events. "Some of this has no relationship to the abduction but it may go to motive,"

July – SD PD open investigation into Blake's embezzlement of funds

??? – Grandmother died

Oct – Blake learns of inheritance

Dec – house in Wenatchee purchased

Jan 10 – Medical equip rented by Sarah (?)

Jan 12 – Friday – Jeremy last seen by Sarah 9:30 p. m.

Jan 13 – Saturday – Jeremy discovered missing by Sarah

Jan 13 – Medical equip delivered to cabin

Jan 15 – Williams starts watching arrivals and departures

Jan 16 or 17 – Williams sees boy (Jeremy?) with Blake

Jan 18 – Storage unit rented by Sarah (?) – Sarah's car inside – Patagonia Jacket

Jan 18 – Thursday – Hendricks hired

Jan 19 – Friday – Some woman (Claire?) takes Jeremy – Bentley

Jan 20 – Saturday – 2nd boy seen – actor? w/his mother?

Jan 20 – Saturday afternoon – Hendricks starts working at house

Jan 25 – Thursday – 13 days missing – Sarah arrives at house

Jan 29 – Local police receive 911 call from Sarah

Jan 31 – Wednesday – 19 days missing – FBI notified – Blake arrested

Feb 1 – Today – 20 days missing

The other agents had gathered to listen and watch.

One spoke up. "There's a lot of gaps."

Andy nodded. "Yep. Let's hear your thoughts. We know about the gambling and the embezzlement. But what's his plan? Why and how is Blake concealing the kid? If he's after the money, why didn't he just murder the wife?"

One of the agents said, "If the wife is dead, the kid inherits, not Blake, right? So, he has to keep the wife alive and get her to give him the cash he needs. Then he can figure out something else for next time, and you know with a gambler there is always a next time."

Another observed, "By threatening the kid, he can convince her to do anything."

Andy flipped the whiteboard marker in his hand, considering the options. He asked, "Why did he take the kid on January twelfth or thirteenth, and then drug Sarah for ten or twelve days? What was happening in all that time?"

"Well, if he's trying to create a false reality and make her look crazy, losing your kid for a couple of weeks looks pretty crazy?"

Sarah cleared her throat. Everyone looked toward the sound and froze.

Michele spoke first. "How long have you been standing there?"

"Long enough. I know Rodney better than any of you. He was an abusive, manipulative asshole. During the divorce, he did everything he could think of to discredit me and it almost worked. He knows all of my fears and weaknesses and he knows how to exploit them. From the time we met, he controlled all of my thoughts and my actions, and I let him. He kept me separated from everyone I knew, except my mother. She was completely taken in by him and never believed that he could be abusive. Instead, she took his side in every argument."

Sarah looked around the room. "Where's Judy? She knows what has been happening since he brought me to this house."

Andy said, "She's interviewing Blake right now. They're going to move him to Seattle. I'm headed back to the station to take a crack at him about the abduction and your imprisonment before we lose sight of him."

"Can I talk to him?" Sarah asked. "He is so sure that I'm weak and afraid that he may slip up and brag about what he's done. I think he's trying to make me believe that I've hurt Jeremy and that he's the only thing standing between me and prison."

Sarah straightened and looked directly at Andy, her gaze steady and confident. "If he wants my inheritance, he needs me alive and he needs custody of Jeremy, to get his hands on it. He'll try to prove I'm unfit, an alcoholic or abusing drugs. He's counting on me being too confused and weak to fight him in court."

Andy didn't answer, asking instead, "What kind of abuse?"

"What difference does it make? Is one kind worse than another?" Sarah rubbed her forehead.

Andy waited.

Sarah relented. "Every kind. His temper is always close to the surface. Everything has to be done his way. He didn't let me work. He threw away my clothes and only allowed me to wear what he bought. I had a locket that my grandmother gave me that disappeared when I refused to stop wearing it. He hated it when I saw Claire."

She stopped and closed her eyes for a moment before she finished. "When the doctor said we'd probably never be able to have children because of Rodney's low sperm count, he raped me and I got pregnant. I thought things would be better, but after Jeremy was born they were worse. I was never good enough for him or for my mother. I tried to leave and he beat me up. Yes, I drink too much sometimes, and I hate him. But I don't hate my son. I am a good mother."

"And yet you did get divorced, and now Jeremy is missing."

Sarah sagged against the wall, her knees giving way as she trembled. "That bastard has taken him. I know it. If you can't get the truth out of him, let me try."

"Tell me about Claire. Why is she helping Rodney and not you?"

"I don't know," Sarah sobbed.

Michele shuffled through photos spread across the table. Picking out an enlargement, she studied it carefully and then handed it to Andy. "This is the photo from the cabin with Claire. It's dark outside and the reflection in the window behind Claire clearly shows Rodney taking the picture. Jeremy is partially behind Rodney, hugging the giraffe."

"So?" Andy asked.

"I don't think Claire is smiling at Rodney. I think she's talking to Jeremy, and I think Jeremy is crying."

Sarah rushed to Michele's side and grabbed the enlargement. "Look," she said, thrusting the image at Andy. "She's right."

Michele picked up a second enlargement. "This is the one of Claire and Rodney. It's taken in front of the fireplace at the cabin. You can't see who's taking the picture but it's not a selfie, and it's too straight on to have been taken by a small kid. I think there was another adult in the room."

She handed the picture to Andy. "And before you ask Sarah if she was there, look at the right-hand side. That's an open doorway to Sarah's bedroom. Unless I missed my guess, you can see the end of a hospital bed."

Andy examined the image carefully. He shook his head. "That bastard is twisting Claire's wrist and I bet he's demanding she smile."

Agent Weller held out his hand for the photos. "I can enhance those," he said, leaving the room.

The phone rang. Andy snatched it up. He listened a moment, hung up, then reported to the group. "That was Jeffers. Whoever rented the storage unit, it wasn't Sarah. They used Sarah's credit card, but the description doesn't match. Both witnesses said they'd never seen either Sarah or Claire before and stated the woman was older, at least sixty, with short red hair."

Sarah pointed at the whiteboard. "My mother drives a Bentley."

Andy drew an arrow from Lydia Ross to the Bentley.

"And, she's about my height and kind of looks like me. She has dyed red hair, but maybe she wore a wig and rented the storage unit, too."

"On it, Boss," one of the agents said and left the room.

"Let's not jump to any conclusions here," Andy cautioned. "But having you make a statement to the police tonight might be a good idea. They'd be asking you for what you witnessed that makes you believe Rodney abducted Jeremy and held you hostage."

"I can do that." Sarah smiled for the first time all day.

"Do you want an attorney?"

"No, I want to talk."

***

After consulting with his FBI team, the Seattle PD, and the local police, Andy agreed to allow Sarah to accompany him to the Wenatchee City Jail, where Rodney was being held pending charges. While Sarah gave her witness statement to the Wenatchee police, Andy would interview Rodney.

As they drove, Andy explained, "In addition to the charges of embezzlement and money laundering that Seattle is pressing, Rodney may be charged with three additional felonies: parental abduction, false imprisonment, and adult endangerment. These felonies are state, not federal crimes, unless state boundaries were crossed."

Sarah nodded, her eyes wide.

"What we need to file these charges is enough evidence to convince the state attorney that we have a case against Blake. When I interview him tonight, I plan to push him to admit that he knows where Jeremy is. I know you want to demand answers from him, but we need to protect our evidence. You will be a state witness when the case comes to trial. So, we have to be careful."

"Can I listen?"

"No." Andy shook his head. "A police interrogation is private. No one will be in the room except the suspect, his attorney, and the interrogating officers. While we are interrogating Rodney, other officers will take your statement. We may use your statement to further question Blake."

"Will you also question Claire and my mother?"

"Yes, we've sent the police to your parents' home to pick up your mother and bring her down to the station. We have a BOLO out for both your mother and Claire."

They entered the station and Andy directed her to a row of chairs. "Wait right here and an officer will be out directly. Okay?"

Sarah managed a half smile and Andy walked away. She leaned her head against the wall and waited.

"Sarah?"

Her eyes flew open. "Claire!"

The policewoman at the counter looked up, interested.

"Oh my god, Sarah. I saw you on the news. What happened? Have they found Jeremy?"

Sarah burst into tears and jumped to her feet. "Where is he, Claire? What have you done?" Sarah grabbed Claire's arm and hung on tight. "Officer, get Agent Andy Jones. This woman kidnapped my son."

The policewoman pressed buttons on her phone and asked for assistance.

Claire stood frozen, not struggling to get away. "I didn't kidnap Jeremy. I love that kid. I'm his godmother."

Police with drawn guns burst through the door.

Andy arrived, took in the scene, and said, "Everybody calm down." He looked between Claire and Sarah. "Miss Hamilton, I assume. We've been looking for you." He took her arm. "Come with me. We need to talk."

Sarah started to follow, but Andy shook his head. "You need to give your formal statement before you talk to Claire or Rodney, remember?" He escorted Claire through the door and down the hall. Sarah watched as they disappeared into a room.

A tall, gray-haired man introduced himself and his young partner as Detectives Zarndt and Espaniola. Sarah shook their hands, still numb with the surprise of seeing Claire appear. She walked with them down the hall and into a room. They offered coffee or water. Sarah declined. When everyone was seated, the woman began. "Sarah—may I call you Sarah?"

"Sure."

"Do you understand that the statement you are about to give will be recorded, both audio and video, and may be used in future court proceedings?"

Sarah nodded.

The detective gave her a warm smile. "Please give audible answers if you can."

"Yes, I understand that you are recording."

"Alright, in your own words, tell me what you remember about the night of January twelfth of this year."

So, once again Sarah told her story, answering every question as completely as she could. They led her through all of her memories, sometimes asking the same question in various ways. Sarah forced herself to be patient, remembering Andy's words about needing her evidence to be able to charge Rodney and Claire with felonies. Claire had sounded so sincere when she asked about Jeremy. Was it possible she hadn't been involved?

When the detectives were satisfied that Sarah had told them everything she could, they walked her to a different room. They knocked on the door and at a barked response, entered. Claire looked up, her face pale and sad. "Oh, Sarah. I'm so sorry. I've been such an idiot."

"Just tell me where Jeremy is," Sarah spoke through a clenched jaw, afraid to let her emotions show.

"I would if I could. But I don't know. I was only in the cabin that night because Rodney called to say that your drinking was out of control and he needed my help. When I got there, Jeremy was hysterical. Lydia—"

"My mother?"

Claire nodded. "Lydia was there and you'd been sedated. Rodney said the doctor had called an ambulance to take you to detox and then you'd have to go to rehab. I wanted to see you, but Rodney insisted I take Jeremy and get out of there so he wouldn't have to see his mother taken away. I'm sorry, but I did exactly what they asked."

Sarah remained quiet, keeping her gaze focused on Claire.

"I know how terrible he's been to you in the past, and yet I believed him. We went into Pateros and waited for Lydia and Rodney at the coffee shop. Jeremy tried to tell me that something was wrong, but I didn't understand. He said his dad was really mad that his mom wouldn't write her name on a piece of paper and that Grandma Lydia had been yelling and that Gaffy was scared. I bought him an ice cream sundae and calmed him down by saying sometimes grown-ups get mad at each other but that everything was fine."

Sarah cocked her head to one side and studied Claire.

"I've been a terrible friend. I wanted to call you so many times, but when you told me to go away and leave you alone last year, I was hurt and angry."

"Where have you been? Why show up now?"

"I left for my vacation the next morning. I've been in Australia since January 15th. I saw the appeal you made on the American news and I knew it was Rodney—I just knew it. I caught the next flight to come and be with you. On the plane, I realized that I should have gone to the police in Sydney and told them what I knew had happened that night in the cabin. As soon as we landed in Seattle, I drove straight here and stumbled on you in the lobby."

"We pulled her flight and passport information. Claire was traveling alone," Andy added.

"Can you ever forgive me? I've been such an idiot."

Sarah pressed her hand to her forehead and rubbed between her eyes. "All that matters now is Jeremy. Where do you think he is?"

Andy said, "Blake is still claiming that he is innocent on all charges. He alluded to his debt being the result of his ex-wife running up his credit cards."

Sarah sputtered.

"Don't worry—no one believes that story."

A tap on the door interrupted them. The door opened, and Judy and Jason walked in. Judy did a double take as she recognized Claire.

Jason let out a low, "Whoa."

Judy recovered her professional demeanor and said, "No one is home at the grandparents' house. The neighbors say they're on a cruise. She didn't know which cruise line, but we'll find them. The Bentley is in the garage, along with a Mercedes. We're going to move Blake now. Do you want to talk to him before we leave?"

Andy considered. "I don't think it'll do any good. But I want to try one more thing." He turned to Sarah and Claire. "If you ladies are okay with it, I want them to bring Blake past this room. He doesn't know that Claire has turned up, and seeing her may shake him."

Sarah and Claire spoke at the same time.

"Of course."

"Sure."

"We'll try to make it look accidental," Andy explained. "You'll be exiting this room with me as they walk by."

"You got it. Give us five minutes." Judy withdrew and Jason stationed himself in the hallway, ready to signal Andy for the exit.

Andy played with his phone. Sarah fixed her eyes on Jason. Claire reached for Sarah and squeezed her hand. Sarah returned the squeeze.

At Jason's signal, they rose and walked to the door.

Sarah stepped out first. Her look of shock at seeing Rodney's approach was real. She yelled at him, "God damn you, Rodney. Where is my son?"

He sneered. "That's for me to know and you to find out."

"Asshole," Claire said, stepping up next to Sarah.

Rodney's steps faltered. His face paled and then flushed red as he glared at Claire. "What's that bitch doing here? This is all her fault. She's always poking around and causing trouble. She should arrest her, not me!"

"That's enough, Blake. Move along," Judy prodded.

When Rodney and his escorts had turned the corner, Andy said, "I think that sounded like a confession. He as good as admitted that he knows where Jeremy is."

Jason nodded.

Sarah linked arms with Claire and tried not to scream at the police to hurry up.

"We need to find the grandparents, ASAP." Andy turned to the detectives. "Let's get someone to take Sarah to the command center and we'll get busy."

"May I go with Sarah?" Claire asked.

Andy looked at Sarah. When she nodded, he agreed.

***

During the drive back to Rodney's house, Sarah and Claire were silent, each busy with her own thoughts. Twilight filled the yard with shadows. The searchers were gone for the day, but the press lingered. Sarah averted her face and hurried to the door as flashes went off.

Inside, the house was bustling with activity. Sarah hurried directly to the command center. "Did Jeremy call?" she asked.

Weller shook his head.

Michele greeted them and introduced herself to Claire. "We have dinner set up in the kitchen." She turned to Sarah. "The police have suggested that you speak to a psychologist about your memories of the night Jeremy disappeared and the days that are missing. She's here now if you're willing to meet with her."

"Yes, of course. I'll talk to anyone who may help find Jeremy."

"That's great. I'll let her know. She'll meet you in the room that Blake used for his office. You get yourself something to eat and take a little break."

"I need to use the restroom, but I don't need anything to eat. I'll be there in a minute." Sarah slipped off her coat and threw it over a chair. "Claire, were you ever at this house?" she asked.

"No. I thought Rodney still lived in Seattle."

"Me, too." Sarah's eyes glazed with tears.

Claire pulled her close in a hug. "Oh sweetie, I'm so sorry," she whispered. "They'll find him and that monster will get what he deserves."

***

Sarah steeled herself as she stepped into the office. In stark contrast to the living room, this space remained untouched, eerily resembling the moment when Rodney had issued his threats.

She shuddered.

A tall, older woman stepped forward and held out her hand. "Hi, Sarah, I'm Janet Smyth. I'm a forensic psychologist with Chelan County. If you are willing, I'd like to help you recover some of your memories." She smiled warmly. "Please, sit down."

Sarah ignored the outstretched hand and stayed silent, appraising the woman, looking for reassurance that she might be helpful or at least trustworthy. Satisfied, she sat herself on the sofa and clasped her fingers together.

"I'd like to use hypnosis to help you remember. Would that be okay?"

"I've never been hypnotized," Sarah said, her voice tentative and unsure.

"I'll help you go into a light trance and ask you questions. When we are through, you will remember everything you've told me."

Sarah looked skeptical.

Janet smiled. "It's not like in the movies. It's just a tool to allow your brain to remember. If you agree, I'll ask the questions, and the session will be recorded and witnessed by your liaison officer and one other agent. How does that sound?"

"When?"

"Right now, if you're ready."

Sarah flinched and rubbed her temple. "Okay, let's do it. Can you make the headache stop?" she asked.

"I'll try," Janet said. "Get comfortable, and I'll get our witnesses."

***

Sarah leaned back against the sofa and listened to the tapping of Janet's pen on the coffee table. Her eyes drifted shut.

The wind picked up and she shivered in the cold. "Ajax, find Jeremy!" she shouted. The dog whirled and dashed away. Fear clenched her heart. Something was very wrong...

***

The tapping sounded louder. Janet's voice interrupted, "Sarah, I'm going to count to three. When I reach three you will come fully awake. Your headache will be gone. You will remember everything. One, two, three."

Sarah jerked and opened her eyes.

Janet said, "You did very well, Sarah. Tell me what you learned."

"Rodney and my mother took Jeremy!" she blurted. "I know they did. They planned it together. I heard them do it." Tears spilled from her eyes and she dashed them away. "Rodney needs money and my mother was helping him, wasn't she?"

No one spoke.

Sarah continued, sorting out her jumbled memories as she talked. "On Thanksgiving, Jeremy and I went to my mother's house and I heard her on the phone with Rodney. She said she'd help him. She told him to calm down, that there were other ways to get me out of the way. Mother wouldn't tell me what the call meant. She called me a terrible wife and a worse mother. My dad was there, but he just stood in the hallway shaking his head and looking sad—like he always does when Mother is mad. I took Jeremy and left before dinner."

Sarah closed her eyes in concentration. "Between Thanksgiving and Christmas, Jeremy and I were happy. It was the first time we didn't have to go to mother's for the holiday. Then, on New Year's Day, Mother drove over and told me Rodney needed my help and that I owed it to him because he'd had to put up with so much trouble from me. We said some terrible things to each other and I made her leave,"

Sarah twisted her hands together and tried to sort out the images that were filling her mind. "I remember that Mother and Rodney were at my cabin, trying to make me sign a voluntary commitment form. I heard Claire, but I was in bed and I couldn't talk." Puzzlement filled her eyes. "There was no storm. How is that possible? I was in the storm but it wasn't real." She drew in a deep breath. "But Jeremy is missing. That is real?"

"Yes, right on all counts. Because of the strong drugs Rodney gave you that night and over the course of the next twelve days, he was able to implant the memory of your drinking too much and neglecting your son. None of that is real. The vivid hallucination of Jeremy being lost in the snow is an implanted memory that Rodney used in an attempt to control you." Janet paused. "What else do you remember?"

"Oh my god! My mother helped him." For a second Sarah froze. "It's true, isn't it? She wants him to have Jeremy and my grandmother's money. Why would she do that?"

"I don't know, but the police will figure it out. Everything you learned tonight will need to be verified before it will be admissible in court. But your memories will help the police find Jeremy."

Janet moved to sit next to Sarah on the sofa. She placed her hand over Sarah's. "Over the next few weeks more memories may surface. I believe Rodney may have used drugs to control you during your marriage. I would encourage you to get help with handling these memories. I can refer you to a specialist who will help you."

Michele asked, "Are you okay? What can I do to help?"

"Hurry up and find Jeremy. If he's home, I can deal with everything else."

"I believe you can," Michele said. "You are amazing." She frowned. "I can't imagine going through what has happened to you. I'm sorry I ever doubted you."

"So, I'm not a suspect anymore?"

"Absolutely not, but we will need to document and verify everything you said under hypnosis."

Janet held out her hand and pulled Sarah to her feet. "After this case is over, call me anytime you need to talk. When someone has experienced years of abuse, the effects are long lasting."

Sarah touched her temple. "My headache is gone."

***

In the kitchen, Sarah pushed her food around on her plate and managed a few bites. Shouts erupted from the command center. Dropping her fork, Sarah rushed from the table and bumped into Agent Weller. He hugged her tight.

"We got a voice message from a kid." He dropped his arms. "Come listen."

Sarah ran. Claire and Janet scrambled after her.

The volume was turned up on the computer. A robotic voice announced the date and time, and then a child's voice said, "Mama. Where are you? I called and called. I want to come home now. Grandma says I can't, but I want to. I miss you and I can't find Gaffy. If you feel better, come and get me. I don't like it on this big boat. Please come."

Ajax rushed into the room, barking furiously.

"Jeremy," Sarah whispered. She placed her hand on the computer screen. "Play it again," she demanded.

And they did.

Over and over, Sarah listened. Each time whispering, "I'm coming, Jeremy. Be brave a little longer."

CHAPTER TWENTY-NINE

NOW DAY 9: Friday 02/02

Midnight came and went. Claire had gone upstairs to sleep in one of the guest rooms, but Sarah dozed on the sofa in the command center, jerking awake each time a call came in.

At 3 a.m., Judy reported that Steve Ross had been located at a hotel in New York City. Sarah came fully awake at the news. "So, Rodney was right: he's not on the cruise with Lydia. Why is he in New York?"

"Don't know yet," Judy admitted. "NYPD is knocking on his hotel room door right now."

Only minutes later, Andy had the information on the cruise ship and its current location off the coast of Spain. The command center hummed with the increased activity as the FBI coordinated with the State Department and with the Policía Nacional in Spain.

Weller called out to Sarah, "I have a call on the line from your dad. Do you want to talk to him?"

Sarah scrambled to her feet and grabbed the headset. "Dad?"

"Sarah, I'm so sorry. I never would have believed Lydia would turn against you like this. She told me you'd been drinking heavily and couldn't care for Jeremy. She said she was helping by taking Jeremy with her on her cruise."

"And you believed her?"

"I did. When I saw you at Thanksgiving, you seemed unstable, and you have had problems in the past," Steve said.

"I heard Mother planning something with Rodney. I wasn't unstable or drinking; I was angry."

"I can see that now, but at the time I believed your mother. In January, Rodney came to the house, beside himself with worry, and told us you'd been committed to a long-term treatment center and that he had his son living with him full time. I didn't doubt anything Lydia said until a week ago." He paused, waiting for Sarah to say something.

When she didn't, he continued, "I've told the police. I overheard her talking to you and telling you not to call again, that we wouldn't help you. I was very upset. We had a big row, but she convinced me, like she always does. I agreed when she said it was for the best that she take Jeremy with her and give you time to get better. The next day, when I took them to the Seattle airport for their flight to Spain, she gave me her cell phone, explaining that she'd purchased a prepaid phone to take with her overseas. She said it would be cheaper and better than our roaming plan."

"Was Jeremy at your house?" Sarah asked.

"Just for a few days. He was with Rodney when you went to rehab and then Rodney had to go out of town on business a week or so before the cruise date. Jeremy talked a lot about missing you and Gaffy, but your mom kept him busy, and he was excited about going on the cruise."

"Didn't you think anything was wrong? Didn't you want to see me if I was in rehab?"

"Of course, I wanted to see you, to make sure you were okay. But Lydia said you weren't allowed visitors or phone calls for the first thirty days. I am sorry, Sarah."

"That doesn't matter right now, Dad. Just tell me what is happening now."

"Okay. The day after Lydia and Jeremy flew to Spain, I remembered your mom's phone, and when I took it out of my briefcase, I must have joggled it somehow. The photo gallery opened and I saw pictures of Claire and Rodney at the cabin. Those two never got along, so it made me suspicious. I checked your mom's recent calls and she was talking to Rodney a lot, way too often to make sense. There were a lot of strange, cryptic text messages, too. I knew something was wrong, but I didn't know what to do. I tried to call you, but your phone didn't answer. I called Lydia, and she told me it was none of my business."

Steve sighed. "Then I called a police detective I know and asked a few questions. He told me that they have an open investigation on Rodney and that Detective Judy Hendricks was the lead. It wasn't hard for me to get her number, and while I didn't want to get your mom in trouble, those pictures made me pretty sure something bad was happening. I figured Rodney and Claire were in on it."

"And you sent the photos to Judy's phone?"

"I did. I had to fly to New York, for trial prep. When I arrived, I turned off my caller ID so they'd come from a blocked number. I knew they'd trace it sooner or later but if your mom was innocent, I wanted to give her a chance to come clean. I tried to reach her, but she never answered. I figured the phone service on the cruise was bad."

Steve's voice broke as he said, "Sarah, I know I haven't supported you against your mother. I'm really sorry for that."

Sarah sighed. "She's hard to go against, Dad. I get it. But right now, I just want to get Jeremy home and safe."

"I'll be in Seattle tomorrow and I'll come over to Wenatchee immediately."

They said goodbye and hung up.

Claire handed Sarah a cup of coffee. "Everything okay?" she asked.

"It will be when Jeremy is home."

"Listen up, everyone," Andy said. "The Policía Nacional are approaching the cruise ship now."

***

The thumping sound of a helicopter less than one hundred feet above the stern of the cruise ship drew the attention of passengers, who paused to look up. Crew members quickly cleared the area below, directing everyone to stand back.

"Grandma, look at that! The police are here!" Jeremy shouted, pointing excitedly.

Lydia paled, color draining from her face as she gathered her sun hat and book from the lounge. "Come on, Jeremy. We need to get ready for dinner," she urged, trying to pull him away.

Jeremy paid no attention. He dodged his grandmother's hand and wiggled his way to the front of the curious crowd. Transfixed, his eyes glued to the hovering blue-and-white helicopter emblazoned with *Policía Nacional* as its door swung open.

Slowly a man in a harness descended to the deck. He landed, unsnapped the harness, and signaled for the harness to be lifted. The ship's captain stepped forward and extended his hand to greet the newcomer. Though the whir of the helicopter drowned out their conversation, it was clear the captain had anticipated this arrival. Excited murmurs rippled through the passengers.

Jeremy turned to share his excitement with Lydia and was surprised to see her leaving the deck. "Grandma!" he yelled. "Wait for me."

Reaching the door, Lydia found her way blocked by crew members.

Jeremy rushed up. "Grandma, did you see that man come down from the helicopter? It's amazing. I want to do that."

"Mrs. Ross," a stern voice broke through the noise, causing both Jeremy and Lydia to turn. The man from the helicopter and the ship's captain approached.

Lydia drew herself up, eyes flashing with anger. "What is it, Captain?"

Instead of the captain answering, the second man said, "I'm with the Spanish Policía Nacional. We have been asked by your government to detain and return you to the United States. You will need to come with me." He placed his hand firmly around Lydia's bicep.

"Stop that," she demanded, struggling to get free of the restraining hand. "I'm a United States citizen." Lydia realized the crowd had grown quiet, straining to hear what was going on. She dropped her voice. "You can't detain me."

"Under the extradition treaty between our countries, we can. The Guardia Civil boats are approaching now. They will take you into custody. Your embassy has been informed that you are being transported to Madrid."

"What is it you think I've done?"

"The Guardia Civil will inform you." He moved her forward, through the door and inside the cruise ship away from the watching eyes.

The captain smiled down at Jeremy. "Come along, son. I believe you are going to get a chance to ride on a speedboat."

***

Andy announced, "The kid is safe." Everyone in the command center applauded. Sarah burst into tears and Claire grabbed her in a tight hug.

Sarah pulled away from her and hugged Andy as she wiped away her tears. "Where is he? Can I talk to him?"

"Jeremy has been placed under the protection of International Social Services. It's afternoon in Spain, so I'm sure the ISS will allow him to talk to you soon. Our state department has assured the Guardia Civil that Jeremy will be safe with you, his custodial parent. They will arrange a flight as quickly as possible. Because Jeremy is a minor, a social worker will travel with him. It's a long trip, but within twenty-four hours, he'll be home."

"What about Lydia?"

"Your mother is in custody, awaiting extradition on an international parental kidnapping charge. Blake will be arraigned today, on kidnapping charges, false imprisonment, endangering a minor and an adult, embezzlement, and anything else the DA can think of. They are both going to face prison time."

Sarah's eyes closed momentarily as she exhaled in relief. Her knees buckled. Michele slipped an arm around her and guided her to a chair.

Sarah settled into the chair as the weight of the news began to sink in. Claire knelt beside her, concern etched on her face. "Are you okay?" she asked softly, watching as Sarah's breath steadied.

Sarah opened her eyes, glancing at Michele. "I just…needed a moment," she replied, voice shaky. She felt a mix of relief and anxiety—relief that Rodney and her mother were going to face the consequences of their actions, but anxiety about how Jeremy's life would be impacted by the legal battles ahead and the emotional repercussions of the events of the past month.

Claire squeezed her hand, offering her support. "You're not alone in this."

Ajax pressed against her legs and laid his head in her lap.

Sarah felt a flicker of hope in the midst of chaos. Together, she and Jeremy would face whatever came next together.

EPILOGUE: 7 Months Later

Sarah pulled her Subaru into a space in the west parking lot of Seattle's Commodore Park. As she killed the engine, Jeremy scrambled from the back seat, waving his arms and yelling, "Grandpa, Grandpa, I'm here!" He ran toward Steve's waiting arms. Ajax leaped from the car and ran beside Jeremy, barking happily.

Steve grinned at his grandson and gave him a hug. "Hi, kiddo. What's new?"

Jeremy laughed. "You always say that, Grandpa. But today I do have something new. Watch what I taught Ajax to do." He pulled a whistle from his pocket and blew two short tweets.

Ajax dropped to the grass and rolled over.

Jeremy blew one tweet and Ajax sat up, ears cocked, ready to perform. "Pretty good, huh?"

"Very good. I'm proud of you both."

Jeremy pumped his arm in the air and shouted, "Yes!" He grabbed Steve's hand. "Let's go to the fish ladder first. Mom says the coho are running. I bet we see a million."

"Hold on a minute. We need to check with your mom."

Jeremy spun around and waved at Sarah, who was unloading picnic supplies from the rear of the SUV. "Mom, hurry up."

Sarah handed a bag to Claire and waved to Jeremy. "Come help us unload."

"Okay. Come on, Grandpa. Mom says we gotta work." He grabbed Steve's hand and pulled him to the vehicle.

Sarah smiled as they approached. She stepped to her father and gave him a brief hug. "You're looking good."

"Thanks, you too." He reached into the SUV and lifted out the cooler. "Where do you want to set up?"

"It's such a nice day, I thought we could just picnic on the grassy slope over there." She pointed to the left. "Choose a spot where we can watch the boats go through the locks." She handed Jeremy a blanket and said, "Go with your grandpa and help him choose a good place."

"You got it, ma'am." Jeremy saluted. "Let's go, guys."

"Wait." Sarah stopped him. "Ajax needs his leash." She pulled the leash from the car and held it out.

Jeremy dropped the blanket on the curb and grabbed the leash. The dog sat down on the blanket and waited for Jeremy to attach the leash to his collar. Then they hurried back to Steve and the three set off together to find the perfect picnic place.

Sarah shaded her eyes with her hand and watched them leave.

Claire handed the last bag to Sarah and slammed the hatch. Seeing the sadness on Sarah's face, she asked, "You okay?"

Sarah caught her lower lip in her teeth and bobbed her head. "Yes, I'm okay. I still don't like letting him out of my sight." She sighed. "My therapist says it'll take a while."

As the women strolled toward the grassy hill overlooking Ballard Locks, Claire asked, "How's Jeremy doing?"

"Better than I am," Sarah admitted. "At first, he hated the idea that we weren't going to live in the cabin anymore. But after he realized we can still spend time there whenever we want, he calmed down. He likes our new house in Ballard. There are a bunch of kids on our block that he plays with, and we take Ajax to Golden Gardens almost every day. We met his teacher last week and he's excited about going to second grade."

Sarah stopped and faced Claire. "And you only live a few miles away, so that's good." She resumed walking.

Claire asked, "Any news on Lydia and Rodney?"

"Both of them have been charged with multiple felonies and denied bail so they have to stay in jail until their trials. I should feel safe. And I do—most of the time. I think Jeremy does, too. But he still sleeps with Gaffy, and sometimes he asks if I'm still sick and if I'll have to go to the hospital again."

Claire pulled Sarah close in a side hug. "Lydia's trial is soon, isn't it?"

"Yes, next month. My attorney thinks she'll plead guilty, claiming she was only doing what any good mother and grandmother would do when presented with the story Rodney fed her. I know that isn't true. Or at least not completely true. I'm not sure why she always thought Rodney was so perfect. But it doesn't really matter. If she pleads guilty, she'll probably only get a sentence for time served and then probation, but we'll file a restraining order to keep her away from Jeremy and me."

"What about your dad?"

"He's filed for divorce and is buying a condo only a few blocks from us. My therapist suggested we do some family counseling sessions together. I think we are getting to know each other. He's really different without my mother controlling everything. He feels very bad about never standing up to Lydia. But I never did either. The therapist has helped me see that my relationship with her was just as abusive as mine with Rodney. I'm learning a lot of ways to cope that don't involve alcohol."

They reached the picnic place Steve and Jeremy had chosen and dropped their bags on the blanket.

"It's perfect, right?" Jermey asked.

Sarah nodded.

"Can Grandpa and I go see the fish before we eat?"

"Yes, you may."

Steve smiled at the language correction. Sarah grinned back and shooed them away.

Claire sat on the blanket and leaned her back on the cooler. "What about Rodney and the two accomplices that helped him drug you?"

"Do you mean the doctor and the nurse from the cabin?"

Claire nodded.

"The woman is a discredited RN, but my attorney thinks she'll serve a very minimal sentence and probably probation because she's been willing to tell the police about Rodney. They know who the guy is that was impersonating the doctor. He's part of the loan shark's team but he's disappeared and they are still looking for him. As for Rodney, it sounds like the financial crimes trial will be first and then the kidnapping trial. Joe says that there's no way he'll see the light of freedom for a long time. I hope he's right."

"Agent Joe Weller?" Claire raised her eyebrow.

Sarah blushed and nodded.

"Do I smell a romance blooming?"

"No way! Trust me, I'm not ready to start dating. We're just friends. He helped me set up all the computer stuff at the new house so that I can work from home. And sometimes, we run into him at the dog park. He has a German shepherd, too. Lucky, his dog, knows lots of tricks and Jeremy asked him how to teach some tricks to Ajax." Sarah shrugged one shoulder. "Last weekend he fixed a window that I couldn't get open, so I invited him to stay for dinner."

"Got it." Claire grinned. "Friends with tools and muscles are good to have."

"Exactly." Sarah blushed, and Claire laughed.

"Did you ever figure out how Ajax got all the way from the cabin to Rodney's house in Wenatchee?"

"Since he can't talk, we have to guess, but we think he followed Rodney's car from Pateros that night. Joe says dogs can pick up on the unique scent trail left behind by a vehicle, so he wouldn't have needed to keep up. It may even have taken him a few days. Williams testified that Ajax was hanging around the entire time he was watching the house."

"If I had the brains of that dog, I'd never have believed Rodney," Claire said.

Sarah laughed. "If I had the brains of that dog, I'd never have married Rodney. But then I wouldn't have Jeremy, and that would be sad."

She sobered. "But from here on out, no one will be able to control me. I'm going to take my time, make my own decisions, and be the best mother I can. Life is too short to waste it on regrets."

HELP AND UNDERSTANDING ABUSE

If you need help – Reach Out – Help is available.

National Abuse Violence Hotline
Call: 1-800-799-7233
Website: thehotline.org

Domestic violence is a pattern of behaviors used to gain or maintain power and control. At The Hotline, our frame of reference for describing abuse is the Power and Control Wheel created by the Domestic Abuse Intervention Project in Duluth, MN. The Power and Control Wheel diagram below assumes she/her pronouns for survivors and he/him pronouns for partners. However, the abusive behavior it details can happen to people of any gender or sexuality.

Moreover, the wheel diagram shows tactics abusive partners use to keep survivors in a relationship. The inside of the wheel makes up subtle, continual behaviors over time, while the outer ring represents physical and sexual violence. Thus, abusive actions like those depicted in the outer ring reinforce the regular use of other, more subtle methods found in the inner ring.

If you are experiencing abuse, please reach out and ask for help.

ACKNOWLEDGEMENTS

Writing a book is a journey filled with challenges, insights, and moments of inspiration, and I could not have traveled this path alone. I am deeply grateful to all the incredible individuals who have guided and supported me along the way.

To my writer's groups, thank you for your invaluable feedback, encouragement, and camaraderie. Your insights have helped shape my work, and our shared passion for storytelling inspires me every day.

I extend heartfelt thanks to my editor, Lisa Wolff, for her meticulous attention to detail and unwavering belief in my vision. Your expertise and dedication have elevated my writing in ways I couldn't have done alone.

To my publishers, thank you for believing in my stories and providing me with the platform to share them with the world. Your support has been essential in bringing *Twisted Lives* to life.

I must also express my appreciation to my friends, who have provided endless encouragement and understanding during moments of self-doubt. Your belief in me means more than you can imagine.

Finally, to my loyal readers, your enthusiasm and passion for my books fuel my desire to write. Thank you for sharing my work with your friends, for inviting me to speak at book clubs and events, and for being a part of this incredible journey. Your support is the heartbeat of my writing, and I look forward to continuing this adventure together.

With all my gratitude,
Tamara Merrill

ABOUT THE AUTHOR

Tamara Merrill is an award-winning novelist and short story writer with a diverse portfolio that showcases her literary talent. She has published one children's book and seven novels—including bestselling historical fiction; *Shadows in our Bones*, and the *Augustus Family Trilogy: Family Lies, Family Matters, Family Myths*, and psychological thrillers *Just One More* and *Twisted Lives*. Her numerous short stories are featured in  print magazines, online platforms, and fifteen anthologies.

As an award-winning author, Tamara enjoys meeting her fellow readers while speaking at book clubs, in person, or during online meetings and at book fairs.

A passionate advocate for the craft of writing, Tamara frequently speaks at writers' events and teaches writing skills within the adult education system. Her dedication and extensive experience have made her a sought-after speaker and educator, enriching the literary community in the process.

Currently residing in Coronado, CA, and Wickenburg, AZ, Tamara balances her time between writing, reading, and painting. Her passion for storytelling brings her joy and fulfillment, showcasing her belief that reading and writing can transform lives.

To learn more about Tamara and her work, visit her website at www.tamaramerrill.com, or follow her on Facebook at TamaraMerrillAuthor and on Instagram @tmerrillauthor, on X @TamaraM19005826.

BOOK CLUB - Readers Guide

Tamara Merrill is an avid, opinionated reader, so it should come as no surprise that she loves book clubs, and is active in several book clubs, in both AZ and CA.

As an author, Tamara enjoys talking about any and all of her penned books at book clubs around the world.

She is available to speak at your book club or library event. In-person at locations in the greater San Diego, CA, or Phoenix, AZ areas. Online via ZOOM or other meeting apps, anywhere and anytime in the rest of the world.

You may contact her through email at Tamara@TamaraMerrill.com

IDEAS INCLUDING FOOD AND DECORATING TIPS - to help you make your book club meeting special, for this or any other of her books, are on Tamara's website www.TamaraMerrill.com under the Book Club tab, and are listed in her books,

FOOD AND A FEW DECORATIONS ARE FUN!

1. Make Twisted Trees by placing bare twiggy branches in vases. Or make wire trees using this DIY YouTube from Paper, Scissors, Glue.

   https://www.youtube.com/watch?v=JJ3r2Xwq8Ro

2. Using poly-batting, or other Christmas snow products, create snow by arranging batting on a table in piles. Arrange your Twisted Trees in the snow.

3. Add a child's toy dog (Ajax is a German Shepherd) to your scene.

4. The Twisted Trees are a fun favor if you make one for each member.

5. Add a sign to your treat table that says:

   Eat and Drink at your own Risk or **Beware of Drugged Food and Drink**

Twisted Lives does not focus on food. But here is a list of the food mentioned in the book and a few ideas of what to serve.

Wine - whatever you like - but the wines mentioned in the book are:

1. Maryhill Zinfandel
2. Gérard Boulay Clos de Beaujeu Sancerre 2019
3. Sauvignon Blanc
4. Chardonnay
5. Burgundy

Alcohol mentioned:

1. Johnnie Walker Blue
2. Gin

3. Vodka

Food mentioned:

Papaya – Sarah received only a single slice, but you could add papaya to a salad or cube it on a skewer with cheese and berries. Or make shrimp and papaya skewers.

Chocolate Tower – Pudding cake is ideal. Or a Bundt cake made in a castle pan. Or chocolate truffles stacked up. Anything goes because it's chocolate!

Lamb Chops – No ideas here. Not sure I'd serve lamb chops at a book club meeting but let us know if you do.

Baked Salmon with Caper and Lemon – Crostini topped with smoked salmon and softened cream cheese you have seasoned with dill and lemon juice, salt and pepper to taste. Garnish with fresh dill sprig and capers.

Coq au vin – make the real thing or just buy a bucket of wings.

Peanut Butter Sandwich – Teeny, tiny sandwiches. I bet people would love them! Make the sandwich. Cut the crusts off and then cut them into bite-sized triangles.

Cookies – No need to be fancy. Everyone loves cookies!

Grilled Cheese Sandwich with Tomato Soup – A cup of good tomato soup – although to be traditional use Campbell's Cream of Tomato – and teeny, tiny grilled cheese sandwich. (See Peanut Butter Sandwich for details).

Pot Roast – Check with your Grandma. I haven't made a pot roast in years. Although, now that I think of it – try a crostini with thin sliced roast beef and Dijon horseradish sauce, topped with a piece of shaved parmesan cheese and maybe a couple of capers.

Boeuf Bourguignon - Make an appetizer using small bites of the classic ingredients, like tender pieces of beef braised in red wine, mushrooms, carrots, and pearl onions, served on small crostini, puff pastry squares, or even mini skewers.

Discussion Questions

1. What did the title TWISTED LIVES suggest to you? Did the story live up to your title expectations?

2. Sarah and Claire are best friends. What defines that type of relationship for you?

3. Was Sarah's relationship with Claire healthy? Why or why not?

4. Did you suspect that Claire was complicit? If so, when did it begin? When did it stop?

5. Do you believe in love at first sight? How long do you feel is an appropriate time to know someone before marrying?

6. Is jealousy a sign that you are loved? How about if you are jealous of your partner?

7. Do you understand Sarah's inability to break away from Rodney? Why or why not?

8. Recognizing abuse is often difficult. Why did Sarah deny that her relationship with Rodney was abusive?

9. The warning signs of abuse don't always appear overnight and may emerge and intensify as the relationship grows. The one sign shared by most abusive relationships is that the abusive partner tries to establish power and control over their partner. What was the first sign that Rodney was an abuser?

What was his one behavior that made you the most angry?

10. How much did the age gap (15 years) between Sarah and Rodney contribute to their problems? What do you consider an ideal difference in the ages of people in a relationship?

11. The nine most common types of abuse in a relationship are physical, emotional, sexual aggression, financial, digital, sexual coercion, reproductive coercion, stalking, and spiritual. How many types of abuse did Sarah suffer?

12. What defines a healthy relationship?

13. Did you recognize the signs that Sarah's mother, Lydia, was also an abuser? Is her father, Steve, an abuser or a victim of abuse?

14. Judy Hendricks doesn't believe that Jeremy is missing. Did you believe from the beginning? If not, when did you begin to believe Sarah?

15. Did Sarah's finding motherhood difficult affect how you felt about her as a person? Did you find her likable? Is she weak or strong?

16. Everyone in this story drinks alcohol to some extent. Do you believe Sarah has a "drinking problem"?

17. What was the most memorable scene for you?

18. Ajax is a special character in the book. Why did Merrill choose to include him?

19. Last but always fun, if this book were to be made into a movie, who would you like to see in the lead roles? Rodney? Sarah? Claire? Lydia? Judy Hendricks? FBI agent Joe Weller?

BOOKS BY TAMARA MERRILL

AUGUSTUS FAMILY TRILOGY – A three-volume family saga that covers one family's lives, loves, and scandals from 1937 to 1980. **FAMILY LIES** 1937-1944, **FAMILY MATTERS** 1944-1960, and **FAMILY MYTHS** 1960-1980.

SHADOWS IN OUR BONES - based on, real people and real events, this book explores the impact that a racial incident in Maine, 1912, has had on descendants and society. DNA testing, racial tension, family dynamics, and eugenics are all examined in this award-winning read.

JUST ONE MORE - A psychological thriller, the story of one young woman caught in a terrible situation. Her friendship with the crows provides Ari's only support system and survival may not be possible.

SHORT STORIES by Tamara Merrill appear in fifteen anthologies and online.